'Beautifully written... conclusion. Perfect for...'
HELLO! MAGAZINE

'[A] surprisingly delicate, tenderly absorbing tale... [with] shades of Dodie Smith.'
YOU MAGAZINE

'Thoughtful and dark.'
THE TIMES MAGAZINE

'A modern day Nancy Mitford.'
SIR ELTON JOHN

'Brimming with secrets, scandal, shame – and snow.'
THE SUN

'This touching, atmospheric story...has echoes of *I Capture the Castle* about it.'
THE SCOTTISH DAILY MAIL

'Fans of Downton Abbey will love this.'
DAVINA McCALL

'Jolly, posh and madcap but with a dark side as the heroine vacillates between carefree childhood and world-weary adolescence.'
THE DAILY EXPRESS

'Captivating.'
WOMAN & HOME

527 894 84 8

Susannah Constantine is a television presenter and journalist. She lives in West Sussex with her husband and three children. She has co-written nine non-fiction books with Trinny Woodall. *After the Snow* is her debut novel.

After *the* Snow

SUSANNAH CONSTANTINE

ONE PLACE. MANY STORIES

HQ
An imprint of HarperCollins*Publishers* Ltd
1 London Bridge Street
London SE1 9GF

This paperback edition 2018

4
First published in Great Britain by
HQ, an imprint of HarperCollins*Publishers* Ltd 2018

ISBN: 978-0-00-821967-3

For Betty Anderson

And for Sten, Joe, Esme, Cece and Helen

Chapter One

Blinking her eyes open against the new day, Esme could tell that it had snowed. She knew by the luminous shards of light that pierced her curtains and brightened her bedroom in a strange, muffled glow. It was silent, not a sound inside or outside The Lodge. No birds singing their morning chorus, no cars grumbling along the lane, not a breath of wind to rattle the ancient windowpanes. She couldn't even hear the housekeeper, Mrs Bee, clattering about in the kitchen making breakfast.

Esme breathed in the cold air and felt it prickle down her throat, imagining tiny ice crystals disappearing into her body. With a great whooshing noise, she released a cloud of silvery breath that billowed in the air like the smoke from a great dragon. As she burrowed back into the warmth of her crumpled sheets, her feet hit an unexpected obstacle and her tummy clenched with excitement. It was Christmas Day.

Wiggling her toes against the weight of her stocking, lying heavy as a wet sandbag at the end of her bed, it felt as if Father Christmas had been generous and her father's shooting sock crackled with the promise of unopened presents. Flinging back the sheets, Esme leapt up, pulled on her dressing gown and flicked on the electric heater before jumping back onto her bed. Holding her father's sock by its toe, she shook the tightly packed presents from the hand-knitted wool. This Christmas there would be eleven, one for every year that she had been alive. She counted as each strangely shaped packet of colour tumbled onto the eiderdown, some starting to come undone as they fell. Father Christmas had done a terrible job with his wrapping this year. Some of the paper had been put on inside out and there wasn't a sliver of sticky tape in sight. Pulling out the last lumpy presents jammed at the bottom of the stocking, her fingers fumbled around the unmistakeable shapes of a tangerine and some foil-wrapped chocolate coins. She had posted her letter to the North Pole a few weeks ago, neatly written on her father's headed notepaper. The one thing she longed for was a new riding hat, but that was too much to expect from Father Christmas. Perhaps her parents would remember. She really had tried to be as good as possible this year, but still always seemed to be in trouble. Like the time she had borrowed her mother's hunting whip; her mother didn't even ride any more, so Esme didn't think she'd notice but her father did when he saw it was missing from the umbrella stand where he kept it as a showpiece. After telling him she had no idea where it was, he had found it hidden under her bed. Thunder followed. She wished she could be more like her big sister, Sophia, who always seemed to know what to do and how to behave. Or at least how not to get caught.

Esme picked up a small package, the wrapping paper cheerfully wishing her a 'Happy Birthday'. It was hard to the touch and much heavier than she expected. Ripping off the paper, a china figurine of a dachshund sleeping in its basket fell into her hand. Exactly like the one her mother had sitting in her bathroom! She christened the figurine Doodle, and put it carefully to one side to open the next present. Esme gasped as she unwrapped an antique china plate. It looked very old and incredibly valuable, with the remnants of an old breakfast encrusted upon it. Her father would be fascinated to see this piece of history as he loved antique shopping when they were in London. He'd know if the plate had once belonged to a wealthy lord, in the olden times.

Picking up the next present she squealed with excitement as she felt its shape beneath her fingers. Tearing it open, she stroked the hard bristles and thanked Father Christmas for providing her with a dandy brush for her pony, Homer. The brush was just like Lexi's. Lexi was her best friend and the daughter of the Earl and Countess, who lived at the top of the hill in their castle. Descended from Italian royalty, the Countess made everyone refer to her as the *Contessa*, although Esme had never heard the Earl refer to his wife with anything but her English title. Lexi stabled her pony, Jupiter, with Homer at Shere Farm – or in *foster care*, as Lexi put it, because the castle stables were reserved for her mother's racehorses.

Esme loved driving up to Scotland for the holidays, when she could spend time with her pony and Lexi. The rolling Highlands felt a million miles away from the hustle and bustle of London. She pulled the brush through her hair, thinking how easy it was going to make removing the encrusted mud that stuck to Homer's fetlocks like bloated ticks. He would be the smartest, shiniest pony on the hunting field. She couldn't wait to show Jimmy, the groom who ran the yard; he was always grumbling about the state of her beloved Homer.

The metal wires of the electric heater clicked and creaked,

glowing red, red hot. Esme's room was heating up nicely. In fact, she'd almost forgotten the snow that lay outside. Sliding off her bed, she tiptoed over to the window and pulled back the curtains. She scratched the frozen condensation and peered out at the magical world beyond the glass. It was as if The Lodge sat within a giant snow globe, enormous clouds of the palest grey sprinkling snowflakes across a white land, blanketing its secrets in a quiet stillness. Opening her window just a fraction, Esme allowed a snowflake to land on her palm and watched it melt into a tiny puddle.

She hoped the Boxing Day hunt wouldn't be cancelled. It was going to be the first time Homer didn't have to be on a leading rein. Jimmy had told her she was a good enough rider to manage on her own now. Homer would have tinsel plaited through his mane and tail and Esme would add some to her new hat. Excited, butterflies quivered in her tummy. But even if the hunt was called off, out here in the countryside it would be replaced by tobogganing and she could exchange Homer's saddle and bridle for a harness to pull the sleigh.

Returning to her presents, Esme wondered whether Father Christmas had given Homer a sheepskin saddle pad to keep his back warm. He hated having cold leather next to his skin and it made him buck until it reached body temperature. Up until now, Jimmy had used an old dog blanket, which was nowhere near as smart as the quilted pad Jupiter wore. None of Lexi's riding things were hand-me-downs or makeshift. She said it was because she didn't have a big sister but Esme knew it was because her family had more money than hers.

The other presents would have to wait until later. Esme was desperate to step into the enchanted world that waited beyond The Lodge's walls and she knew that once her parents were awake, she'd be trapped inside until the Christmas service at Bonnyton Church. She grabbed some warm socks and stepped into the corridor.

Beyond her room the rest of the house was still sleeping. Pressing her eye to the keyhole of her sister's room, she could see a copy of *Cupid Rides Pillion* lying open on the floor. Sophia was addicted to Barbara Cartland novels and was in love with the idea of falling in love. Each book provided a new hero that might one day sweep her off her feet. She must have fallen asleep reading last night and Esme knew not to wake her if she didn't want a verbal bashing. Boarding school had made Sophia moody when she came home and she didn't want to do the same things as her little sister any more. When she was on holiday she wanted to be in London hanging out with her glamorous friends and their older brothers rather than at The Lodge.

Esme had mapped out a soundproof route past her parents' bedroom years ago when she began sneaking out in the early hours to meet Lexi in their secret place in the woods. As she tiptoed down the corridor now she automatically avoided the creaking floorboards that would give her away. It was so quiet she could even hear the mantel clock chiming in the drawing room. Creeping past the kitchen into the back hallway she pulled on her wellington boots and lifted her Red Indian elk-skin coat off its peg. Her father had brought it back for her after a trip to Canada and it was her favourite present of all. The soft leathery outside was decorated with brightly coloured beads in pretty patterns. It had a slightly sweet, pungent smell to it – not like a rotting old rabbit carcass, but more like something dead that hadn't yet started to fester. Her father had given her moccasin slippers, too, but she had quickly learned that they weren't much use outside.

Esme slid back the rusty iron bolt of the back door and placed one booted foot on the fresh snow. She watched as it sank into the deep, powdery mound. She felt a sense of delight at making the first footprint in this untouched world. Her Advent calendar had come to life, the glittering icicles and twinkling marshmallow rooftop filling her with a sense of hope. Maybe the snow would make Mummy happy today. A tiny robin flicked his tail, its red breast and black beady eyes bursting from the white canvas that lay before her. He looked at her, unafraid.

'Happy Christmas Mr Robin.'

'Tut tut tut,' it replied, before shooting off its branch and onto the washing line.

Esme hugged herself, daring to believe that this was going to be the best Christmas ever. Her mother couldn't possibly feel sad when she saw how beautiful the world outside looked. And then Daddy wouldn't have to be on guard and she and Sophia could enjoy themselves. Scooping up a handful of snow she nibbled at the powder, marvelling at its strange, metallic taste. Then, dragging her boots through the snow, she set off towards the gate and the world that lay beyond it. She looked up towards the castle, hoping Lexi would be on her way to meet her at the pond.

Culcairn Castle was like a fairy-tale castle with high, strong walls and three enormous round towers that rose right up into the clouds. You could tell it had been built to keep the baddies out. It was a very famous castle in Scotland – so important that the Culcairns had opened it to the public. Lexi told her that it had a quarter of a million visitors a year, which seemed like loads, especially if they all came at once. There would be none today though. It was closed in the winter.

Esme blew into her hands as she continued to the pond. Kicking the surrounding snow in search of a rock, she lifted the largest she could manage over her head and smashed it onto the ice. It bounced. Tentatively, she inched onto the frozen water. The slippery surface creaked but not enough to cause alarm. She tried to skid but her feet were like two tiny snow ploughs that created miniature drifts. She remembered the time Lexi had fallen in and she had lain flat on the ice to distribute her weight and haul her friend out. The water was only knee-deep, but it was good practice for a real-life drowning situation.

Esme started to count in her head. She and Lexi had an agreement that if the person who you were meeting hadn't come by 500, then you could leave. Sometimes she would get to 500 and be about to leave and then see Lexi come running towards her, her long hair in her eyes and her clothes in a tangle, laughing with pleasure that Esme was still there. Sometimes it was almost like there was an invisible thread that bound them together, each knowing what the other was doing.

But today there was no sign of her. 498... 499... 500. Esme finished counting, imagining her friend opening her stocking, her smile even bigger as she discovered what was in each package.

It really was very cold. Cold enough to freeze the breath from her nostrils as well as her mouth. Pangs of hunger gnawed at her stomach. She waited a few seconds more. Perhaps Lexi was snowed in? And anyway, she would see her at the Christmas service with the rest of her family. It was time to head back to the house. As she turned, she saw a rusty ball of fur streak across the snow. Most people would have mistaken it for a fox, albeit a pale version with white socks.

'Digger! Happy Christmas. I can't wait to give you your present!'

Ignoring her, Digger dashed round the snow in demented circles.

'Stop showing off,' laughed Esme.

Digger's arrival meant that Mrs Bee was up and breakfast was probably waiting. Today was not a day to be late.

Esme went straight into the kitchen to find Mrs Bee. The housekeeper's name was actually Mrs Bumble but ever since she could remember Esme and her sister had called her Mrs Bee. She could hear the clink of cutlery coming from the dining room but the housekeeper was nowhere to be seen. A delicious smell of roasting turkey filled the room and an orderly line of Pyrex bowls, overflowing with potatoes, carrots and Brussels sprouts, sat on the Formica tabletop, while baking trays brimmed with chipolata sausages, bacon rashers and round patties of stuffing. Esme stared in delight. It was hard to imagine how just half an hour in the oven could crisp the patties into Esme's favourite part of Christmas lunch, drenched in steaming satin-smooth gravy poured from the silver sauce boat.

In the middle of the table stood Mrs Bee's majestic Christmas cake. Freshly iced, it bore a remarkable resemblance to the snow-covered world outside, its thick, white frosting smothering what lay beneath. As a final touch, a miniature

Father Christmas in his sleigh had been positioned in the centre. After snapping off a sugared icicle, Esme skipped out of the kitchen and ran upstairs to get dressed.

Pushing open her bedroom door she saw Mrs Bee staring at the dirty china plate from her stocking. Startled by Esme's arrival, she looked up.

'Esme!' she said. 'Where on earth have you been? Your mother and father are already having their breakfast. Och and look at you! That snow is melting all over the carpet. How could you have gone out in this weather? And in your wee nightic. Come on, your father will want to leave for church soon. You know perfectly well he hates to be late.'

'Don't be angry, Mrs Bee, it's Christmas! And look at all my presents. How lucky am I? Look, this little dog is just like Mummy's.'

'Is this a dandy brush I see?' said Mrs Bee, her tone softening as Esme ran towards her.

'Yes! Homer will be so pleased. Although I don't think I'll be able to visit him today, will I, with the snow? Oh, Mrs Bee, happy Christmas! I can't wait to show Mummy my presents.' She was about to ask her what she had found in *her* stocking when she remembered again that poor Mrs Bee had no family of her own to give her presents; thoughtfully, Esme had decorated an old cake tin with pictures of pretty flowers cut out from a discarded copy of *Country Life*.

'Your present from me is under the tree, Mrs Bee,' she reassured the housekeeper.

'Och, how lovely!'

'I can't believe it's a proper white Christmas. It's made everything just perfect.'

Mrs Bee swept Esme's hair back from her forehead. 'I'll be staying nice and warm indoors today, Esme. The snow gives me chilblains. Now, what're you going to wear for church?'

'I want to wear a dress. The cream-and-white one. It's my favourite,' Esme said, dropping onto the bed. She stroked the sparkling silver tinsel adorning her headrest. Suddenly, an idea popped into her mind that made the prospect of wearing a dress even more enjoyable. 'I know, Mrs Bee – I'll make this tinsel into a halo! Just like a Christmas angel. Daddy will love it!'

'Oh, he will, darling. I can just imagine his face when he sees you dressed up all pretty.'

Esme pulled on her dress and stood still as Mrs Bee coiled the scratchy foil around her head. Peering at her reflection in the mirror she clapped her hands together. 'Just like an angel!' she said. Her clear blue eyes shone with excitement. Her long blonde hair fell over her shoulders, the tinsel covering a jagged fringe she had cut with the kitchen scissors in a bid to hide a chickenpox scar above her left brow. A rosy bloom from the cold flushed her cheek.

Mrs Bee smiled back at her. 'Now, off to breakfast with you. That's enough dilly-dallying for one morning.'

'Thanks Mrs Bee!' Esme said. She couldn't wait to show her new outfit to her family.

Her parents and sister were eating breakfast at the large oak dining table, silent, just like any other day. The only noise was the muffled sound of Christmas carols coming from Mrs Bee's radio in the kitchen.

'Happy Christmas, everyone!' said Esme, giving her mother a big hug.

'Happy Christmas, darling,' her mother said softly, returning her daughter's embrace with one that felt as light as air. She gave a listless smile.

Esme's heart sank. This morning was a bad morning. Couldn't her mother just try to be happy on Christmas Day? She decided to help her along.

'Have you seen the snow, Mummy? It's so beautiful and all ready and waiting for you, like a big white carpet with crystals everywhere. You'll love it and I can't wait to show you. I've already been outside to test it out for you and it's all soft and welcoming...' She broke off as she caught Sophia's look and her father's clenched jaw. It was no good.

'Happy Christmas, Daddy,' she said, trying to make him feel better. 'Do you like my halo?'

'It's lovely, darling,' said her father, his voice spiky, 'but you aren't an extra in a pantomime. You've nearly missed breakfast. Quickly now, sit down and have something to eat. And before we leave, I want you to take that silly tinsel off.'

Esme looked over at her sister, praying at least she would tune into their unspoken pact of trying to make their mother feel better. It could be exhausting but sometimes, between them, they could make her smile and join in, if only for a few moments. Occasionally, there were whole stretches when their mother was very, *very* happy, excited about the smallest thing, but even then she could suddenly stop mid-sentence and drift away again.

But Sophia looked gloomy, as though she had already given up, and her tone was spiteful.

'You can't wear that, Es,' agreed Sophia. 'It looks silly. We're going to church not a fancy-dress party.'

Sophia, also blonde and blue-eyed, was dressed almost entirely in navy blue, the wall of colour only broken up by a white frilled collar.

'Well you just look like an old maid,' said Esme, rapidly blinking to stop tears from falling. She looked forlornly at her plate: half a grapefruit, a boiled egg and one piece of toast. Mrs Bee always made sure that breakfast on Christmas Day was disappointingly small so as not to ruin the family's appetite for her Christmas feast.

Esme glanced at her mother. She was concentrating on her grapefruit, eyes downcast as she methodically put one segment after another into her mouth. Her spoon rose timidly before each bite, the juice making her cough. Sip of tea. Wipe of lips. Back to the slow process of eating.

'Diana, can you pass the butter?' her father asked.

Esme's mother didn't react and she knew her father was testing her to see if she would. Sophia looked at her sister and pursed her lips. In a protective reflex, Esme passed the pat of Anchor across the table.

Mrs Bee always said that her mother had her 'head in the clouds' when she wasn't listening. It was like she was dreaming with her eyes open, her mind far away in another land.

'Thank you, Esme,' her father said, smearing a thick layer of butter on his toast, smartly topped with a big dollop of marmalade.

Esme watched as he took an enormous bite and looked over at his wife. She'd noticed him doing that a lot lately, even more so than usual. He often seemed worried about her but sometimes he seemed cross that she was so distant. He tried to make her happy by giving her the most beautiful things, even when it wasn't a special occasion. Esme loved watching her mother open the old brown leather boxes with *Phillips of Bond Street* in gold writing embossed upon them. Mrs Bee always said that the best things came in small packages, but when bad days became bad weeks even these gifts didn't pull Esme's mother out of the grey mist in which she lost herself. Her father bought them to make her happy and when she wasn't grateful Esme felt sorry for him and made up for her mother's lack of interest by telling her what amazing taste her father had.

'Mummy, you haven't shown us your present from Daddy yet. What did he give you?'

Her parents always gave their presents to each other before breakfast.

Her mother blinked dramatically, as if she was shaking off a deep sleep. 'Sorry, sweetheart?'

'Your present – from Daddy. What did you get?' Esme asked again, busily cutting her toast into soldiers.

'Oh, my present. It's a lovely brooch, darling.'

'What's it like?'

Her mother absently spooned up another grapefruit segment.

'Mummy?'

'Yes, darling.'

'What's the brooch like? Is it pretty?'

'Well, yes, of course it is.'

'May I see it?'

Her mother looked at her as if she was noticing her for the first time.

'Darling, why have you got that silly tinsel on your head?'

Esme reached up and tugged at the halo in her hair. 'Oh, nothing. I thought you'd like it.'

'Esme, that's enough talking,' her father cut in. 'Finish up your breakfast and run upstairs to collect your smart coat. We need to leave in a few minutes.'

Sophia rolled her eyes. 'Who cares if we're a few minutes late, Daddy? It's only a bloody church service. Just because you want to get there before the Earl and Contessa.'

Her father never usually cared about being late. It was only when the Culcairn family were involved that he got grumpy about timekeeping. Esme thought it was strange because he didn't seem to like the Earl, though her mother always came alive in his company. She often smiled at Lexi's father, even if it wasn't a good day.

'Don't swear about church, Sophia. If we are late, we won't get our pew. Now get going, Esme. You will have to leave the rest of your breakfast.'

Her mother's eyes didn't flicker. She was the one who was going to make them late. She hadn't even got her lipstick on and she never went anywhere without her lipstick and powder, even on bad days.

But at least she might liven up when she saw the Earl.

Chapter Two

The journey to Bonnyton Church was a precarious one at the best of times. Narrow, windy lanes bordered by thick thorn hedges made it impossible to see any cars coming in the opposite direction. Today, Esme's father drove at the pace of a tortoise through the treacle-like snow. He sat rigid, hands clasping the steering wheel, cigarette hanging from his lips, his face getting redder and redder as he became more and more agitated.

He doesn't want to be late, thought Esme, because he doesn't want anyone else sitting near the Culcairn family. But Esme knew they weren't important enough to get the front pews on Christmas Day.

Sophia nudged Esme and wiggled a gloved finger. Esme stifled a giggle. The simple gesture always managed to close the five years between them. A wiggling finger meant a wiggling willy. Esme wiggled hers in response. Sophia then flicked a series of V-signs at her father's back. Esme copied her. She felt protected by her sister once again and knew her earlier meanness about the tinsel halo was only because of the bad atmosphere at the breakfast table.

When they finally arrived at Bonnyton the bells had just stopped pealing, which meant they were late. The congregation would be preparing to stand for the arrival of Father Kinley and the choir. The parking space where the family normally left their car had been filled, but her father's stress levels gave him permission to double-park, blocking the back entrance to the graveyard.

'Not their bloody space, anyway,' he muttered, his dead cigarette still attached to his mouth.

The snow along the church path had been compacted into an icy carpet by earlier arrivals and the large oak door to the entrance was already shut. When her father lifted the latch the noise sounded like a gunshot in the hushed silence inside the church.

As the family stood in the doorway, Esme breathed in the familiar smell of pine but quickly hid behind her sister as everyone turned, their disapproving faces dampening her relief of having arrived just in time. The church was completely full, every pew jammed with people, buttocks spilling over into the aisle. Henry and Lucia, the Earl and Contessa of Culcairn, sat at the front and only the Earl gave them a smile. Lexi waved at Esme furiously, despite her movements being restricted by a horrible tweed coat. She pointed to her matching beret, crossing her eyes and sticking out her tongue in disgust. There was nothing pretty about what she was wearing; it was just prim and frumpy and Esme knew how Lexi hated being made to dress like an 'old lady'.

Mrs Hornbuckle, the hunt secretary, had already sprung up from her chair and was tipping hymnbooks into her father's arms. She led the family to a pew at the back, hidden in the shadows. Esme could see disappointment etched on her father's face. Her mother seemed less concerned, her head still up in the snowy clouds.

Standing on tiptoes on her hassock, Esme saw that Lord William and Lady Mary-Rose Findlay were sitting behind the Culcairns. Lord William was a very important man, with whom she had never had a proper conversation, but Lady Mary-Rose was one of the funniest women Esme had ever met. She swore all the time and told very naughty jokes. Esme thought she ought to have her own comedy show on TV. She looked back at Lexi, sat next to her older brother, Rollo, and sister, Bella. Esme loved Bella but didn't know Rollo as well because he was the same age as Sophia so spent more time with her. Esme and Lexi thought they fancied each other. Sophia always blushed when Rollo's name was mentioned and they always seemed to go missing at the same time when Esme's family visited the castle. Next to them were their parents, the Earl and Contessa. Everybody else was rubbing shoulders, squashed up on the short benches, but the Contessa had lots of room around her. Even her husband sat a few inches away. If Esme were next to Lexi's mother, she would avoid sitting too close to her as well, just in case touching her brought bad luck. She never opened umbrellas indoors either and always crossed herself if she saw a single magpie. The Contessa worshipped Rollo but never seemed very interested in her daughters, which made going to Culcairn Castle lots of fun for Esme as she and Lexi could do whatever they wanted – once they got past Nanny Patch and the nursery maid.

Esme jumped as the Contessa suddenly turned around and fixed her with a stare that hit Esme like a slap, her cheeks smarting and flushing in response. The Contessa looked like an Italian movie star with her scarlet lips, high cheekbones and dark glossy hair pulled into a sleek chignon, but despite such beauty, her cold, coal-black eyes always made Esme feel unsettled.

Everyone stood for the first carol, 'Once in Royal David's City'. A young boy had taken centre stage at the altar. His angelic voice rang through the church, alone and pure. The organ cranked air into its pipes, coming to life. Esme's mother, who had been on her knees praying since they arrived, stood and swayed, although not in time to the music. She must be praying very hard, thought Esme, as her eyes were red and watery. Luckily Esme's father knew the words to the carol by heart because he was staring at her mother and not the hymnbook. Esme looked past him to Sophia, who gave her a knowing look.

Esme loved the Bonnyton choir. The Munroes never went to church in London; her father said that was for 'commoners' who had nothing better to do than pray. The only choir she had to compare it to was the one at her school in Kensington and it seemed to her that country choristers were much better than city ones – probably because the air was cleaner. She looked out for her favourite singer, a large woman who, even in her vestal robes, appeared magnificent. Esme loved watching as her mouth opened wide like a frog to let loose a surprisingly exquisite voice. She always made a great effort with her make-up, today wearing turquoise eye shadow, black eyeliner, vibrant pink lipstick and a bold swipe of blusher on each cheek. Esme's mother rarely went to such lengths with her face, wearing only a soft pink lipstick and pearlescent powder. Mrs Bee maintained that Diana's beauty came from within and she didn't need anything smothered over her freckles to bring it out.

Esme's thoughts were interrupted at the sound of her father's deep, booming voice, now drowning out those of the rest of the congregation. He was proud of his singing and loved to show it off, much to her and Sophia's embarrassment. Tilting his head back, his nostrils flared as he inhaled deeply in readiness for the next verse. On this Christmas morning, his left nostril held a large bogey in its depths. Esme took the handkerchief from his pocket and handed it to him, poking a finger up her own nose to indicate the need for extraction. The carol ended and her father blew his nose, checking the handkerchief's contents before returning the crumpled cotton to his pocket.

'Let us pray,' commanded Father Kinley.

A grumbling sound spread through the church as the congregation pulled out their hassocks from under the pews and dropped to their knees. Esme's mother was the first to kneel, her dark curls falling forward like a curtain. She was being terribly pious today, Esme thought, wondering whom she was praying so hard for. Or maybe she was having a little nap. Her mother found it so easy to sleep anywhere; watching TV, having lunch and even once when she was driving. Luckily, she had been on her own and hadn't been going too fast when she hit the tree as she was coming back from the village shop. Lexi's father had found her and brought her back home, her white face even paler than usual. She hadn't driven for a long time now.

The congregation rose as the organ sounded the first note to the next hymn, and her father's singing began in earnest. Her mother was definitely asleep because she didn't stand up and suddenly, as if struck by lightning, this made Esme very angry. She kicked her mother hard on the calf and, like a new-born foal, she scrambled confusedly to her feet before starting 'Once in Royal David's City' once more.

'Mummy,' Esme breathed, ashamed of herself for hurting her mother. She pointed to her hymnbook. 'That's the wrong hymn. We are singing this one now.'

Her mother looked at Esme with an empty expression, then slowly turned the pages to the right carol, picked up the chorus and sung in perfect pitch along with her fellow worshippers. She rocked back and forth to the music, like a swing in the breeze. Esme saw her father's hand stretching past her sister, searching for her mother's arm. Discretely, he tugged his wife past his daughter to position her next to him.

'You're on my foot. Get off!' Sophia whispered, shoving her mother angrily.

'For God's sake, Diana,' Esme's father hissed. 'Pull yourself together.'

Esme hoped no one around them could see what was going on. Diana stopped singing and stared ahead, emptied of life once more.

Father Kinley began his address and Esme tried to listen but found herself looking instead at the other mothers in the congregation, wondering if they were empty or full of life. She didn't have any good friends at school because she didn't invite any of them to her house for fear her mother might behave strangely. But she had been to Lucinda Burgess's house and she wished that they could swap mothers. Lucinda's mother wasn't a beauty like hers but she made up for it with colourful clothes and big earrings. She fussed over her children; kissing and cuddling them, making them laugh.

Snatches of tales about the poor and needy, the homeless, soldiers fighting in unpronounceable countries, the Prime Minister and Her Majesty the Queen, drifted past her. Then, as he always did when he neared the end of his sermon, Father Kinley began to list the local villagers who had gone on to the next life, saying how much the community would miss them. Once, Father Kinley had come to The Lodge. Her father had stood awkwardly at the front door while he had asked how Mrs Munroe was getting on. It was only when Mrs Bee asked him to come inside that her father remembered his manners and offered him a cup of tea. He hadn't stayed long and Esme had been made to come into the drawing room and play him a piece on the piano. Her father hadn't said much and her mother had been upstairs resting. Father Kinley had not come back to visit since then.

'Pray for their families, dear friends,' he was saying now, 'at this time when family is everything and the loneliness that their dearly departed has left becomes all the more painful.'

The blood of shame rose into Esme's cheeks. Wanting another mother was like wanting your own dead. And she didn't want that. Father Kinley was referring to the butcher's daughter, Karen, whose mother had died of cancer. That was sad enough but then Karen had been sent away because the shock had broken her father's heart and he had died too. Esme's mother was like a yoyo but at least, she thought, she had a father who could take care of them. With Mrs Bee's help, of course.

She looked over to her father. He was holding on to her mother as if he was about to haul her off to jail. She tried hard not to be cross with her mother because between her father and Sophia she got quite enough crossness already; it was important that she and Mrs Bee topped her up with kindness.

Outside the church, Esme tried to spot Lexi as the Culcairn family left through a side door – like they were a famous pop group leaving the stage, she thought, smiling. Sophia went off to find Rollo like a starstruck groupie.

'Merry Christmas,' came a familiar voice.

Esme looked up. It was Jimmy, a mound of freshly fallen snow collecting on his cap. Her mother brightened and smiled at him.

'Jimmy! Happy Christmas. How are you?' Diana said.

'Well, I'd be a lot bleeding happier if it weren't for this bloody snow. I had to come here by sleigh, didn't I? And how are you, Mr Munroe? Broke, I'd imagine. How many diamonds did Diana get this year?' He roared with laughter at his own joke. Esme's mother smiled, too. She loved Jimmy because he made her laugh. Somehow he managed to be rude to everyone then get away with it. Esme wondered if it was because he didn't care what people thought of him.

'Jimmy!' said Esme. 'Guess what? Father Christmas gave Homer the smartest brand new dandy brush.'

'Like we don't have a thousand of those already,' said Jimmy. 'But at least yours won't have most of its bristles missing.' He ruffled her hair. 'You looking forward to the Boxing Day meet? Homer's going to buck like a randy whore when you get on his back – he's practically jumping out of his skin in his stable.'

Jimmy had made an effort with his appearance this morning, thought Esme. His thinning hair, which he cut himself with horse clippers, was smeared across his bald patch. The few strands left stuck to his scalp in lines like a cattle grid. His tweed jacket hung off his narrow shoulders and the top button of his shirt was missing, a mishap he had tried to disguise with a pony club tie that hung like a bow around his neck.

'I still want to go to the meet, though, Jimmy,' Esme said, eagerly. 'We can do what we did last time it snowed and put butter on his hooves to make sure it slips right off. I asked Father Christmas for a sheepskin numnah. That would have stopped him bucking but I don't think I was good enough last year.'

'No you bloody wasn't,' he cackled. An explosion of spittle blew out of his mouth in a great wheeze, some of it landing on Esme's cheek, which she quickly wiped away with her glove.

'You'll believe anything, Esme. Maybe pigs really can fly. If a rug stops that horrid pony bucking, I'll give you ten pence. You should have seen him this morning when I put him out. His tail went up and he farted his way around the field like a rocket. When you get on him tomorrow it won't be the doctor you'll be wanting, it'll be the bloody undertaker!'

27

It was her father's turn to guffaw at Jimmy's outburst this time, which surprised Esme.

'Oh come on, Jimmy,' he said, patting him on the back. 'Give the damn pony a lunge or get on his back to wear him out before Esme rides him. Look at you, you're probably only a stone heavier than her.'

'Oh, right,' Jimmy said, annoyed. 'So it's fine for me to end up in a bloody coffin?'

'Come now, my lad,' said her father, like he was talking to a disobedient but beloved gun dog. 'It *is* what we pay you for.'

'I'd like to see *you* sit on the monster. You wouldn't last five seconds before you were in a heap on the floor, crying for your old nanny.'

'Jimmy, I'll have you know that I was a fine rider as a boy. I galloped faster than the wind when I was on the hunting field.'

'And now the only wind you have is the hurricane that flies from your arse!' said Jimmy, laughing.

Esme's mother started giggling. She was becoming a little too animated in Jimmy's company. Her mood was starting to fizz beyond normal jollity and Esme could tell that her father wanted to get her away from Jimmy before words started to spill from her mouth.

'Esme, darling, why don't you go and find your sister so we can get going to the castle? We don't want to miss out on the mince pies.'

'Jimmy ought to come with us,' said her mother. 'Or at the very least join us back at The Lodge for…'

'Time to go, darling. We'll see you tomorrow, Jimmy,'

her father said, pulling his wife away before she could invite Jimmy for lunch.

The back road up to the castle was always difficult – riddled with potholes it was impossibly steep and windy – but because it was Christmas it hadn't been gritted so was even harder to navigate. At first, the Munroes' car crunched through the snow with little complaint, but as soon as they started uphill, the weak motor began to protest. It was used to smooth tarmac and wasn't happy trying to adjust to conditions that were better suited to a tractor. Like a spoiled child digging its heels in the snow, it ground to a halt. Esme's father cranked on the handbrake but it was no use on the icy surface and the car began to slip backwards.

'Shit,' her father muttered, gripping the steering wheel hard.

Esme looked out the back window as the car slid into the deep ditch at the side of the road, the final crunch of the bumper as it hit the bank forcing her onto her sister's lap.

'Ouch, Esme, get off,' Sophia said, pushing her sister back onto her seat. She hadn't found Rollo after the service and was impatient to get to the castle.

None of them was remotely hurt or even surprised. Her mother was facing forwards as if nothing had happened and her father still held the steering wheel in a vice-like grip. Taking the back road up to the castle had been a stupid idea, but on days like today, when a wide circle of the Earl and

Contessa's friends made the trip, Colin preferred to use the private gates like the Culcairn family.

'Shit, shit, *shit*,' Colin said.

Sophia started laughing into her scarf, quickly bending her head down so that their father couldn't see her in the rear-view mirror. Esme started sniggering too. A great fog of nauseating fumes from the exhaust pipe was now seeping into the car.

'Turn off the ignition, Daddy,' said Sophia, regaining some sort of control.

'Oh, right. Yes. Well I suppose there's only one thing for it now; we'll have to walk.'

It was easier said than done. The car had fallen into the ditch at an angle that made the doors feel extremely heavy. Sophia managed to push hers open with her feet, scramble onto the snow and then pull Esme out after her. Together, they opened their mother's door and held it while she and their father dragged themselves out. Esme watched as her mother's expensive navy heels disappeared into the powder like hot rods through wax. Her stockinged legs now had a cast of snow that rendered her totally immobile. Esme didn't know how her mother could stand it; the cold was so intense that her own legs had begun to ache.

'Well, Daddy, you've really done it this time,' Sophia exclaimed. 'Not only have you chosen to crash on the back drive, which no one will be travelling up because they aren't stupid, you've also managed to pick a spot that is still miles from the castle and just as far from The Lodge. By the time anyone finds us we'll have frozen to death.'

'Sophia, don't exaggerate. It will only take us twenty minutes to walk to the castle,' her father said.

'Maybe on a normal day. You seem to have forgotten the three feet of snow we'll be wading through and our lack of huskies and a sledge.'

'Darling, there isn't three feet of snow and anyway we haven't got a choice. Either we get a move on or we stay in the car until tomorrow when the newspapers get delivered.'

'*Tomorrow?*' Esme gasped. 'But we'll miss Mrs Bee's Christmas lunch!'

'Exactly, darling. So let's start walking.'

Esme took her mother's hand, which was stiff with cold. 'It's all right Mummy, I know the way. Follow me.'

Sophia and her father strode off ahead, carving great tracks into the snow with their confident strides. Every time she looked they seemed further away, disappearing like ghosts into the fuzzy whiteness. Suddenly it didn't feel like an adventure any more. She wished that her mother would just speed up a little bit so that they could catch up, but with every step it felt as if they were going even slower.

Esme tugged on her mother's hand. 'Come on, Mummy, we need to walk a bit faster or we're going to lose them.'

It was bitterly cold. The sort of cold that penetrated deep into your bones and made you feel as if you would never be warm again. She thanked God for not allowing heating in churches, otherwise she wouldn't have been wearing so many clothes. Even so, her legs and feet were going numb from wading through the snow. Snowflakes were beginning to clump together on her mother's mink coat like the fur of a great polar bear.

'Mummy, are you warm enough?' she asked, shivering.

'It is very cold,' her mother replied, her voice muffled through her scarf.

'I know. My feet are like ice cubes. Just think – you can wriggle them in front of the fire when we get to the castle. We must get there, Mummy.'

'But I've lost my shoe, darling.'

'Your shoe? When?' Esme turned around, surprised. 'Why didn't you say anything?'

'I don't know.'

'Stay here, Mummy,' she sighed. 'I'll go back and get it.'

Releasing her mother's hand, Esme followed their steps back down the road. But the further she went, the shallower the footprints became. New snow filled the freshly made holes, covering any trace of her mother's navy heel. Walking into the wind now, the snowflakes hit her face like a thousand tiny needles. It was hard to see anything; all the trees marking the side of the drive had disappeared and everything looked unfamiliar and eerie. Esme bowed her head and tucked her chin into her coat, not knowing what to do. Looking back, she couldn't even see the shape of her mother the snow was falling so heavily.

'Mummy!' she called. '*Mummy!*'

She began to run back up the hill as best she could, trying not to panic. Even with her eyes closed, she'd be able to find her way to the vast gates that marked the private entrance to the castle, but she wasn't sure her mother could do the same.

Maybe she couldn't wait any longer with only one shoe,

thought Esme and as she trudged up the hill she comforted herself by imagining her mother already standing by the fire in the drawing room with a big blanket around her shoulders, sending someone out to find her.

After what felt like miles of walking, the castle finally rose into the sky before her and she soon reached the drive. There were already a lot of cars there and she could hear the party in full swing. As she pushed open the front door she wasn't sure whether it was a blast of warm air or a sense of relief that washed over her.

Pulling off her own sodden boots, she noticed her sister's coat had fallen off its hook and landed in a dark pool of water on the rush matting.

Serves her right for not waiting for us, Esme thought, although she still picked it up and placed it alongside her own coat on the cast iron radiator.

The sound of laughter and clinking glasses trickled down the hallway from upstairs. She knew all her family would be safe and warm in the drawing room, probably each already on their third mince pie. She ran up the corridor and bound up the staircase, two steps at a time. At a drinks table on the landing stood the Culcairns' butler, Mr Cribben. He was taking a deep swig from a crystal decanter, which he hurriedly put down. He wiped his mouth with the sleeve of his tailcoat.

'Esme! Merry Christmas. Would you care for a drink?'

'Yes please, Mr Cribben. A bitter lemon please. Have you seen my family?'

The butler snapped the lid off a small Britvic bottle with a silver opener disguised as a duck's head.

'Yes,' he hiccupped. 'I believe they are in there already.'

'Thanks, Mr Cribben, and happy Christmas to you too.' Esme took a gulp of her drink, the bubbles getting up her nose and making her cough.

Entering the warm glow of the drawing room, she peered through the throng of guests, trying to find her family. This was the grandest reception room in the private side of the castle and Esme's favourite. It was so big that it had two marble fireplaces and not one but two enormous Christmas trees. Both were festooned with silken bows and golden baubles, real candles flickering dangerously close to the thick boas of tinsel. Piles of extravagantly wrapped presents lay beneath them.

Esme saw Sophia and Rollo talking under some mistletoe and wondered if they might be about to kiss. Cheerful faces, many of whom she recognized, occupied ornately carved sofas and chairs upholstered in pale-blue silk. She caught sight of the Earl talking to Father Kinley, Lord Findlay in conversation with Lord and Lady Robert Fraser, then her father appeared, breaking away from the crowd, gripping a steaming cup of mulled wine.

'Darling, there you are. What took you so long?' he asked, crossing the carpet and ruffling her hair.

'Why didn't you wait for us, Daddy? Mummy lost her shoe and I couldn't find it. Is she here?'

'Oh, I'm sure she's here somewhere,' said her father, gesturing his hand around the room. 'Probably powdering her nose after being out in the snow for so long. Why don't you go and find Lexi?'

Yes, Lexi, Esme thought, excitedly. She squeezed into the

crowd, parting ladies' skirts with her hands as she tried to get to the back of the room where the children usually played. Lexi was her best and only real friend. Unlike the girls at her London school, Lexi liked to do the same things as her. They weren't interested in pop stars or boys and didn't give a monkey's about how they looked. As long as they had each other and their ponies, they were happy.

'*Rraaaah!*'

Esme jumped as two hands covered her eyes.

'Lexi!' Esme squealed, spinning round and putting her arms around her friend. 'Oh Lexi, happy Christmas! Isn't the snow *amazing*?'

'I know! But are you OK? Sophia said your car crashed into a ditch and you had to walk all the way to the castle.'

'Yes, it was a terrific adventure, Lexi, and most of it I had to do on my own because Mummy went missing! But Daddy says she's probably powdering her nose now – have you seen her?'

'No, not yet,' said Lexi.

'Oh look!' It was Bella. 'Sausage rolls.'

Bella was born hilarious, wise – and thalidomide. Esme's mother had told her that thalidomide was a pill that some women had taken to stop feeling sick when they were pregnant because the doctors hadn't known it was dangerous or that it would make babies' arms stop growing. Esme was amazed how well Bella managed without arms. She had even stopped noticing sometimes.

'Happy Christmas, Bella,' said Esme. 'Do you want me to get you one?'

'Not one, stupid. Ten – at *least*!'

The girls pushed their way over to Mr Cribben, who was swaying through the room carrying a precariously balanced silver try laden with the shortcrust pastry parcels. Grabbing a handful, half of which Esme gave to Bella, she and Lexi then retreated under the grand piano so that they could talk properly.

'What did Father Christmas bring you, Lexi?' Esme asked, through a mouthful of crumbly pastry.

'Well, the best present was a stable rug for Jupiter, embroidered with his name! Oh, and I was given a subscription for *Horse and Hound* so we can see where all the pony club events are in the summer.'

'Amazing!' Esme grinned. 'Let's try and get our pictures taken jumping a *huge* hedge when we go hunting. Didn't you say they were sending a photographer up here for the New Year's Eve meet?'

'Yes, definitely. Papa will be attending so at the very least we'll get a photo if we stand next to him. Homer and Jupiter will be famous!'

'Oh and I almost forgot! Lexi, Father Christmas gave me a dandy brush just like yours! Homer will look so handsome in the photos.'

Lexi smiled back at her and said in a deep voice, 'Lady Alexa Culcairn on Jupiter and Miss Esme Munroe on Homer taking their own line at Smythe Thorns.'

'We'll be the talk of the town!' Esme said, gleefully.

Stuffing another sausage roll into her mouth, she peered out from under the piano, half expecting and vaguely hoping to see her mother drying out by the fire. She heard her father's bellowing laugh from across the room. If he didn't seem worried about her mother, then everything must be all right.

Lexi and Esme continued their unspoken mission to finish off all the sausage rolls, sipping their bottles of bitter lemon between bites.

'Did you see Rollo and Sophia under the mistletoe? Maybe they'll fall in love and get married?' said Esme.

'And then we really *will* be proper sisters! Perhaps we can be bridesmaids together. Let's go and draw our dream dresses,' said Lexi. 'I got some new Caran d'Ache in my stocking.'

After riding horses, drawing made-up outfits with Caran d'Ache colouring pencils was Esme's favourite thing in the world to do and she was saving her pocket money for a new tin.

Just then, the other conversations in the room fell away at the sound of the Earl's voice booming out, and Esme looked up, startled.

'What do you mean you left her in the snow? How could you be so bloody irresponsible, Colin?'

'Esme was with her and I assumed she was already here and powdering her nose,' Esme heard her father reply.

'You've already been here for nearly an hour! Diana would never spend that much time on her appearance, so where the hell is she?'

Esme froze. Where *was* her mother? It was her fault, she should have looked harder – until she found her.

'Stop shouting, Henry,' said the Contessa. Then, in a quieter tone, 'Colin, I can't believe you left Diana like that, especially with her being the way she is right now.'

'It's not as though she hasn't been here before!' said her

father. 'And like I said, Esme was with her. Sophia and I were only just ahead. Never crossed my mind that she might get lost and I don't suppose she is now.'

'No, Colin,' replied Henry, his voice hard. 'She might have frozen to death out there. I will go and search for her myself.'

'Oh Henry,' said the Contessa. 'Don't be so utterly ridiculous. We have all these guests here. Just send Miller.'

Esme crawled out from her hiding place and rushed to her father's side. She wished Sophia was with her but she was probably somewhere with Rollo and his friends, smoking or doing whatever it was they did in her smoochy novels.

'Daddy! We should go and find her. It's all my fault. I lost her like the shoe.' She looked up at her father, holding her breath and tears.

'Esme, you lovely girl,' said the Earl. 'Why don't you and I go and find your mother together? Colin, Lucia, you stay here and *enjoy* yourselves.'

And without giving anyone a chance to say anything more, the Earl took Esme by the hand and walked out of the drawing room, leaving her father, the Contessa and many of the other guests open-mouthed.

Chapter Three

Mr Miller, the chauffeur, was waiting at the bottom of the front stairs, with a basket in hand.

'Your Lordship; tea and flapjacks. The car is just outside.'

'Thank you, Miller. No need to drive us, I will manage perfectly well. Esme, put your coat and boots on. What fun – a Christmas adventure!'

But Esme noticed that his jolly tone was not reflected in his eyes. They were darting about nervously and he looked worried, even though he was trying to cover it up. Grown-ups often didn't tell the truth when they were worried. Was it about her mother? Or was he still cross with her father for not seeming to care?

The castle door flew open on turning the brass handle. Snow whipped inside, a frozen rage slicing through the oil-fired warmth. The blizzard had intensified. Esme pictured her mother curled up in a ball, like a frightened rabbit. At least she was wearing a fur coat. That's how Eskimos kept warm and it was even colder in Greenland. But was mink as warm as sealskin? What if she had fallen asleep? Would she hear them calling?

Mr Miller wrenched the Land Rover door open and as Esme climbed in the wind slammed it shut, almost catching her leg.

'Where shall we start looking? I mean, Mummy could be anywhere. She might be buried under a snow drift.'

'Don't worry, Esme,' said the Earl. 'I think I know where she might be. She doesn't like big parties, so I think she will have gone somewhere she can relax. She just forgot to tell you.'

Of course! He was right. Her mother could be terribly forgetful, especially on bad days.

The Earl wound down the window and yelled over the rumbling diesel engine, 'Miller, will you call the yard and tell Jimmy we're on our way?'

'Yes, Your Grace.'

'Oh, and tell Mr Munroe that I will drop Mrs Munroe and Esme off at The Lodge. If you don't mind, you will have to take him home in the Range Rover.'

'Is that where you think she is?' asked Esme, at once relieved and puzzled.

'Yes, I know it. Isn't that where you escape to when you're sad or just want to get away?'

'Yes, I do,' said Esme, wondering how the Earl would know. 'I go and talk to Homer if I'm unhappy or scared. Do you think Mummy is scared?'

'Your mother's mind works in mysterious ways, Esme. She probably thought it was quicker to go to the yard than face the steep drive up to the castle.'

Winding the window back up, the Earl suggested Esme pour them both a cup of tea from the flask in the basket. Esme felt grown up, sharing the responsibility of being part of a search party for her mother.

'So what was the best thing Father Christmas brought you this year?' he asked.

'Oh gosh, I loved all my presents but if I had to choose the most exciting it was probably the towel that he used to dry his reindeer. It was still wet!' She laughed.

'Goodness. How fascinating. That just goes to prove that Father Christmas is alive and kicking.'

She was surprised by how comfortable she felt being alone with the Earl. She wasn't at all shy with him like she sometimes was with grown-ups. She pulled the flask from the wicker basket and unscrewed the lid, releasing a hiss as the compressed heat escaped from its container. A steaming muddy waterfall flowed into the mugs, each decorated with the Culcairn foxhounds. As they drove, the beam from the headlamps cut a slice of amber through the speckled grey twilight. The snow was falling so thick and fast it was almost impossible to differentiate individual flakes.

'Goodness,' said the Earl, 'I bet you haven't ever seen snow like this before, Esme. I haven't seen it this thick since I was a boy. I remember taking that sleigh – you know, the one on show in the main entrance – for a turn down the drive. My brothers and I used it as a toboggan. We got into so much trouble! Not only for touching a piece of history – Queen Victoria once sped around Scotland in it, you know – but also because it was so heavy it broke Robert's leg when he fell off head-first.'

Esme could picture them, wild and laughing, using all their boyish strength to pull the thing out from the arch of the great stone hall, its runners scraping over the flagstones.

She knew exactly which sleigh he meant. It now sat unused and roped off from tourists tempted to hop in.

'Good Lord, there's your car Esme. How on earth could your father have ended up in the ditch like that?'

'It just sort of happened.'

A warm chuckle escaped the Earl's throat as he looked at the abandoned car in the snowy trench. It was almost unrecognizable, so deep was the snow covering its roof and clinging to its windows, bolsters of white like sagging bags under tired eyes.

As they passed The Lodge, Esme saw a faint glow of light from the kitchen window. She could just make out Mrs Bee at the sink and waved, in case the housekeeper could see them.

'Who are you waving to? Mrs Bumble?'

'Yes. I feel sorry for her having to work on Christmas Day.'

'But I'm sure she does it gladly to help your mother.'

'Yes. She loves Mummy so much. Says she's the kindest lady in the world.'

'I'd agree with that, Esme. Does your mother ever do the cooking?'

'In our London house she does. But sometimes she burns things as she forgets to take food out of the oven. Once she left a cottage pie in for a whole night! Daddy said it looked like dog poo.' Esme felt immediately guilty for telling tales about her mother. 'But most of the time she makes us lovely food.'

The village appeared before them, unfamiliar with all the houses thatched in snow. As they passed the cottages Esme imagined the families inside; happy, cozied up together, Christmas lights twinkling and brightly wrapped presents nesting under baubled firs. That should have been her family. Instead, here she was with her best friend's father, scouring the countryside for her mother.

Driving past the village shop she caught a flash of red; mistletoe hanging by a noose of tartan ribbon above the door. A chill gripped her. What if her mother wasn't at the yard? She might not have made it that far. Again, Esme imagined her stuck in a hole, stiff with cold like the frozen carcasses Digger sometimes found.

Leaving the village behind, the Land Rover started to climb the steep incline. She wondered how they were going to make it up the hill. It was very cold now. She daren't speak as she could see how hard the Earl was concentrating to keep the car on the road. She studied his profile. She had always liked his face. Greying hair that was swept back off a high forehead, strong nose and thin lips. His eyes had unusual flecks of yellow and orange but if asked what colour they were she'd say green. She noticed that his eyebrows were lower than usual, set in a frown – not cross but more concerned, unlike his jaunty tone of voice.

'Now, Esme, here comes the tricky part.'

'Will we get up the hill, do you think?'

'My dear, of course we will. This old thing can get anywhere. It's a marvellous lump of metal. Come on, why don't you sit on my knee and help me drive? Don't think I don't know about your and Lexi's little escapades in the Triumph.'

Esme felt her face flush at being caught out for driving the little green car around the estate. She waited for the reprimand, but it didn't come.

'Come, sit on my knee. This bit of road is really wiggly, and four hands will be better than two.'

Hesitating, she shuffled across the bench seat and onto his lap. He felt warm and safe, as did the steering wheel when she placed her hands on the black plastic, next to his. Her father never even let her sit in the front of the car, let alone on his knee to help drive. She had once got on his lap but he had told her to get off. 'You're not a dog, Esme.'

'All right: lean forward, the car needs all the help it can get. Come on, old friend, you can do it. *Push!*'

He eased his foot down on the accelerator and they lurched forward, wheels spinning as the engine roared, heaving the car forward. With ox-like strength and almost human willpower, they made it over the brow of the hill and shot forward along the now-level road.

'Well done, Esme! I couldn't have done that without you.'

Flushed with pride, she couldn't wait to tell her father and Sophia how she had helped rescue their mother.

'Now, you'd better hop back, what with being on a public road. It wouldn't do for us to get stopped by the police. We'd all miss Christmas lunch and I'd be terrified to be on the end of Mrs Bee's wrath if her turkey went to waste.'

As they drove into the stable yard an avenue of noble horses peered out at them with a lazy interest. Jimmy's livery was home to sixteen hunters and it always made Esme feel proud of him that four of them belonged to the Prince of Wales. Many people wondered why a Prince chose Jimmy's place to keep his horses when he stayed at the nearby Balmoral, especially when it was so messy and chaotic. But Esme knew as well as the Prince that Jimmy was the best rough rider in the Highlands and when the horses were presented at the meet, their owners knew their horses' coats would be gleaming and that they would gallop like machines because they had been ridden out every day of the week and schooled over natural fences. You couldn't put a price on safety when hunting, and a bit of muck here and there was far better than a broken neck.

Esme crossed her fingers and prayed that her mother was there. As they entered the main house, she could hear wild laughter coming from inside and one of the voices definitely belonged to a woman.

Climbing over various dogs and high-top boots dull with unbuffed polish, the smell of wet fur and drying leather filled the small kitchen. She and the Earl walked into the living room to find Jimmy and Diana doubled up with mirth and holding tumblers – the ones Jimmy collected with his Green Shield Stamps from the petrol station. Esme was so relieved she felt like crying.

'Oh darling, you're here,' said her mother, looking at the Earl, and for a moment Esme felt confused. She had expected to see her mother as she had been when they were separated; slow, confused and unsure.

'I knew it wouldn't take long for you to find me. Henry, you are far too clever. Will I never be able to hide from you?'

'This is not a joke, Diana. Your daughter was extremely worried,' said the Earl.

'Esme, sweetheart,' said her mother, 'you know me: free as

a bird and with a will of my own. I tell you, Henry, I could bloody kill my husband for leaving me alone in this weather. But then again, if he hadn't I would have had to endure drinks with all your ghastly friends. Instead, Jimmy has been filling me in on all the gossip. Poor Mrs Polk was left for dead out hunting yesterday. Knocked clean out after a fall. When she came round she thought she was at a cocktail party and started offering the whips drinks. It's too funny. Imagine: "Tim, would you like red or white?" while she's covered in mud and blood pours from her nose. She'll be mortified, should she remember. She does so love the *importance* of her position as chief gate-shutter, poor love.'

It was a long time since Esme had heard her mother utter so many words at once.

'Diana, I… *We* were worried. Esme and I have come to take you home.'

'Yes, Mummy. I thought you were lost,' said Esme, finding her voice.

'Sweetie, I'm fine. And angel, you are adorable to come and rescue me. You care, I know you do, darling, and I'm sorry if I worried you. But look, everything has worked out perfectly. Come here and give me a kiss.'

'You didn't *seem* fine, Mummy, and if you were then why did you leave me on my own? Why didn't you tell me you'd changed your mind and were coming here?' All of a sudden Esme felt overcome with sadness, as if her mother really didn't care about her at all.

'Well, I didn't think I was and when I lost you I got confused and went back to the church. And there, would you believe it, was darling Jimmy.'

Esme looked at Jimmy for an explanation.

'That's right. I left my wallet and had to go back to fetch it,' he said.

'That's not strictly true. Jimmy put five pounds in the collection box by mistake so he returned to take it back. Isn't that right, Jimmy?'

'Well, yes, but I replaced it with one pound. I'm not that much of a tight-arse.'

'So there we go. Come, Esme, come and sit next to me. Am I forgiven?' She looked at the Earl as she said this.

Reluctantly, yet unable to resist, Esme went over to the sofa where her mother enfolded her in her arms.

She kissed her and whispered, 'Darling Esme, my darling, darling little squirrel.'

'Oh, Your Lordship,' said Jimmy, as the Earl let out a big sigh. 'Just sit down and have a drink. It's Christmas for goodness's sake. Come on Esme, what would you like? There's some ginger beer in the fridge or make something yourself with the soda siphon.' Jimmy's accent was as thick as the smell of alcohol in the room.

The Earl accepted a glass filled with a golden liquid that shone through the crystal.

'Happy Christmas, to us all. So nice to have the family together,' Jimmy said, roaring with laughter.

Esme left the room to fetch her drink. Jimmy's kitchen was as familiar to her as her own. She had been going to the farm since she was four, when she first started hunting. Jimmy had taught her to ride and took her and her fat Shetland pony on the lead rein until she was confident enough to ride to hounds on her own. In those days her mother would drive her to the meet and follow the hunt, forever concerned that she might have an accident. Jimmy had no such qualms. As far as he was concerned Esme was made of rubber and would bounce if she took a fall.

She wondered now how her mother could go from being so quiet and sad to being so cheerful. Her moods could change unbelievably quickly; in church, Esme had been scared she was going to faint. But anyway, at least she was happy now. She was always happy with Jimmy.

Esme poured herself a pint glass of fizz, grabbed an apple from the chipped fruit bowl and, after grabbing her coat, went outside into the yard, causing a sleeping lercher to yelp as she accidentally stepped on its paw.

'Sorry, Mumfie. Didn't see you there.'

From the stables, there came a collective whinny from horses always on the lookout for their next feed. A whiskery nose poked up, just visible above its door. It was Homer, standing on tiptoes to make himself noticed, Esme thought. He was pleased to see her. Suddenly she felt as if a balloon had been let out in her chest.

Was Homer the only one in her family who was pleased to be with her? Even on Christmas Day it seemed her mother would rather be with Jimmy. Her father had been happy for her to go alone to find her mother and she hadn't even *seen* Sophia at the castle. At least Lexi and the Earl had been kind to her.

'Hello, fella. Happy Christmas. Did you miss me? Have you had a nice day? Did Jimmy give you extra oats? You good boy. You know that Father Christmas bought you some lovely things. A curry comb and a dandy brush to make your mane all silky. And you won't have to have a cold saddle next to your skin now 'cause you have a brand new sheepskin saddle pad. Imagine that? Here's a fella; a lovely juicy apple for you.'

The pony took the apple from Esme's hand in one giant bite. He rolled it around his mouth in an attempt to gain a good grip so he could crunch through the slippery skin. It popped back out. Esme nuzzled his nose with hers, his warm, sweet-smelling breath thawing the red spots of cold on her cheeks. Stiff whiskers, newly clipped and spiky, prickled her skin. His pretty honey-brown muzzle shone gold against his copper coat.

'Too big for you, huh?' she said. 'Here, let me take a bite for you to make it easier.' Esme put the slimy apple to her lips and took as large a bite as she could. Juice spurted out as her teeth pierced the taut skin.

'There you go, boy. That's better, isn't it? Who's my darling boy?'

Homer had disgusting manners, she thought. He ate with his mouth open, turning the apple sap to foam as he chomped away, making loud sucking, squelching sounds and bubbles. Round and round went his jaw in methodical turns to reduce the flesh to pulp.

'Good boy. I'll come back and say goodbye.' Esme patted her pony and walked away.

Back in the farmhouse it seemed a party had kicked off. The Earl had joined in the merriment and was sitting on the sofa with Esme's mother nestled in the crook of his arm, shoeless feet curled up underneath her. Jimmy sat on his 'throne' with Mumfie on his lap. His face was red and his eyes were creased with joy.

Esme went to sit on the footstool by the coal fire. Too big to be a lap dog, the lercher jumped down and lay beside her, his head and half his body on her knees.

She looked at the scene before her. Every time her mother turned to the Earl her eyes seemed to come alive. It was almost shocking in contrast to the detached, milky gaze reserved for her father.

'Oh, and I'll tell you another thing, Your Lordship,' Jimmy was saying, 'the next time you come to the meet, don't go fannying around on your feet. It's about time you got on a bloody horse. I tell you, if the Prince of bleeding Wales can stay on, you can too. Stop being such a prissy little girl and get your arse in the saddle.'

'Jimmy, you're a nightmare; my hunting days are over. Diana, tell him to stop bullying me,' said the Earl, smiling. He flicked his wrist from his sleeve and looked at his watch. 'Goodness, it's nearly two o'clock. We'd better be off.'

'C'mon, Your Lordship. Don't go yet. One more for the road.'

'No, Jimmy, you are very kind but I must get Mrs Munroe and Esme back home. We're already very late.'

'Oh, Henry, just one more, then we'll go. Come on, how often do we get time like this? Esme, darling, be a love and call home. Tell Mrs Bee we are on our way.'

Esme was torn between the prospect of lunch and presents and the fun of this little group. She felt like one of the grown-ups now, especially as Sophia wasn't there to enjoy their secret party, and it was a relief to see her mother full of life and humour again so she went out to the hall to the phone, its disc whirring after her small finger dialled each number.

'Mrs Bee? It's me, Esme. We're leaving now. I'm with Mummy. Lexi's father is going to drive us home.'

'Esme! Is your mother all right? Where did you find her?'

'It's a long story, Mrs Bee. I've had a real-life adventure.'

'Adventure or not, lunch is going to be ruined! Your father and Sophia are already back; Mr Miller dropped them off an hour ago. They'll be relieved to hear you've found your mother. Will she be needing a hot bath?'

'No thank you, Mrs Bee. She seems very warm,' said Esme. 'We've been having such fun. Oh, and I told Homer about his presents – he whinnied with happiness.'

'He was probably telling you that you're late for lunch!'

'Don't worry, we'll be back soon. Tell Daddy. Bye, Mrs Bee,' she said, before hanging up.

Esme put on her coat again and ran outside. Jimmy and the Earl were already helping her mother into the Land Rover. She was singing 'Roll Me Over in the Clover' far too loudly, Esme thought.

Jumping into her seat, she turned and waved goodbye to Jimmy as the Earl drove out of the stable yard.

'Mummy, are you drunk?' she asked.

'Oh darling, I'm not drunk. I'm just happy it's Christmas. Darling Henry, I do love you so.'

Maybe she *was* a bit tipsy but Esme knew something else was not right. Her mother had been so sad this morning and was now very, very happy. When she had two moods so close together it was only a matter of time before she sank into a deep sleep, a lifeless stranger unable to recognize her own children. It was always the same. Esme's excitement about Christmas lunch and presents around the tree evaporated; her mother was about to ruin it all.

❄

Arriving at The Lodge, Esme and the Earl helped Diana to the front door, where Mrs Bee was waiting to let them in.

'Mrs Bee, I'm sorry we're late. Such a relief that Diana has been found safe and well. Now you can all enjoy your delicious lunch...' The Earl's apology stopped mid-flow as he took in the sight of Colin, veins on the sides of his neck pulsating; he was clearly struggling to control his rage.

'Henry, what in God's name happened? I've been worried sick, and with good reason. Look at her!'

Esme took in the sight of her mother and all at once wanted to protect her and the Earl from her father's anger. She stood next to her and put her hand in hers.

'If you hadn't left us, Daddy, Mummy would have been OK. And if Lexi's papa hadn't gone to look for her we might not have found her,' Esme said.

'Yes. Yes, of course. I am grateful to you, Henry,' said Esme's father, guiding the Earl towards the door. 'Diana... She's not faring too well at the moment so I think it's best you stay away from her. For the time being...'

'Whatever is best for her,' said the Earl.

'Now, Mr and Mrs Munroe,' said Mrs Bee, stepping in. 'I suggest you go to the drawing room with a glass of champagne and wait for me and the girls to bring the food.'

This simple order and the housekeeper's calm delivery put everything back to normality. It was Christmas. They would have lunch and open their presents. The day would continue as it had always done. Or at least that's what Esme hoped, given that she never really knew from one moment to the next what mood her mother would be in and how the next few hours would play out.

The sisters sat around the kitchen table while Mrs Bee busied herself making the final preparations to the meal. The whirring sound of the cooker turned into that of a Force 5 gale when the oven door was opened to remove the picture-perfect turkey.

'Och, that weighs the same as an eighteen-month-old baby!' exclaimed Mrs Bee, grunting as she heaved the bird from the roasting tin onto a large white Wedgewood platter on the table.

'Why was Daddy so horrible to the Earl?' asked Esme, still preoccupied with the adults' terse exchange. 'At least he tried to find Mummy. Poor thing; she could have died and been buried in the snow and we wouldn't have found her 'til the spring. It's only because of Jimmy that she isn't a human icicle.'

Sophia peeled a strip of crisp skin off the plump turkey before her and curled it around her extended tongue. 'Mmm...' She licked her fingers. 'You always try to protect Mummy, Es. She wanted to go to Jimmy's instead of the castle. She wanted the Earl to rescue her. And now she's made us all late for lunch and Daddy is pissed off. End of story.'

It was true. Esme *did* always defend her mother, and her mother, when she wasn't sad or asleep, did the same for her.

'Come on, girls, help me get the lunch in. Esme, will you get the bread sauce and the sprouts?'

Out they trooped, all pomp-and-ceremony, Esme leading the way into the dining room, where her father had already taken his position at the head of the table. He stood up and relieved Mrs Bee of her fowl, now garnished with glossy sausages and rolled bacon rashers. Esme was relieved to see her father smiling.

'This looks wonderful, Mrs Bee. You are a marvel. Shall I sharpen the knife?'

With that, he took up his weapons, the sharpener in one hand and the long thin carving knife in the other. Using theatrical sweeps he ran the blade back and forth against the file before replacing the sharpener with the fork, with which he stabbed the turkey while allowing his foil to glide through the plump breast on the other side. Thin slices of meat fanned out symmetrically as they fell away from the bird, each piece of moist white flesh edged with a half-moon of brown skin. Little puffs of steam rose up, filling the dining room with a smell exclusive to Christmas Day.

Esme was starving. She piled her plate high and poured over so much gravy that it slopped onto the table.

'Oi, Esme!' shouted Sophia. 'Don't take all the gravy – it's not soup.' She snatched the sauce boat from her sister and tipped the rest onto her own plate.

'You've finished it now, Sophs. What about Mummy and Daddy?'

'There's more on the side, stupid.'

'Then don't get cross with me for taking it all!' Then, in a fit of defiance, Esme picked up her plate and tilted it towards her, slurping up some of the thick meat juice. 'There,' she said. 'It won't spill now.' She looked over to her mother, who had returned to her breakfast self.

'Esme! Manners, please,' said Mrs Bee. 'Now eat up.'

Christmas Day was the one and only day that the house-keeper ate with the family and she did so reluctantly. Esme thought it was because she felt embarrassed by not having any smart clothes to wear apart from the cardigans her parents gave her every year.

'Quite right, Mrs Bumble. Especially as you've been up since the crack of dawn preparing it. Would you like a small glass of champagne?'

'Well, maybe just a wee one.' She held up a crystal port glass for Esme's father to fill. It only took one sip for her face to take on a deep, purple blotchiness.

Esme raised her glass. 'Merry Christmas, everyone.'

'Merry Christmas!' chimed her father, Mrs Bee and Sophia.

'This is delicious, Mrs Bee,' said Sophia, scooping up a forkful of peas. 'Mummy, aren't you going to eat your food? Mrs Bee has spent hours cooking it.'

This was a deliberate dig. Sophia knew full well that their mother hardly ate a thing when her mind went elsewhere. At least she would never starve because she made up for it on her good days. Esme had never seen one person able to eat so much at a single sitting. Mrs Bee sometimes had to cook her extra food.

When everyone had finished, Mrs Bee got up and cleared the plates, scraping the leftovers on top of the pile.

'Digger can have these,' she said, putting the plate of scraps onto the floor.

Esme called for her dog, who scurried into the dining room and wolfed the lot down in time for Mrs Bee to pick up the clean plate and take it with the others into the kitchen.

Moments later, she returned with a platter of fire: the Christmas pudding made in November for maximum flavour. Esme had stirred the batter and made a wish. The flames died down as the alcohol burned away, leaving behind a mound of glistening sweetmeat.

Helping herself to the first slice, Esme picked out a tiny parcel of tin foil from her pudding and unwrapped it. 'A shilling!' she squealed, holding up the hot coin.

'Well done, darling,' said her father.

'Look, Mummy!' Esme's shoulders sank as her mother remained silent, not even looking up at the coin.

'How wonderful!' said Mrs Bee.

Esme felt silly for expecting her mother to react to her lucky shilling. She licked the coin clean, popped it into her pocket and shook off her disappointment.

'Daddy, we haven't pulled the crackers!' she exclaimed, rising from her seat in anticipation.

'Goodness, so we haven't. Sit back down and we'll do it now.'

'We can't watch Her Majesty without our paper crowns on,' she said, smiling.

The small group crossed arms, a cracker in each hand to form a chain, and pulled. Her mother's hand in hers held no resistance, so Esme leant across and she and Sophia pulled each other's.

Sophia groaned and then read out her joke. 'Why did the lobster blush?'

'Because it saw *The Queen Mary's* bottom. That's so old,' groaned Esme, copying her sister, although she actually thought that the picture of Queen Mary in her frilly underpants was very funny.

They all put on their paper crowns, Esme carefully placing one on her mother's head. It sat lopsided and made her look like a forgotten toy.

'All right, plates down. Time for presents!' announced Esme's father, as they finished their puddings.

Normally, presents were opened before the Queen's Speech, but the Queen had given a written address instead this year, following a documentary that had aired about the Royal Family a few months previously. Esme was disappointed that they didn't get to see Her Majesty, although she supposed she always looked the same. An embroidered dress and pearls, a stiff hairstyle and a small smile. Without the Queen, the world would stop turning, Esme thought. She wondered why she never wore her crown in public. If she were the Queen, she'd make sure she put it on every day. Her father always said that Queen Elizabeth was a handsome woman but not nearly as attractive as her sister, Princess Margaret. Maybe people said the same thing about her and Sophia, but Esme didn't think that either of them was particularly *handsome*. That was for boys. Lexi had mentioned that the Princess was coming to stay at Culcairn Castle in a few days' time, so she could decide who was the more attractive sister then.

Mrs Bee ushered everyone into the drawing room, where Esme dropped down next to the gigantic Christmas tree. Every year, her father would go about the dressing of the tree in the same meticulous fashion, while she and Sophia passed him the decorations. First the lights, which were small and white, had to be wound from the top down, ensuring that each layer of branches was equally illuminated. Then came the tinsel; finely woven pieces of silver had to camouflage every inch of the ugly white wire to which the lights were attached. Once this had been achieved – which took a good two hours to ensure perfection – glass baubles collected from all corners of the globe or handed down to them from past generations were hung equidistant from each other in order of size and colour. Holding the tree steady was the sand–filled bucket in which it stood, which was wrapped in golden paper that splayed out around the base in a skirt. An assortment of mismatched gifts lay in the pool of shimmering paper. There was nothing haphazard about the Munroes' Christmas tree; it had to be visually faultless and decorated in the best possible taste.

Esme's father was very artistic and loved to paint. Many of his paintings adorned the walls of The Lodge and their house in London. Esme thought that if he spent all his time painting rather than organizing the transport of important paintings all around the world he would be much happier.

He loved to talk about art and knew so much about it. Esme loved to sit alongside him whilst he painted, drawing her own pictures and listening to him recounting tales of great artists.

As her father began to hand out the presents, Esme felt a familiar embarrassment that they had so much and Mrs Bee had so little. Even though Mrs Bee frequently told her 'I'm short of nothing but money'. Quickly, she handed a present to the housekeeper, which Mrs Bee duly unwrapped.

'Oh, thank you, Mrs M,' said Mrs Bee, delighted with her cardigan. She looked over to Esme's mother, who was sitting listlessly in a high-backed embroidered chair. 'Why don't you hold the bag for the wrapping paper?' she asked her.

Seeing that Mrs Bee was trying to engage her mother, Esme picked up the bag and held it out. 'Mummy, hold the bag open so we can get the paper in easily.'

Diana picked up the other handle in slow motion.

'Come on, wakey-wakey – it's not bedtime yet,' said Sophia, giving her mother a prod.

She stirred and looked over at Esme. 'Darling, you'd better get a pen and paper so you can jot down who's given you what – for your thank-you letters.'

Esme hopped up and ran to the desk, flipping its lid back in search of a sheet of writing paper and a biro. Plonking herself back down she waited to be passed her first present.

Darling Esme, Happy Christmas, lots of love Aunt Nancy, read the label.

Aunt Nancy was the youngest of her mother's three sisters. Her father was also from a big family, with three brothers and one sister. Because there were so many of them and none had a house large enough to accommodate the whole family at once, they would try to meet up elsewhere in the summer holidays instead. Esme loved spending time with all her cousins. But that didn't happen very often. Both sets of grandparents had passed away before Esme was born. She envied Lexi and her extended family, who all lived nearby.

Aunt Nancy always gave good presents and this year was no exception; she had given Esme *The Mandy Annual. Mandy* was Esme's favourite comic, the one she spent her pocket money on each week.

'Sophia, look – this one's from your godfather, Bill,' said Mrs Bee, handing her a beautifully wrapped parcel.

Esme knew it would be something elegant and perfectly chosen. Her father's oldest friend from his school days at Eton was seriously rich and very generous because he had no children of his own.

Sophia squealed as she unwrapped an Afghan coat from its tissue. It was a thing of real beauty. Embroidered down the front, a bit like Esme's Red Indian jacket, it had shaggy sheepskin cuffs and frog fastenings that gave it a Russian flare. Sophia hugged it and spun around the room, using the coat as her flamboyant dancing partner. Her face was alight with joy as she grinned and twirled around and around.

'Oh Es, look at this! Isn't it the most divinely wondrous thing you've ever seen? Feast your eyes! Darling Bill is the *best*! Daddy, are you furious? I know you think that only drug-taking hippies wear this sort of thing but I love it; you'll have to blame your best friend for being so utterly, utterly adorable! He is the best and kindest fairy godfather in the world!'

Her father laughed. 'You'll get arrested wearing that around here. You might as well go and live on a commune and hug trees. I need to have words with Mr Bill Cartwright. He is incorrigible. Don't wear it anywhere near me. People will think I have a commie as a daughter.'

'Oh Daddy, you're so square. I shall wear it day and night.'

'You'll soon tire of it. But you'll never get bored of *our* present to you.' With that, Colin handed her a large, heavy-looking square package. Sophia ripped off the paper.

'Oh Daddy, I can't believe it!'

It was a red record player with a lid that doubled up as a speaker. Esme knew her sister had wanted one of these forever, collecting all kinds of music for the time she could play the records on her own turntable. Esme hoped that her present from her parents would be just as exciting. Perhaps, just perhaps, it would be a velvet hunting cap from Patey's. Her mother had pointed out the rip in her old hat so knew she needed one. Esme was old enough now to wear one without a chinstrap. Knowing it was her turn next she sat expectantly, her tummy fluttering with excitement.

Her father rummaged through the dwindling pile of gifts.

'Diana, where is Esme's present?'

'It should be there. Is it not?'

'You said you wrapped it last night. Darling, Mummy bought your present. Diana, go and see if it's upstairs.'

Dropping the bulging Harrods bag, Diana rose slowly and left the room.

'Darling, Mummy will find it – don't look so worried. She told me she had bought you something wonderful.' Colin glanced up at Mrs Bee.

'Open this one from me,' said the housekeeper, hurriedly, to Esme.

'Thank you, Mrs Bee.' She looked down to hide the hot tears that welled in her eyes and started to fall on to the parcel with a tell-tale splash as she tore open the wrapping paper.

'Mrs Bee, these are just what I need. Thank you so much! They're even better than the ones I lost and will keep my hands cozy out hunting. Thank you.'

She got up and hugged Mrs Bee as though her life depended on it. The housekeeper hugged her back, Esme's tears concealed in the crook of her neck.

'Here we go, darling, here's your mother,' she said.

Esme peered over Mrs Bee's shoulder to see her mother standing in the doorway, empty-handed and dry-eyed.

Chapter Four

Esme wrenched herself from Mrs Bee's embrace, barged past her mother and shouted for Digger. She pulled on her wellies, grabbed her coat and ran into the cold twilight, ignoring her father's appeal for her to come back. This was turning out to be the worst Christmas ever and she needed to get away, to be in her secret place. Hot tears froze against her skin as she tried to catch her breath.

It wasn't even the present. Her mother had *forgotten* her. Why hadn't her father taken charge like he had with Sophia? It wasn't that Sophia was her parents' favourite because they usually treated them both equally and she was pleased that her sister had got the present she wanted. She also knew she was luckier than lots of other children, but it made her feel small, invisible even, that they had forgotten to buy *her* a present.

As Esme walked through the orchard the moon cast enough light for her to see her way into the thick woods surrounding The Lodge. She felt safe and her tears subsided. The trees were her allies, keeping her hidey-hole secret from her family. Lexi and Sophia knew where it was and Esme wished her sister were here with her now. Only *she* would really understand how sad Esme was feeling.

She strode across the hardening snow, Digger bounding

alongside her, her boots and his paws leaving barely a trace. Despite the ghostly white covering that changed the wood into a foreign landscape, she had no trouble finding the entrance to her place of escape. Hidden behind a thicket of ancient brambles and rampant foliage, she pushed her way through and opened the crudely made door.

The old Victorian summer house had lain derelict when Esme chanced upon it one day when searching for Digger, who had gone missing on a wild rabbit chase. She called the summer house her 'secret place'. It was her home from home, somewhere she could escape to when she was upset. Here, she was in charge and could do and feel as she liked.

She lit a candle that had been stuck onto an old saucer and was lying on the windowsill with a box of matches.

The room was filled with a tidy collection of bric-a-brac. Over the years Esme had siphoned off unwanted bits of furniture from The Lodge barn. There was a chair, a little table, a couple of rugs, a rusty portable barbeque, firelighters, matches, an old saucepan and a row of tins filled with teabags, sugar and digestive biscuits. The walls were festooned with cobwebs. In one corner there was an upturned crate draped with a fading chintz cushion cover. Carefully laid out on top of this makeshift counter sat a selection of Esme's possessions. Sliding the chair across the floor, Esme sat before the crate and picked up a lace handkerchief with the initials *D. L.* embroidered in one corner. She wiped her eyes, her tears joining the stains of her mother's from long ago, marking the linen with crinkly little circles. There was no point in crying; it wouldn't change anything. Her mother had really done it this time. Esme had forgiven her too often and to have forgotten her at Christmas was unforgivable. She would save up her pocket money and buy a new riding hat herself. Maybe she could take some money from her mother's purse? It wouldn't be like stealing because she should have spent the money already on her hat.

Feeling better knowing that she could be clever and brave enough to do things on her own, she straightened the lopsided candle that was spilling wax onto her table. She cast her eyes over her things and picked up an almost-empty perfume bottle, pulled out the stopper and inhaled the fading scent. Like the rest of the ornaments in the summer house, it captured the essence of her mother; this smell was exclusively hers.

It was funny how all her fears and worries disappeared as soon as she entered her little house. Here she could make up whatever she wanted and everything could be just perfect. A sense of ease washed over her as she started building a fire in the barbeque, to the excitement of Digger, sitting alongside her. Paper, firelighter, coal and kindling laid in that order, just as Mrs Bee had taught her. Once lit, Esme wrapped herself in one of the rugs and settled down on the beanbag she had nicked from the playroom.

'Digger, come on, up you come.'

The dog hopped up onto her knee and licked the salty droplets off her face, tucked his nose in the crook of her elbow and let out a big sigh. The potted fire flicked friendly shadows around the room. Esme looked up at the photo of her mother that she had taken from the house. It was beautiful; a society portrait taken before Esme was born. Legend had it that a very famous man who made films had 'noticed' her mother. He wanted her to star in his new feature about a lady who had saved children from an orphanage run by a wicked man who made them dig for diamonds and emeralds in a dangerous mine. *This* was the mother Esme held in her mind's eye, the one she could remember from when she was younger. The mother who made her feel secure, told her not to be afraid. The one she could confide in with all her fears and secrets. This was the mother she spoke to, the one she longed for her to be now.

Esme knew her mother loved her but it was complicated. She thought about the time recently when she'd made Esme dare her to go to the shops with a bra over her blouse. But Esme had noticed that often after doing such wild things her mother crashed down again, becoming even more unhappy. Her mother took pills every day and Sophia had told her that she'd overheard Mrs Bee tell Mr Quince, the gardener, that these were to help 'make her demons quieter'.

But here, in her secret place, her mother could be anything Esme wanted her to be. She picked up an imaginary hat from the side and turned it around.

'Oh, Mummy,' she said, 'this is the hat I've dreamed of having. How did you get the right measurements for my head? I always thought that you had to actually *go* there to be measured up in person. Just feel how soft the velvet is. Oh and look, they have even sewn up the tails of ribbon at the back. I've always done that myself, but those hadn't been made *especially* for me! Oh, silly me! You took my old riding hat and gave it to Mr Patey to get the right size, didn't you? I thought so. How clever you are – and I didn't even notice it missing. I really, really love it and I will look after it so well. I promise. After hunting I'll scrape the mud off then steam the velvet over the kettle and brush it 'til it gleams. Oh thank you, thank you so *so* much, Mummy!'

Her mother smiled with her eyes as she looked down from her picture, propped up against the wall.

'So, Digger, now that I have my hat,' said Esme, 'let's make a nice cup of tea.'

Stepping outside into the cold, she packed the little saucepan with snow, her pink hands turning white. She placed the saucepan over the barbeque so the snow would melt. It took three goes of packing and melting to get enough water for a decent cup of tea.

'Mummy?' she asked the photograph. 'What are you going to wear for New Year's Eve? I think you look prettiest in your dress with the big pink flowers and wide sleeves. I love that dress so much. You look like you're floating like a butterfly in it and you can wear the brooch that Daddy gave you, too. I haven't decided yet but if you wear that I will wear pink as well and we can be like twins! New Year's Eve is so much fun.'

The water was bubbling away with gusto. Once Esme had made her tea she curled up next to Digger and sang softly to herself. She looked up into the caves of the roof, where shadows moved in the flickering darkness. It was quite snug now. Her body began to relax, succumbing to the warmth.

Awaking with a start, stiff with cold, Esme took a while to remember where she was. As soon as she realized, she leapt up, made sure the fire was out, folded up the rug and, tugging at Digger's collar, dragged him out into the frozen wilderness. She had no idea what time it was but without a backwards glance she ran through the trees, branches snagging at her hair and clothes.

'Oh God, they're going to kill me,' she muttered.

She sped down the hill towards The Lodge, now in almost complete darkness, bar the drawing-room windows, from which light escaped between gaps between the drawn curtains.

She tugged at the front door but it was locked. Running round to the back of the house, she tried the cloakroom door. It too was locked. She unlatched the tall wooden gate that separated the garden from the courtyard, and mounted the two steps to Mrs Bee's own door.

'Mrs Bee, Mrs Bee, it's me!' she whispered desperately, then knocked softly on the door. 'Mrs Bee, it's me – Esme.'

No response. Walking backwards she looked up to see if the housekeeper's light was on. Darkness. Did everyone think she had come home and was tucked up in bed? She ran around to the front of the house again, Digger at her heels. Light glowed through Sophia's curtains. Esme dug into the snow for a handful of earth then threw it at the window. A smattering rattled the glass but her sister didn't appear from behind the curtains.

'Sophia?' Esme could hear the faint melody of 'Let It Bleed'; Sophia must be trying out her Christmas present.

Glancing across to the window of the room where her mother would be sleeping, away from her father, she chucked a handful of pebbles at the glass. Nothing. Suddenly remembering that Mrs Bee always left the sash window in the larder open a fraction, she ran round to the side of the house, Digger dancing and yapping at her heels.

As if she were getting out of a swimming pool, Esme pulled herself up onto the icy ledge, pushed open the window and climbed through. She looked back at Digger and realized there was no way she could pull him up so she slipped quietly into the back hallway to let him in through the door.

There didn't appear to be anyone waiting for her to come back and the only person she was sure must still be awake was her father. Slowly, Esme turned the door handle to the drawing room. She could hear canned laughter coming from the television. Her father was lying on the sofa, a big box of chocolate at his side.

'Daddy?'

He jumped at the sound of her voice. 'Oh, Esme, darling – you gave me a shock. Shouldn't you be in bed? It's a bit late for you to be up. Run along with you. And don't forget to brush your teeth.'

Esme stared at him, appalled. Hadn't anyone even *noticed* that she'd been missing since she'd fled the room in tears? Did he even remember why she had been upset in the first place? Clearly not. She might just as well have slept all night in the summer house! Digger would have kept her warm. Next time she would run away. That would show them. She wanted to jump up and down and scream to get a reaction from her father.

'Um, night then, Daddy,' she said, willing the tears not to spill onto her cheeks.

'Night-night, darling. Sweet dreams.'

She was dismissed. Still dressed in her coat and boots, she turned to leave, wiping her eyes with her sleeve, then asked, 'Where's Mummy?'

'Darling, she went to bed a while ago and said she was going to read. I'm surprised she didn't put you to bed before. Night, angel, see you in the morning.' He gave a small wave and rummaged through the chocolate papers before popping a rose cream into his mouth, followed swiftly by taking a deep pull on his Rothman cigarette.

Esme went up to her mother's room. She put her ear to the door. It was quiet. She turned off the landing light to better see if the light from her reading lamp glowed through the keyhole. It did. She knocked quietly. Nothing stirred. She knocked a little more forcefully then pushed the door open. But her mother was asleep, fully clothed on top of her bed. Tiptoeing over to the bedside table, she put her hand out to see if she could stir her and accidentally knocked over a glass of water. It splashed all over the floor.

'Damn!' she said. 'I'm sorry, Mummy.'

But her mother didn't stir. She looked at her sleeping face, eyes fluttering under closed lids. She was breathing deeply and evenly. A good night's rest was the cure for everything. Tomorrow would be a better day.

Esme knocked on her sister's door.

'Hello?'

'It's me. May I come in?' Esme entered without waiting for an answer. Sophia was sitting on her bed riffling through a box of records.

'What are you doing?' she asked, hoping her sister might have noticed her absence.

'Just putting the albums in alphabetical order.' She looked up at Esme.

'Es, have you been crying? Where have you been? I couldn't find you.'

'I went to my secret place for a bit.'

'I'm not surprised,' said her sister, kindly. 'I can't believe Mummy didn't get you a Christmas present.'

Having her disappointment confirmed and recognized by Sophia made Esme feel even more upset. She started to cry.

Sophia put the box of records on the floor. 'Oh, Es. Poor you. Come here.' She pulled her down to lie next to her. With her arms around her little sister, she stroked her hair. 'Don't worry. I've got some money saved up and I'll buy the hat for you. Do you want to choose a record to play?'

'The Hollies?'

'The Hollies it is. You know Mummy didn't mean it.'

Esme nodded her head, which Sophia gently moved from her shoulder as she slid off the bed.

'Come on, why don't I brush your hair before you go to bed? One hundred strokes, like the maids used to do for their mistresses in the olden days.' Sophia pulled out the small padded stool at her dressing table. 'Come sit, m'lady.'

Esme giggled.

'Blimey, what have you been doing? Climbing through every hedge on the estate backwards?' Tugging at the knots as gently as she could, Sophia brushed her sister's hair into a glossy sheen. 'You have lovely hair, Es. Nice and thick and shiny, just like Homer.'

'But without the straw in it.'

'Well, I don't know about that,' said Sophia, pulling out the remnants of a bramble. 'I swear you were a little woodland creature in your past life.'

Esme thought about this. Maybe in her next life her mother would be normal.

'OK, that's it. You'd better get to bed now otherwise you won't wake up for hunting.'

'Thanks, Sophs,' said Esme, giving her sister an extra-strong hug. 'Sleep well.'

'You too.'

Chapter Five

Awaking from the depths of slumber, Esme slowly opened her eyes and stretched. She let the comfort of sleep keep her in its embrace, sighed contentedly and turned onto her side. But then she saw her hunting clothes in a neat pile, topped by her old riding hat. It was the Boxing Day meet, she remembered excitedly. Refusing to let the absence of her longed-for new hat spoil her day, she kicked her way out of her blankets and yawned loudly.

At eleven o'clock sharp, she and Homer would be trotting up to the castle to join her fellow riders for port and sausages before they set off to find a fox. This was her favourite meet of the year because it was more for show than purpose – like a pantomime. Everyone would decorate their bridles with Christmas ribbon so their mounts looked extra smart to impress the large crowd that would come to watch from surrounding towns and villages. It was the first time she was going to a meet in the snow because if it hadn't been Boxing Day it would have been called off and they would have just followed the hounds on foot.

Wearing her hunting kit made Esme feel grown up and proud. She had devised a set way of dressing: her jodhpurs before her woollen vest and white shirt, her pale-blue striped pony-club tie before her socks. Finally, she put on the yellow felt waistcoat that had belonged to her grandmother. It was a perfect fit, both smart and comfortable with small brass buttons and a silk back. She had already cleaned her boots on Christmas Eve, hoping as she scrubbed that she would have a velvet hunting cap from Patey's to complete her Boxing Day meet attire.

There's no time to be sad now though, thought Esme. On hunting days, she needed a full cooked English breakfast and hoped Mrs Bee hadn't forgotten. She ran down to the kitchen and was relieved to see the housekeeper plating up eggs, bacon, haggis, a potato scone and some fat sausages.

As she ate her way through the delicious food, she felt anxiety begin to rise. It was a pity Sophia had lost her nerve after breaking her arm in a fall so didn't ride any more. Esme suspected that if Rollo hunted, her sister might have at least come to the meet, but she had no interest now and preferred to stay at home. Anyway, she was going skiing with her friend Grania in a few days' time, before she went back to school.

'Esme, love,' said Mrs Bee, 'have you had enough to eat?'

'Oh yes, thank you Mrs Bee. It was delicious. I couldn't eat another thing. Do you think I should say goodbye to Mummy? Is she coming today?'

'I'd leave her be for the moment,' said Mrs Bee. 'But don't worry, she wouldn't miss the castle meet for anything. You know that, love.'

'But I'd better go and say goodbye to Daddy. It's time for him to get up anyway.'

'All right, sweetheart. Why don't you take his tea and the papers up for him? He'd like that.'

On the way upstairs and despite the housekeeper's advice, Esme went in to check on her mother. Her clothes were folded on a chair and she was almost entirely hidden under her bedclothes with just a few strands of hair escaping out onto her pillow. Esme gave the crown of her head a kiss and whispered, 'See you later, Mummy.'

Closing the door quietly behind her she went on to her father's room. He was already sitting up in bed.

'Ah, darling. Did you sleep well?'

Esme nodded.

'And what's this? Have you brought me breakfast in bed?'

'Just tea and the papers. I'm going down to Jimmy's now. Mrs Bee is taking me. Daddy, you are coming to the meet, aren't you? And you will bring Mummy, won't you?'

'Yes, of course, darling. Now, run along – you don't want to keep Jimmy waiting!'

He was right. Jimmy waited for no one when it came to hunting – not even the Prince of Wales, Esme remembered.

❄

When she arrived at the stable yard Lexi was already mounted on Jupiter, who stood nervously chewing at his bit.

'Esme! I've missed you. How was your Christmas? Papa told me that your mama was down *here*, after all that kerfuffle. Is she all right? You and Papa are clever to have found her. Look what I got for Christmas.' She stood up in her stirrups. 'A saddle! Brand new with suede kneepads and everything so I can grip better when he bucks. Isn't it gorgeous? What did you get?'

Esme blinked. She hated telling lies, especially to Lexi, but she couldn't say her mother had forgotten to buy her anything.

'Mummy and Daddy gave me a new riding hat. From Patey's. It's brown velvet and fits like a glove because Mummy snuck off with an old hat so they could make one the same size. Isn't she clever? I didn't even notice.'

'Why aren't you wearing it?'

'Erm… Mummy said the snow would leave marks on it. Anyway, today isn't really a proper hunting day. Just the meet. I want to save it for a big Saturday.'

Esme could tell that Lexi thought the Boxing Day meet was the ideal time to wear it. She quickly changed the subject. 'Look at Homer,' she said. 'See how smart he looks. Like he's going to a ball!'

Lexi laughed. 'He does! So does Jupiter,' she added, patting her pony's neck.

'Why aren't you on your horse, Esme?' came a voice from the stables.

'Morning Jimmy.'

'It'll be *good afternoon* soon. Get on your wreck of a pony,' he ordered.

As Esme tried to mount him, Homer shied away, moving around in circles.

'Stand still, Homer,' she said, hopping to keep up. '*Jimmy*, he won't stand still.'

Jimmy strode over and grabbed the pony's bridle. 'Now *stand*, you little bugger. *Stand!*'

Jimmy helped Esme into the saddle of the now-still horse, got on his own mount and set off with the girls down the road.

It only took a few seconds for Homer to start misbehaving.

'For God's sake, Esme, can't you keep the bleeder under control? Stay on the verge. Jesus! The little faggot's going to slip and break a leg. Oi! Be careful! Keep off the sodding road!'

'I'm trying!' shouted Esme.

She was using all her strength, balance and seven years' riding experience to keep a highly volatile Homer off the sheet ice that glossed the tarmacked road ahead.

'Homer! Be careful, you stupid idiot.' But her words fell on deaf ears. He knew he was going hunting in the same way Digger knew she was going to take him rabbiting before they had even got outside. Esme imagined all the horses gossiping and winding each other up into a fever of excitement whilst they were being brushed and polished. Homer was normally pretty placid but this morning he was hysterical. Even the extra-strong bit in his mouth had no effect; the galvanized steel must be hurting him as she yanked on it but he paid no attention. Every time he veered onto the road his trot became short and staccato, as though not caring that he might slip and crush Esme's leg. Getting to the meet as fast as he could was all that seemed to matter.

Esme wished they could have used the horsebox. She was going to be exhausted before they even got there, but because it was so snowy and the castle close by, Jimmy had said they would hack.

After a while, Homer began to settle, giving Esme a chance to notice the glorious day. The snow that had yesterday been such a hazard now lay like a shimmering offering for the Boxing Day meet that Lexi's parents were hosting. As ever, Esme's stomach flipped as she saw the castle, high and poetic, like in a fairy tale. Today its windows were glinting as if to welcome the crowds and its stone walls, usually cold and unfriendly, took on a warmth, coloured by the full beam of the sun.

The steep drive up to the castle was lined with people. As Jimmy, Lexi and Esme approached they could hear their cheerful greetings. Everyone was cold but everyone was smiling. There were lots of non-countrified brightly coloured clothes, smart boots and Sunday bests alongside the tartan kilts worn by the locals. Esme was relieved that Homer was now trotting excitedly, so she could just about keep him under control.

Up by the castle wall stood the gathering horses. John Blakely, the hunt master, was the boss today and Esme caught a glimpse of him surrounded by people. He beamed when he saw Jimmy.

'Merry Christmas, Jimmy! I see you've got your lady friends with you today. You old bastard; you always get the pretty ones.'

'Morning, Master!' chimed Esme and Lexi in unison.

Esme loved listening to John talk. He always had something to say about people in the village.

'Merry Christmas, Lady Lexi, and a happy new year to you, Esme. Goodness, Homer looks a bit fresh this morning. Jimmy, have you been feeding him extra fuel?' he said, looking at Homer's neck and loins, white with frothing sweat.

'No, John. Jesus, if I gave him oats he'd be farting his way across the Channel by now, no word of a lie. That little pony gets excited if I even *show* him oats. A bit like you with Joyce's ankles, even though they're as thick as pig shit.'

A deep growl of laughter escaped John's mouth and Esme knew a juicy story about Joyce would follow.

'And not just her ankles, Jimmy. I bumped into her in Brantridge when I was Christmas shopping for the wife. Goodness me. She was dressed for summer; short skirt and a *very* revealing blouse under her coat. Looked like she needed warming up. Offered to do it myself. She wasn't happy. Not happy at all.' He laughed again.

Mrs Bee didn't like Joyce. Said she was *common as muck*. Esme couldn't wait to tell her how silly she had been, wearing summer clothes when it was snowy.

'Esme, Lexi, come on – let's go and find your parents and a glass of port. I've got a right thirst. John, we'll see you later.'

Kicking their ponies and shoving them forward, the girls and Jimmy headed towards the heart of the meet, where the hounds were congregated.

The contrast against the snow of the red berries on the holly bushes and the scarlet tail ribbons on the horses made Esme stop and look around her. It was only when Homer suddenly swerved to avoid a kick from Father Kinley's vast piebald that she returned to concentrate on the job in hand.

It was always a surprise to Esme to see a dog collar instead of a white silk hunting stock on one of these occasions. What would the vicar do if his horse was injured during the hunt? The dog collar would be useless as a substitute bandage, unable to suppress blood spurting from a wire-ripped vein, and would do nothing to protect the vicar's neck from being broken.

Esme had been shown how to tie a stock early on. They were just like cravats but weren't only for show; if tied correctly and with enough pressure they could save lives. Instinctively, her hand went to check her own hunting stock's tongue was tucked neatly into her jacket and that the knot sat centred over her Adam's apple.

Patting Homer on the shoulder, Esme followed Lexi and trotted up to say good morning to Punch, the whipper-in. Punch was funny – a young Jimmy in the making – so-called because as a little boy he was always being punched by his elder brothers. They labelled him 'Punchbag' and the name stuck, though they dropped the 'bag' when he got bigger. Esme thought this was funny rather than sad because Punch was such a bruiser now. He loved his job, helping the hunts-man to keep control of the hounds, although he was pretty useless at it. Esme and Lexi adored him, laughing like mad as he raced after disobedient hounds that had decided that a hare rather than a fox was on the menu that day.

'Nice to see the toddlers are out with the grown-ups today,' said Punch to the girls now.

'*Lady* Lexi and *Miss* Esme to you, Punch. And we are *not* toddlers, thank you very much,' said Lexi, laughing.

'How is *Mrs* Munroe, Miss Esme?' said Punch.

'Er, she's fine thank you,' said Esme, immediately worried. 'Why do you ask?'

'I saw your mum wandering through the snow yesterday morning. I stopped to ask if she was OK and she told me she was just out for a walk but had a shoe missing. She said she was fine and that she preferred to walk shoeless in the snow. I mean, is she bonkers or what?'

Esme looked down, feeling blood rush to her face in shame.

'Don't be stupid, Punch. She got lost and was just frozen cold. If you walked about in snow, you'd be wobbly too,' said Lexi, springing to Esme's defence.

'Have I put my foot in it? My shoeless foot!' He laughed.

'No Mummy got left behind, that's all. Our stupid car slid into the ditch and we had to walk up to the castle. Mummy lost her shoe and I went to find it and then I lost her. Anyway, I met up with her at Jimmy's and we had the best fun ever,' Esme responded in a rush.

'Sounds a right laugh,' said Punch, raising an eyebrow.

'Oh look, there's Mummy!' said Esme. 'I'm going to say hi. See you in a minute.'

Pulling Homer sharply on the right rein, Esme walked away.

If Punch had seen her mother, why hadn't he bloody well helped her? she thought, furious. Everything that happened yesterday was his stupid fault. Well, he could go to hell! Kicking Homer, she trotted on past Robin the huntsman, who looked magnificent in his pink, brass-buttoned hunt coat, brown-topped boots, white breeches and black hat, the crowd of excited hounds barking beneath him.

In amongst the crowd was Esme's mother. Relief at seeing her spread over Esme. She had made it after all and was talking to Mr Quince, their gardener, and the Earl. She was laughing, her dark hair covered with a silk Hermes scarf, knotted beneath her chin.

'Look who's arrived! Merry Christmas, lassie,' said Mr Quince.

'Happy Christmas Mr Q! Hello Mummy, are you having fun?'

'There you are, darling! Don't you look smart? Oh and Homer, what a handsome boy you are.'

'Good morning, Esme. And how are you on this fine and beautiful day?' said the Earl.

Esme felt her mother's hand on her thigh and all uncomfortable thoughts from her earlier conversation between Punch and Lexi dissolved.

'Really well, thank you,' she said, smiling.

'Glad to hear it,' the Earl replied. 'We were just discussing with Mr Quince here, which trees made the best firewood. You still haven't given us your expert opinion, Mr Quince.'

'Like I said, Your Lordship,' said Mr Quince, 'hardwood is best. Beech or ash.' Then, turning to Esme's mother, 'Do you have enough wood stacked in your shed, Mrs Munroe?'

'Dear Mr Quince, I couldn't ask you to chop another piece of wretched wood, even if our frozen pipes depended on it. You are sweet. You must make the most of this weather to rest. I'm pretty handy with an axe. I'll just chop up that ghastly oak cabinet that Colin's mother lumbered us with.'

'Mummy, you can't!' exclaimed Esme, shocked that her mother would suggest such a thing. 'Daddy said that it's the most valuable antique we have!'

'Being priceless doesn't make it any more attractive, darling. Isn't that right, Henry?' she said.

'I'm not sure Colin would trust you wielding an axe,' said

the Earl. Esme saw him slip his hand around her mother's back.

'How is the arthritis, by the way, Mr Quince?'

'Och, it's terrible, Mrs M. If it's not the damp, then it's the cold that gets into my old bones. But a wee bit of chopping won't do much harm.'

Esme was always moved by her mother's kindness to everyone, whatever their job. She had told Esme how worried she had been about Mr Quince since his wife died last Easter and how she had asked Mrs Bee to cook stews and pies to fill the freezer she had given him from The Lodge.

'No, you must rest, Mr Quince. Don't worry about us; we'll cope. Like I say, there's little for you to be getting on with in the snow. Save yourself for dealing with the damage once it melts. You dear man. Right, how about a nice warming cup of mulled wine to cheer you up? Let me get one for you.'

'You mustn't wait on me, Mrs M,' the gardener's protest was joined by a blush that broke through the thicket of whiskers beneath his cheekbones.

'But of course she must. We all know that Mrs Munroe has a heart of gold, don't you Diana?' said the Earl, now stroking her back. 'You will always be incapable of breathing an unkind word to anyone.'

The Earl was so nice to her mother, thought Esme. She had never heard her father talk to her like that.

'Henry, you really do see me as some kind of Mother Theresa. I can be quite beastly if I need to be. Ferocious, actually,' said Diana, making a mock growling noise.

'As ferocious as a baby rabbit,' teased the Earl. 'Indeed. I have seen that side of you and it is *terrifying*!'

'There you go, Mrs M. His Lordship knows you're soft as butter,' laughed Mr Quince.

Esme saw how much her mother was enjoying herself and felt glad.

As she took a cup of mulled wine from a passing tray and gave it to Mr Quince, she appeared to notice Esme again. 'So, darling, how was the ride up here?'

'Homer was *so* naughty, Mummy. Bucking – and he even reared a little bit. But I stuck on. I think Jimmy was quite impressed. Look at him! He's shaking.'

'You silly boy. Here, have a sausage.' Her mother placed her open palm under Homer's nose and offered up the steaming chipolata, sleek in its honey coating. The pony picked it up, snorting and shaking his head as he chomped.

'Esme, I have never known another pony eat meat. Homer is the funniest thing.'

'Mummy?'

'Yes, darling?'

'Well...'

'What is it, sweetie?'

Checking that the Earl and Mr Quince were out of earshot, Esme continued. 'Well, I came to say goodnight to you last night, but you were already asleep.'

'I know you did, my angel. You were quiet as a mouse and I felt your precious little kiss, but you know Mummy was so tired. After you left, I fell straight to sleep and dreamt of you.'

Esme thought back to the knocking over the glass of water. Her mother must have pretended not to hear it.

'But the spilled water? You didn't get wet or slip this morning, did you?' asked Esme.

'No, darling. What water?'

'Oh, nothing. Don't worry. Mummy?'

'Yes?'

'Do I have to ride back to the yard now, 'cause I really want to follow the hounds on foot. It's a bit of a waste riding all this way and not hunting. The scent will be amazing today.'

Jimmy had told her and Lexi before they left that there was too much snow and it would be dangerous for the horses, while the frozen peaks of mud could hurt their feet. 'A bit like you walking on sharp rocks with no shoes on,' he had said.

'I do agree, darling, and the snow has messed things up a bit. You and Lexi ought to take the ponies down to Jimmy's now, because by the time you get back here for lunch it will be nearly 1.30. You'll have to go at some point; best to get it over and done with.'

'We could put Homer and Jupiter in the castle stables and run back to join the hounds. Jimmy can do the same then he can lead them on Badger when he goes back. What do you think?'

'Well, I don't know… I'm not sure Jimmy will be happy with that.'

'He won't mind. *Please* Mummy.' Esme stuck her lip out, pleadingly.

'Why don't you ask him yourself? He's right here. Morning, Jimmy. How are you?'

'Morning Diana, Your Lordship. How was lunch yesterday? Bet it wasn't just the turkey that was roasted when you two arrived late for your Christmas dinners!' said Jimmy, smirking.

'We all had a marvellous day. Thank you so much for your kind hospitality yesterday,' said the Earl.

'Jimmy?' asked Esme. 'Will you lead Homer and Jupiter back to the yard so that me and Lexi can go on foot with the hounds and be here in time for lunch?' She grimaced, bracing herself for the inevitable telling-off.

'Esme Munroe! Who the hell do you think you are? Lady bleeding Muck? No, you lazy twit, I will not take your effing poncey pony home. I am not your slave. In fact, you know what? *You* can take *my* horse home, so *I* can go hunting on foot and have lunch at the castle. Put *that* in your effing pipe and puff on it. Now, get your high 'n' mighty backside out of here. We are leaving. *Now!*'

'Keep your hair on, it was just a question,' muttered Esme under her breath.

Jimmy gave her a sharp look.

'What about if we – me and Lexi – put our ponies in the stables here and then ride them back after lunch? It's just that if we go back to the yard now, we won't have time to follow the hunt. It *is* Boxing Day, Jimmy. *Please?*'

'Why didn't you tell me about your sodding lunch? I'd planned on taking the horses back and driving to meet the hunt on foot for the afternoon. But no; just because you're off hobnobbing with the toffs you expect me to miss out.' He paused, remembering the Earl. 'No disrespect intended, Your Lordship,' said Jimmy.

'It's not a disaster, Jimmy,' said the Earl. 'You can put… Badger is it?… in our stables too. Then you can go out now and I'll get one of the grooms to run them all down in the box later. Frightful shame for the girls not to go – and you too, of course.'

'Well, Your Lordship, that's ever so kind. You're lucky, Esme, to have such a persuasive and hospitable ally,' said Jimmy with a grin. 'If it were up to me, I'd send you packing. Right, you'd better get that fat donut moving – the hounds will be off soon. Go and find your friend.'

'Oh, thank you so much!' said Esme, looking at the Earl. 'Thank you, Jimmy. Bye, Mummy. Be back soon.' Esme waved to her mother and blew her a kiss as she moved away, but her mother didn't return it because she was looking at the Earl.

'Bye-bye, Mummy!' she repeated, but once again she was ignored, her mother now whispering in the Earl's ear.

Esme kicked Homer in the ribs, which would have hurt had there not been so much fat lessening the impact. He didn't move. Raising both legs as high as they would go, she slapped them down against his flanks and shouted at him. She was angry. What were the Earl and her mother talking about? It must be something very important for her mother not to say goodbye. She wondered whether she ought to tell her father but the lure of the hounds was too exciting so instead she cracked her whip on Homer's bottom and caught up with Lexi.

'Hi!' she said.

'How did you persuade Jimmy to let us go?' asked Lexi.

'It was your father. He told him we had to go and he offered Badger a stable, too,' said Esme.

'You are brilliant, Esme! He would have said no to me. You do seem to bring out the best in him.'

93

The girls got back just as the hounds were moving off. They heard Robin sound his horn and the pack baying. This was the first time either Lexi or Esme had been out on foot; younger children weren't allowed to follow, as they were too small to keep up. It made Esme feel very grown up.

'What happens if the hounds find a fox? How will Robin and Punch keep up with them?' asked Esme.

She had never been so close to the hounds when they were sniffing out a fox. It was incredible to be able to see them working so hard.

It wasn't long before the huntsman gave a series of short, sharp blows, signifying a fox was afoot in a thicket of rhododendrons. Robin instructed his pack to spread around the animal and then close in on it. Their noses went down and tails wagged, on the scent of something interesting.

It didn't take long for one of the hounds to let out a soulful howl followed by an excited yelp that persuaded his fellow dogs to join in. They didn't so much bark as sing. The sound sent thrilling shivers down Esme's spine, not because they would soon kill the fox but because if she were on Homer she would be galloping after them. That was what she loved about hunting: the speed and danger of it all. It made her feel free and forget everything apart from the next hedge to jump.

The hounds suddenly went quiet, like they had been switched off, and then came the growls as they fought over the fox's carcass. She didn't like to think of the poor fox, even though she knew his death would have been swift.

'Wow!' exclaimed Lexi. 'That was amazing. I actually *saw* them kill the fox. Did you?'

'Yes! It was like watching it on TV. Punch did so well keeping the hounds together,' said Esme.

'What a perfect morning. *And* we won't be late for lunch,' Lexi said, looking at her watch.

'We'd better find Mr Trent to take us back to the castle.'

Minutes later, hopping onto the gamekeeper's off-roader with her friend, Esme couldn't wait to tell her parents all about it.

'Hi, Mr Trent. Happy Christmas,' said Lexi.

'And to you, Lady Alexa. Now His Lordship left strict instructions to get you home at top speed. So you girls had better hold on tight,' he said.

Esme grabbed Lexi's waist, who in turn grabbed Mr Trent's. Despite being like a cross between a six-wheeled motorbike and a tank, the Terra Tiger could go surprisingly fast and the girls were at the castle gates in minutes.

'Thanks for the lift, Mr Trent,' said Lexi. 'We would have been in terrible trouble with Mama if we'd arrived after lunch.'

A row of boots lay outside the door.

'After you with the boot jack, Esme,' said Lexi.

Esme hooked her foot into the V-shaped notch and eased her riding boots off, placing them next to the others. Her feet were cold and she couldn't wait to get inside to warm them up.

Amongst the pile of coats in the hall was Esme's mother's scarf, a brilliant burst of colour in the sea of tweed.

Lexi was already sprinting up the stairs. 'Race you, Es!' she shrieked.

Reaching the dining room and its distinctively adult aroma of claret and cigars, the girls flew through the door, laughing, and raced to the two unoccupied high-backs that hooped the dining table.

'Sorry we're late, Mama!' squealed Lexi.

'We've had to start without you,' said the Contessa.

And so they had. The guests were talking, eating and drinking, seated on slippery red-leather, brass-studded chairs that crackled when you moved.

Glancing around the table Esme saw her mother chatting to the Earl. She was backlit by the sunlight streaming through the vast sash windows, flecks of dust circling her hair like a halo. She was laughing, her head close to the Earl's, eyes looking straight into his like she was searching for something. It occurred to Esme that her mother had been with Lexi's father far more than her own today. In fact, she hadn't seen her father all morning and her mother hadn't seemed sad at all. Was it the Earl who made her happy or her father who made her sad? Did she like the Earl more than her father? Maybe it was because he didn't get cross with her.

The food was infamously disappointing at the castle and today's annual Boxing Day lunch exceeded its reputation with a flavourless stew and dumplings. Indistinguishable in colour or texture, both were an unappetizing grey with globs of flour floating in the gravy. Soggy cabbage and lumpy mashed potato completed the bland offering.

'Mmm, my favourite,' said Lexi with genuine enthusiasm, not waiting a second to dive her fork into the mound of food before her. 'This is just what we need to warm us up after our morning. Tuck in, Esme!'

Esme looked down at her food, rapidly congealing on the finely decorated china plate. This was not the kind of stuff she ate at home. But then the Culcairns didn't have Mrs Bee at the helm. Mrs Bee said that because the castle kitchen was down in a 'dungeon' probably no one bothered to pull the chef's socks up. Esme thought Lexi's family had become immune to bad food and cared more about the company and wine than what they ate. She was used to colourful dishes, bursting with flavour. Tentatively, she lifted her fork to her mouth and gagged. *Ugh!* Utterly disgusting slop. How was it that people who were so rich served awful food? It was a standing joke between her parents and assorted friends that they would eat a little something before coming to lunch or dinner at the castle.

Today, though, the sponge pudding for dessert was good. It was *really* good. The golden syrup overpowered the taste of suet and flour. Esme tried to remember how to eat treacle pudding without burning her tongue. The scalding-hot syrup would coat the silver spoon in a boiling glue that she had to scrape at with her teeth before she could enjoy the delicious sweetness beneath. She felt her tongue blister. No matter; Mrs Bee had told her that the mouth healed faster than any other part of the body.

Esme glanced at her mother again, still deep in conversation with the Earl, and wondered if she was ever going to talk to the poor man sat on the other side of her. It was rude of her to ignore him like this.

Then, turning back to Lexi, she asked, 'What shall we do this afternoon?'

'Why don't we build a snowman? A huge, enormous one

with a face and hands and everything. We can use wellies for arms. It'll look so real!' said Lexi. 'You get your scarf and a carrot from the kitchen and I'll meet you downstairs.'

'OK. I'll just tell Mummy,' she said.

Esme looked back down to the end of the table. Her mother was no longer there.

Chapter Six

Esme's stomach gave a small lurch. Lunch had not finished. Well, not for the grown-ups, anyway, and for her mother, this was the part of the meal she always liked best: coffee and chocolates. She rose from the table and set off to find her. As she passed the Earl, now talking to the lady on his left, he raised his hand at her, like a policeman telling a car to stop, but she knew *his* hand was saying a little goodbye.

Finding someone in such an enormous building would be impossible for most people, thought Esme, but she had such a good sense of the place she felt sure she'd be able to find Mummy, so she set off confidently for the drawing room. She peeked her head round the door but it was empty, save for the Contessa's dog, bathing in a warm spot of sunlight. Brian was barely able to move on his short legs with his enormous stomach and balls that skimmed the ground. No one in the family really liked him except the Contessa – and Brian was devoted to her. He lumbered after her like a big fat walrus, ripples of blubber propelling him forward, his long ears and droopy jowls flapping in sync.

'Hello, Brian,' she said. 'Have you seen Mummy?'

The dog's eyes seemed sad, grey with cataracts and circled by warts, as they looked in her direction. Unable to resist,

Esme entered the room and went over to him. He rolled onto his back to allow her to tickle his freckled tummy.

'You like that, don't you, boy?'

He growled with pleasure, his lips flapping open to reveal a set of stained teeth.

'I'm sorry, boy,' said Esme, 'I have to go. Got to find Mummy. Good boy.' She stroked his head then left the room to continue on her way.

A long tapestry, complemented at intervals by other valuable objects and paintings, ran the length of the corridor outside the drawing room. The lack of windows, save for the slits of glass way up high, had kept the corridor dim and the hand-stitched carpet as good as new; sunlight hadn't faded its delicate pastel colouring. Esme touched a marble bust of one of the Earl's ancestors, a beautiful lady. Like everything in the castle it was a stunning piece. This particular work had been sculpted by a famous Frenchman, she seemed to remember being told. She kissed her hand and placed it on the woman's cheek for good luck.

A weak sliver of light escaped from underneath the door of the morning room, enough to illuminate an oil painting in the corridor of perhaps the same woman, riding side-saddle on a chestnut horse. It was her mother's favourite artwork, one she said she wished she owned. The plaque on the frame read *John L. Fernley*. Esme poked her head into the morning room to see the source of light but again it was empty. In the Earl's study, his large desk stood in the centre of three tall windows. It was solid, masculine and piled high with papers. His large leather swivel chair sat vacant. Esme sat in it and spun round just as she sometimes did with Lexi, the seat getting higher with each turn. Once she could reach the desk, she stopped. An ink blotter was covered in writing. She tried to decipher some of the words but the Earl's writing was too scrawly. There was a tall pile of art catalogues. She tilted her head and read the spines; they were all from Christie's. She wondered if the Culcairn family were selling a painting or buying more, although they certainly didn't need any more. The top catalogue cover showed a photograph of a badly painted man. *Francis Bacon*, it read.

Esme hopped off the chair as she heard a man's voice seemingly coming from behind the bookshelves. To her surprise, she then heard her mother's voice and held her breath as she listened.

'It's a future without you that will kill me. What purpose will I have?'

The man's voice responded again, quieter now. Perhaps it was her father? But if so, why were they hiding? Whatever their reason it was clearly a secret. One of the wall panels creaked and, not wanting to get caught, Esme shot into the footwell under the desk just as her mother appeared from behind the rows of leather-bound books and ran out of the room crying.

Esme heard another set of footsteps but didn't dare move or even open her eyes. She waited.

'Esme? *Esme!* Where are you? Oh. Hello Papa. Have you seen Esme?'

It was Lexi.

'No, darling. I'm just on my way back to the dining room. I'll let her know you're looking for her if I see her.'

Esme waited until she could no longer hear the Earl's

footsteps and then scrambled out from her hiding place, causing Lexi to jump.

'What are you doing in here?' Lexi asked. She had a pair of boots and a tweed cap in her hands. 'Have you got the rest of the stuff?'

'Um, no, but I thought we could use a fountain pen for his nose and these drawing pins for eyes,' Esme said quickly, thinking on her feet and gathering a handful of gold buttons from the Earl's desk tray.

'Brilliant idea,' said Lexi.

Esme's heart told her to chase after her mother but her head reasoned that often when her mother cried it only lasted for a short time, then she would mop up her tears and all would be well. The snowman would be a nice surprise for her.

With so much snow it didn't take them long to build a huge snowman. The girls heaved a small snowball for the head onto the enormous torso and pressed the wellington boots into position at the bottom. Lexi took her scarf off and wrapped it around its neck, whilst Esme made its eyes and nose with pins.

'He needs a mouth,' said Esme. 'Shall we use some holly berries?'

They set about picking the red fruit, careful not to catch their fingers on the prickly leaves, and stuck them on in a smile. Putting on the hat with a flourish they stood back and admired their handiwork.

'He looks like Mr Quince!' said Lexi, laughing.

'Mummy will love it!'

The grown-ups were still at the dining-room table when the girls returned, as was the norm when lunching at the castle; they would sit around drinking port until teatime. Everything was just as it had been earlier, but now Esme's mother had returned to her seat. She was in fits of giggles throwing chocolates in the air and trying to catch them in her mouth. Suddenly, her face became sulky, she skipped over to the window and hid behind a curtain, then popped out, shouting, 'Peek-a-boo!' before collapsing once again into laughter.

Esme noticed the Contessa whispering to the man on her right then laughing when she looked in her mother's direction.

Her mother's behaviour could be seen as funny, but instinctively Esme didn't smile, simply joining her father as he said, 'I think it's time we left.'

Thanking the Contessa for lunch, he took his wife by the elbow and guided her out of the room. Esme gave Lexi a small smile and mouthed 'See you later.'

The journey home was grim, the atmosphere heavy. Her mother sat immobile. She didn't speak but Esme could hear the hiss of merriment draining from her as if she had been punctured. Her father muttered crossly under his breath.

'You are an embarrassment, Diana. Can't you see how

your behaviour affects us? Hmm?' He looked at his wife but she was gone.

Flown to her place in the clouds, thought Esme.

Her father turned on the radio and lit a cigarette. Esme was angry with him for spoiling the fun and uneasy about her mother's rapid mood change. Picking at a hangnail, she pulled the hard skin with her teeth. It stung and a tiny ball of blood flowered on her thumb. She sucked it clean.

Mrs Bee was waiting for them. Opening the passenger door, she leaned in to help Esme's mother out of the car. Sophia opened the door for Esme.

'Och, Mrs Munroe,' she said, her voice full of kindness that made Esme want to cry. 'Come in with you. Let's get you into bed with a nice cup of tea. Girls, it's all right, I'll take care of your mum now. Esme, I'm sure there'll be a good film on the television. Sophia, take her into the lounge and get yourselves a piece of cake. Esme, I've made your favourite: coffee and walnut.'

The family traipsed into the welcoming warmth of the entrance hall. Esme wrapped her arms around her mother's waist and pressed her head into her chest. She hugged her with as much strength as she could.

'I love you, Mummy,' she said softly. Her mother made no move to hug her back but Esme knew she could hear her.

'Esme, let your mother go. She needs to rest,' said her father. 'Sophia, why don't you take your sister into the drawing room and sit with her?'

Esme caught him sharing a look with Mrs Bee.

Prizing herself away, Esme kissed her mother's cheek and turned away, towards the drawing room. Looking behind her, she could see Mrs Bee and her father were already helping her mother up the stairs. She kept collapsing, her body going limp, her legs shaking. She looked like a rag doll. Sophia, arm around her sister's shoulders, steered Esme into the drawing room.

'Come on, Es. Sit down and let's see what's on.'

Esme hesitated, wondering if she should tell Sophia what she overheard at the castle.

'Sophs… I need to tell you something. I heard Mummy—'

'Oh God, let's forget her and watch a film. Look,' she said, switching on the television. 'It's a Fred and Ginger one – your favourite. I'll get us some cake.'

A small fur ball came trotting into the room.

'Digger!' shrieked Esme, delighted; her beloved dog could read her mind and always found her when she was upset. 'Oh, Digs, what would I do without you?' she said.

He jumped up onto a faded chintz armchair, where she joined him and snuggled up to watch the film, curled around her dog and a tapestry cushion.

'Here you are Es, get that down you,' said Sophia, handing her a plate of cake.

The comforting smell and Sophia's kindness prompted Esme's instant gratitude; she sat up, took the cake and thanked Sophia, hoping her sister would know it was for more than just the slice of cake.

'Shall we go up and see Mummy after this?' asked Esme.

'I don't think so,' said Sophia. 'Daddy and Mrs Bee will

help her to bed and then she'll probably sleep. She'll be fine in the morning.'

Sophia stretched out in the armchair, her plate resting under her chin.

'I love Fred Astaire,' sighed Esme, watching the flashing images on the television screen. 'He's so talented, I don't know how anyone can move their feet so fast!'

'Oh, Esme,' Sophia said disapprovingly. 'There are lots of men out there who are far more attractive than *Fred Astaire*!'

Esme shrugged, offering her sticky fingers to Digger to lick clean. 'I like him.'

The girls sat in silence, watching the dancers glide across the ballroom in a sea of chiffon and tails.

Esme looked at her sister, whose slice of cake was yet to make it to her mouth. 'Are you OK?' she asked.

'What?' asked Sophia.

'Are you OK?' she repeated.

'Yup. I just find all this black-and-white tap dancing boring. I'm going to call Grania and then go and play some records. Are you all right on your own?'

'OK. See you in a bit.'

Esme wanted to show her sister that she was grown up enough to do her own thing and didn't need babysitting so she went to find her father, who was in the dining room, drawing. Using his pastels he could make his subject come alive with just one tiny smudge on a sheet of paper.

'Can you see, Daddy?' Esme asked, noticing that his desk lamp was pointing at a vase of hyacinths.

'Of course I can, darling – the light creates more shadow,'

he said, squinting and holding up the soft chalk to get the perspective right, just as he had taught Esme.

'Daddy?'

Lost in his work he didn't answer so Esme left, put on a jacket and walked out to the woods, Digger following at her heels.

When she arrived at the old summer house she decided not to light a fire like last time. She didn't want to risk falling asleep again. Instead, as much to keep warm as for something to do, she began to sweep the floor. It was a thankless task as the roof was a source of never-ending dust. A combination of dry rot and hungry woodworms ate away at the exposed beams, sprinkling a fine oak powder over every surface. Esme picked up her mother's photograph and blew the dust off it, making Digger sneeze.

'Bless you,' she said.

By the time she came back, nearly two hours later, Mrs Bee had supper ready.

'Kitchen supper tonight, love.'

She ate her cauliflower cheese alone. Sophia must have taken advantage of their father's distraction with his artwork and sneaked out to the village. She had made some local friends that he wouldn't have approved of – not because they weren't nice but because they weren't 'our sort of people'. Esme didn't really know what that meant but assumed it was people who weren't rich.

Putting her plate in the dishwasher, she collected her mug of Horlicks. 'Can Digger sleep with me tonight, Mrs Bee?'

The dog usually slept in his basket in the downstairs cloakroom.

'Well, I don't see why not. Just this once, love.'

'Thanks! I'll be sure to get up early to let him out. We'll go up now. Will you tuck us in?'

'I'll be up in a minute.'

By the time Mrs Bee came in, Esme was putting on her nightdress.

'May I say goodnight to Mummy?'

'No, darling. Your mother is fast asleep but when she woke earlier she asked me to tell you she'll be "fine and dandy tomorrow".'

Her mother never used that expression so she knew Mrs Bee was just saying it to make her feel better. She looked at the photograph of her mother on her bedside table.

'Mrs Bee?'

'Yes, love?'

'Is Mummy very unhappy?'

'No, love,' she said, picking up the photograph frame. 'Look at her here; that's when you won your rosette at the gymkhana last year. She looks so lovely.'

'It was such fun. Homer beat everyone.'

'Your mother loves you so much but sometimes it's difficult for her to show it. You'll understand better when you're all grown up. If it wasn't for your mummy, my life would have taken a turn for the worse. I count my blessings every day that I have you and your family to look out for.' She gave Esme a squeeze.

Esme wondered if 'looking out' for her mother was sometimes difficult and she wanted to tell Mrs Bee about the episode at the castle but felt that would be telling tales on her mother.

'Right, time for sleep. Night-night, love.'

'Night, Mrs Bee.'

When the door had closed behind her, Esme gathered Digger into her arms. His little body pumped out smelly breath but it didn't matter and his unquestioning presence gave her permission to cry. Sobbing into his fur, she eventually drifted into sleep.

In the middle of the night, Esme woke with a start. She often did so after frightening dreams – when fleeing screeching witches or avoiding falling off the edge of a cliff – but this time there had been no nightmare. Something else had pulled her from her slumber. She suddenly realized that Digger was barking. Peering into the darkness, everything was as it should be; everything, that was, apart from a faint smell of something burning. Switching on her bedside lamp she looked at the time: 3.30 a.m.

How strange, she thought. There's no way Mrs Bee would be cooking this late. Maybe she left something in the Aga?

Climbing out of bed and rubbing her eyes, she walked into the corridor. Thick smoke was coiling its way down the hall. She could hear Digger more clearly now; short, sharp barks and noisy scratching. Running towards the noise and smoke, she found Digger pawing at her mother's bedroom door, desperately trying to get in.

'Daddy! Sophia! Mrs Bee! Quick, it's Mummy! There's smoke coming from her room!' she shouted, before bursting through her mother's door and being assaulted by thicker, choking smoke. Flames licked the drapes hanging around the four-poster bed.

'Mummy!' she screamed, seeing her mother's still form on the mattress. 'Stay there, Digger.'

Holding her breath, she tried to pull her mother from the bed but the dead weight was too much for her.

'What the—?' Esme could hear her father stumbling onto the landing. 'Bloody hell!'

'Daddy, in here!' she tried to shout, but the smoke made her voice small.

'Oh, Christ!' he said, appearing beside her. 'Esme! Help me!'

Coughing, she helped her father drag her mother out of the bed, until finally she landed heavily on the floor. Esme watched her father pick up the lifeless form and carry her mother from the room, before grabbing his pyjamas and following blindly behind him. He slammed the bedroom door shut behind them.

'Esme, go and get the fire extinguisher, quickly!'

She stood paralysed, Digger barking up at her. She picked him up and put the sleeve of her nightdress over his muzzle. Smoke filled the hallway.

Her father shouted at her. '*Get the extinguisher now!*'

She dropped her dog and watched her father bend over her unconscious mother and put his mouth to hers, blowing air into her lungs.

'Diana! Wake up!' he shouted, slapping her cheek. He blew into her mouth again. 'Diana, my darling angel – come on. You can do this. Breathe. Oh God, darling, what have you done? Breathe, my darling. Breathe!'

Esme stood still, staring. She had never seen her parents kiss on the lips before. Then her father looked up, desperation etched on his face, and she ran to the kitchen to fetch the fire extinguisher. Dragging the heavy metal canister up the stairs, she found Mrs Bee sitting on the floor, cradling Esme's mother in her arms, tears running down her cheeks.

'Esme, give me that!' her father said, running towards her. He unclipped the hose, opened the door to Diana's bedroom and sprayed the flames until the fire had gone out.

'I've called for the fire engine, the ambulance is on its way,' Mrs Bee said. 'Now we have to move her. Get her downstairs.' She looked at Esme. 'Darling, your mother is going to be OK.'

But Esme didn't believe her.

Her father looked at Mrs Bee. 'Call Jimmy, Mrs Bumble. Get him to come as quickly as possible.'

'Christ, what's going on?' It was Sophia, still muffled by sleep and coughing at the smoke-filled air. She looked down at her parents, taking in the scene before her.

'Oh my God, *Mummy!*' She bent down over her mother and started to shake her, trying to get her to respond.

In a daze, Esme knelt down next to her mother. She smelt of dying bonfire. Esme held her breath in the hope she could hear her mother's. She felt her father's hand on her shoulder.

'Sophia, Esme, look at me.'

The girls looked up at their father. His face was wet with tears and blackened by smoke.

'Darlings,' he said, his voice shaking, 'You are going outside to wait for Jimmy and the fire engine. Mrs Bee and I are going to stay with your mother. Take Digger with you.'

'Is Mummy… dead?' Esme asked.

'No, darling,' he said, his voice a bit stronger. 'She's sleeping. Mrs Bee is looking after her. I need to go back into her room to check the fire is out. Go now, with Sophia. Jimmy should be here soon.' There was a softness in his voice, like his heart was in his words.

Esme stood huddled with Sophia in the cold night, holding her hand. Jimmy had arrived. He didn't talk as he carried thick coats out of his car. His expression grim, he carefully wrapped them around the sisters, talking to them like he would a nervous horse. Esme was very relieved he was there.

Two beams of white light streaked the blackness. An ambulance, followed by two fire engines, screeched to a halt.

'I'm scared, Jimmy,' said Esme, quietly, her face streaked with ash and tears.

'Your ma's going to be fine, Esme,' he said. 'We're all going to be fine.'

'But what if she isn't?'

'She's got smoke in her lungs. Why isn't she out here, in the fresh air?' said Sophia. She was shaking, gulping in great mouthfuls of air herself, like a fish. She rushed back inside.

'Jimmy, why isn't Daddy bringing Mummy outside?' Esme asked.

'The ambulance men are doing that,' said Jimmy.

Esme began to cry, trembling with a violence that threatened to break her. Jimmy put his arms around her.

'Shhh.' He handed her a Murray Mint. 'The sugar will make you feel better.'

Esme shook her head, clamping her lips together.

'Esme, listen to me. Mrs Bee told me if it hadn't been for you, who *knows* what might have happened? You're a bleeding little star.'

She turned and looked up at him. He was smiling a sad smile.

Esme hugged him. 'It was actually Digger who saved her. He knew. He was there before me,' she said, desperately.

'Well, you're *both* little stars.'

Suddenly there were voices shouting and people running about. Her father was outside and a policeman was urgently asking him questions.

'What time do you think your wife took the pills?' the man asked. 'Do you have the bottle? We need to know how many she took.'

Two more uniformed men emerged from the house, carrying her mother out on a stretcher. She lay unmoving with a mask over her face, her body covered in a holey blanket. Esme broke free from Jimmy and ran over to the stretcher. She took off her coat and put it over her mother to stop the cold getting through the gaps.

A nurse stepped forward and gave the coat back to her. 'Hello,' she said gently. 'What's your name?'

'Esme,' said Esme, sobs still wracking her body.

'Well, your mummy is very lucky that you woke up and found her, to have you as her daughter. You are a hero, Esme, and we're now going to take your mummy to the hospital and get her better. You need to stay here and look after things for her.'

Esme looked around. Everything was blurry and happening so fast. Bright blue lights from two fire engines and an ambulance lit up the scene. Men in uniform, with silver buttons and yellow hats, ran in and out of the house. She watched as her mother was lifted up on her stretcher into the back of the ambulance, her father quickly clambering up after her. The doors closed and the vehicle pulled away.

Chapter Seven

Opening her eyes, Esme remembered everything. She got out of bed and dropped to her knees, putting her hands together in prayer.

'Dear God, please, *please* make Mummy be OK. Please make sure the nurses give her a nice breakfast. Tell them she likes two sugars in her tea and honey with her toast. And tell her I will come to see her as soon as possible. Make Daddy let me go. Thank you. Amen.'

She tried to imagine her mother in hospital. She had never been inside one before, but she had seen them on the television. She hoped her mother wouldn't be scared when she woke up, not knowing where she was, and that the nurses would be as kind as they were on *Emergency–Ward 10*.

Not caring how early it must be, she went to her father's bedroom. The door was open, the room empty. Clothes were strewn all over the floor and his bed was a jumbled mess of sheets and blankets. She went on to her mother's room where a paper sign reading *CAUTION, CAUTION* in bold letters was pinned to the door, its wood blackened by the flames. Venturing inside, Esme saw the bed sheets had been scorched to cinders and were covered in white powder from the extinguisher. Everything had been ruined and she worried what would happen if her mother needed a nightie or her baby pillow. Sighing, she left for Sophia's room, but on finding her sister fast asleep, went in search of Mrs Bee.

'May I come in?' she asked, opening the door.

Mrs Bee was standing at her basin, scrubbing her dentures with a toothbrush. She quickly popped them in her mouth, pressing them into place with her tongue, and smiled at Esme. 'Now I can talk properly. You're up early, love. How did you sleep?' she asked, smoothing her short hair.

'Where's Mummy?'

'She's in hospital, love, where the nurses will be taking good care of her.'

'What about Daddy?'

'He's with her. Keeping her company and making sure the doctors are doing all they can to make her better.'

'I want to see her.'

'Let's see what your father has to say. He's going to call us a wee bit later to let us know what's happening.'

'Has she got her things?'

Mrs Bee paused. She looked tired and even her glasses couldn't hide the bags under eyes. 'She won't be needing much, love.'

'Does that mean she won't be there for long?'

'I don't know about that. We'll know more when your father calls.'

'And what about her room? Why's it got that sign on the door? Is it a crime scene?' asked Esme, thinking about the policemen solving murders and robberies on *Z Cars*.

Mrs Bee gave a small laugh. 'No, Esme, it's not a crime

scene. The firemen just want to make sure it's safe before we redecorate it.'

'It's not going to fall down, is it? I mean, it was a fire, not an earthquake.'

Mrs Bee smiled weakly. 'It's not going to fall down, love, I promise.'

'Wasn't Digger clever? You know he was the one who rescued Mummy? He woke me up because he knew she was in danger, just like a real-life police dog. I'm so proud of him.'

'And so you should be, love,' agreed Mrs Bee. 'Right, shall we go and put the kettle on? I'm gasping for a cup of coffee.'

Despite Esme's father's reluctance to put the heating on, thanks to the Aga the kitchen was always warm. Today was no exception. Drops of condensation slid down the window and onto the sill, seeping into the wood.

Mrs Bee put the kettle on and busied herself. Usually Esme liked to help but today she only felt like sitting; it was as if an invisible force was pinning her down. Her eyes ached as did every part of her body.

'Why don't you make Mummy a card? I'll get your felt-tips.' She went to a drawer in the big pine sideboard, pulled out a Tupperware box filled with every colour in the rainbow and gave it to Esme, then carried on getting breakfast ready.

Esme sat concentrating on making her mother a picture. With a few strokes she drew a little house, nestling amongst the trees, beneath a great big yellow sun at the top of the page. It was a picture of her secret place in the woods; she hoped her mother would like it.

'That's lovely, Esme. You've inherited your father's talent,' said Mrs Bee, sitting down next to her to make her coffee.

Esme watched her put a teaspoon and a half of coffee granules, two teaspoons of sugar and a splash of hot water into her mug. Mrs Bee made it look like such a delicious drink but Esme had never been allowed to try it.

'May I mix it for you please, Mrs Bee?' she asked. Taking the spoon from Mrs Bee's hand she mixed vigorously until the thick, brown mixture turned almost white, like butter icing. 'Is this fluffy enough?'

Mrs Bee peered into the mug. 'Ay, darling. See how it's turned white? That's because you've put so much air into it.'

She got up again to take the screaming kettle off the hotplate, before filling the mug and returning to the table.

Esme watched, riveted, as, slowly and elegantly, white frothy bubbles appeared in the liquid, forming a head of creamy foam, magic happening before her eyes.

Mrs Bee held the cup to her mouth, allowing the steam from the coffee to cloud her glasses.

'Have a taste,' she said, offering her mug to Esme, 'but be careful – it's hot.'

Esme cautiously put her puckered lips to the rim and took a sip. '*Mmm*, I like this,' she said, the bittersweet coffee coating her tongue.

The telephone rang and Esme jumped up to get it. 'Hello?'

'It's OK, Es, I've got it! Put the phone down,' came Sophia's voice.

Esme was tempted to stay on the line but knew her sister

would realize she was still there. Reluctantly, she put the receiver down.

'Do you think that's Daddy?' she asked Mrs Bee.

'Might be. Or one of your sister's friends. Finish your drawing, dear.'

Esme added details to her sketch: light from the windows, a little wooden heart hanging over the doorway. Each time she changed the colour of her pen, she looked up at the door, waiting for Sophia. She wanted to go into the drawing room but knew her sister would be cross if she was speaking to a friend.

'Why's she taking so long?' she asked Mrs Bee, frustrated.

'Teenage girls like to talk,' Mrs Bee replied.

Finally, the kitchen telephone pinged and Sophia burst into the room. 'That was Daddy! Mummy is OK but she's being moved to a hospital in London tomorrow. Daddy's going with her.'

'Och, darling, what a relief,' said Mrs Bee, wiping her glasses with the dishcloth. 'Isn't that wonderful news, Esme?'

'Is Daddy on his way home now?' asked Esme.

'Yes. He's coming to get clean clothes, then going straight back to the hospital.'

'So, may I go with him and see Mummy?'

Sophia looked at Mrs Bee. 'I don't know about that, Es. I'm not sure she's allowed visitors.'

'I'm not a visitor,' said Esme, locking her jaw in determination.

'Stick your chin back in. You look like Desperate Dan,' her sister said.

'Well, I *am* going and no one can stop me. I'll get dressed now so I'm ready if Daddy's in a rush.' She patted her thigh for Digger who was sat, besotted, by her chair and then turned and strode out of the room, her head held high.

'God, she's so bloody stubborn,' Esme heard Sophia say behind her back.

Running to her room, she quickly threw on some clothes, cleaned her teeth and ran a brush through her tangled hair, removing the matted strands left behind in its bristles and putting them in a silken pouch labelled *Hair for Birds' Nests*.

Rushing back down the stairs, the front door opened to reveal her father. 'Daddy!' she cried, flinging her arms around his neck. 'How is Mummy? May I come back with you to the hospital?' she asked, before he had even a chance to catch his breath. He looked worn out.

'Darling, give me a second. I've been up all night and I need some breakfast. The hospital food is terrible.'

As he carried her into the kitchen, Esme hoped that God had heard her prayers earlier that morning.

'We can just have some toast then leave to see Mummy. I'm all dressed and I've brushed my teeth.'

'That's the thing, darling; I'm not sure it's a good idea for you to come,' he said, looking to Mrs Bee for support.

'Perhaps your father is right, love,' she said.

'No, Daddy, I want to come. I'm not scared. I've seen people in hospital lots of times. On telly. Anyway, it will help Mummy get better. It's always nice to have visitors when you're stuck in hospital.'

'But darling, Mummy is in a deep sleep; she won't know if you're there or not. Lots of rest is what she needs to get better.'

'Well then I can just give her a kiss and put my card on

her pillow. Look.' She held up her drawing, the piece of paper now folded with 'Get Well Soon' in her best writing added at the top.

'I can give that to her and you can come and visit when she's feeling a little better.'

'You said I could come. You promised.'

'I didn't promise, darling. When someone is in hospital they need peace and quiet. Your mother had a horrible shock and, well... she didn't even notice *me*.'

Her father was hiding something. Esme knew it and it frightened her.

'I am coming, Daddy, and that's that. You can't change my mind. I'll get someone else to take me if you don't want to.'

'I think...' He fiddled with the belt holding his corduroys, searching for words.

'Daddy, it will be nice for you too, if I come back with you.'

Her father sighed. Esme knew he wasn't going to argue any further.

'Very well, darling. But you must do exactly as I say when we get there. We must stick to the doctor's orders.'

At the hospital, Esme gripped her father's hand as he strode over to the reception. A neatly dressed lady with glasses perched on the end of her nose was chatting to a nurse and didn't notice their arrival. Esme's father planted his hands on the desk and coughed for attention.

'Excuse me for interrupting your coffee morning, ladies.'

The receptionist pushed her glasses up her nose and turned to face Esme and her father.

'No need to get touchy, sir. I've only just come on duty. How can I help you?' she said, bristling.

'I'm here to see my wife,' he said. 'Diana Munroe. She was admitted at 4 a.m. this morning. I was here all night and I've just been to collect our daughter.'

The nurse looked at Esme then back at her friend. 'I'll see you tonight, Angela.' The other nurse stood up and headed away, soon just a silhouette in the fluorescent lighting.

'Let me see,' the first nurse said, shuffling papers. 'Here we go. Diana Munroe. She's in intensive care. Go down the corridor, turn left. The first set of double doors on the right and you'll find the nurses' station.' She looked down at Esme and smiled.

Esme returned the smile and was rewarded by a wink.

'Thank you,' said Esme, trying to make up for her father's impatience as he strode away from the desk and in the direction the woman had pointed.

'You're welcome, sweet thing,' she said. 'I hope your mum gets better soon.'

Esme waved goodbye and ran after her father, her shoes slipping and squeaking on the linoleum floor.

Catching up with him further down the corridor, he turned and addressed her. 'Now, Esme, before you see your mother, I want you to give me a minute to talk to the doctor on my own. We need to check that she's allowed more visitors.'

'But, Daddy, I want to see Mummy *now*.'

'No, darling, you must wait here until I say so.'

A row of six orange plastic chairs with black metal legs were arranged against the wall, beneath a print of Monet's *Water Lilies*.

'Here, darling,' he said, and poured her a cup of water from a plastic jug. 'I won't be long. Sit tight and no mischief please!'

'How long will you be, Daddy?'

'Not long. Be a good girl,' he whispered, before disappearing through a set of double doors labelled *Intensive Care Unit*.

After silently counting up to sixty and unable to wait a second longer, Esme tiptoed after her father. Pushing open the doors, she was hit by a thick smell of disinfectant. She could hear beeping noises all around her and a hissing sound like air being expelled from a punctured tyre.

Looking around the ward Esme saw her father standing by one of four beds, with a man in a white coat holding a clipboard. They were talking quietly and seemed oblivious to the body squirming and writhing underneath the blankets in the bed alongside them. Nurses were checking the ward's various flashing and beeping machines, taking notes, and changing plastic bags attached to tall metal poles.

Esme tiptoed over to her father, unnoticed. A sort of television screen was fixed above the bed, but all it showed was a series of lines, like a graph with letters and numbers. Wires attached to the screen dropped down to the bed below.

Lowering her gaze, Esme reeled back in shock, her hand covering her mouth at the sight of her mother. Tubes erupted from her mouth and hands, making her look like some grotesque sea creature. Her head was thrashing from side to side, her eyes scrunched up in apparent pain. She made no noise but she looked anguished, her dark hair whipped into a matted chaos around her head.

Esme screamed. Her father and the doctor whirled round in unison.

'Esme! What the devil are you doing in here? Get back outside – *now*.'

'But Daddy – *Mummy*!'

'*Get out, now*!'

Esme could hear fear in her father's voice. Pushing past him she pressed herself against her mother's bed, rooting her feet to the ground and holding tightly to the iron bedframe. She stared at her mother and shrieked when her father tried to lift her away, tears running into her open mouth.

'Let go, Esme!'

'Oh, God – Mummy! *Mummy!*'

At the sound of Esme's voice her mother's eyes sprang open, in a monstrous bloodshot glare, each pupil an enormous black pool in a sea of broken veins. A low growl came from deep inside her and her cracked lips peeled back over her teeth in a ghoulish grimace. She frantically lurched towards her daughter, pulling the tube in her neck in the process.

Esme's father's repeated attempts to prise his daughter's hands from the bedframe were proving pointless; every time he tried, she clamped her fingers more tightly around the metal, vice-like, bound by her love for her mother.

'Esme, darling, you must let go. Come on, sweetie. Let go.'

Esme shook her head vigorously, trembling with fright. Giant sobs threatened to break her in two.

'Squirrel, let go.'

'*No!*' Esme screamed again.

Diana snarled savagely in reply, her breath sour with alcohol, vomit and something like turpentine. The smell made Esme recoil and finally release her grip on the bedframe.

This was not her mother. This beast before her bore no resemblance to the gentle woman who had loved and looked after for eleven years. This thing – possessed by a terrible demon – was terrifying. It couldn't be her mother – yet Esme knew that it was. Her mother's soul had fled the evil that had taken over her body, but her illness lay naked before Esme now, plain for all to see.

The shock of this realization subdued her for a moment, but when she felt her father try to guide her away, she scratched, hit, hissed and spat to stop him. If she left her mother, she would die! But then she felt the prick of something sharp in her arm and everything went black.

❄

Esme woke to find herself back at The Lodge, her head on Mrs Bee's lap and familiar warm fingers stroking her cheek. She opened her eyes a little, but her eyelashes felt as if they were glued together.

'Hello, darling,' Mrs Bee whispered, as though she wasn't quite sure if Esme was awake.

Everything felt so slow, her tongue too big in her mouth and her body pinned down by some invisible force. 'I'm so sleepy.' Her voice was groggy.

'I know, love. You've been out for the count all morning. Slept for three hours, you have.'

'I... I don't understand,' Esme mumbled, her speech thick.

'The doctor gave you a wee injection to calm you down. Your father said you were terribly upset. Seeing your mother so poorly – it was all too much for you. Your father should never have allowed you to go.'

Esme felt a gnawing sense of anxiety, like something horrible was about to happen. Mrs Bee started wiping her eyes gently.

'Your poor wee eyes – swollen and stuck together from all that crying.'

Esme realized her eyes were aching, along with every part of her body. 'Mummy?' she asked, suddenly remembering the horrible demon.

'Esme, love, your mother is on her way to London, where they can look after her better. Your daddy's gone with her.'

Esme struggled to sit up.

'There, there, now. Just lie quietly. It's all right,' said Mrs Bee, easing her back down on the sofa and stroking her hair away from her forehead.

Esme started to cry; it was all coming back. 'What's going to happen?' she asked.

'Well, your father thinks it would be nice for you to go and stay with Lady Lexi for a wee while, up at the castle. Take your mind off things. Won't that be nice?' She smiled.

'Will Sophia go with me?'

'Darling, she's going skiing, remember?'

Esme felt numb, her brain unable to process what Mrs Bee was telling her. She closed her eyes. It was all too much.

Over the sound of her racing heartbeat hammering in her ears, she heard a latch click.

'Mrs Bee?'

It was Sophia. Esme opened her eyes once more and watched her sister come into the room. She sat down in the chair next to the housekeeper, prompting the release of a great cloud of dust from the old blanket that covered it.

'Hi, Es, how are you feeling? Woozy?'

'Yes.'

'Not surprising. Apparently, you had to be given a sedative to knock you out.' She paused, then, 'What was it like? Seeing Mummy, I mean.'

'Scary,' Esme whispered.

'It was bloody stupid of Dad to take you. What was he thinking? It makes me so cross.'

Esme's head feeling clearer now, she pulled herself up into a sitting position. She could tell her sister was upset and was trying her best to hide it. She wore her bravery like a suit of armour: clunky and obvious.

'He's trying his best, Sophia. It's been a shock for him too,' interjected Mrs Bee.

'So when will Mummy come home, do you think?' asked Esme.

'Well, that's the thing. Daddy doesn't know and that's why he's organized for you to stay with Lexi at Culcairn. If I wasn't already going skiing I'd probably have been sent off to stay somewhere, too.'

Esme looked between the two women. 'But can't I stay here with you and Digger, Mrs Bee?' Time with Lexi sounded like fun but she needed to be at The Lodge for when Mummy came back.

'No, Daddy insisted you go,' said Sophia.

'And it won't be any fun staying here with me,' said Mrs

Bee. 'I need to get your mother's room shipshape and I have a mound of housework to do and there'll be no one for you to play with. Digger will keep me company. And you know your mummy would much rather you were having a nice time with Lexi.'

'When am I going, then?' said Esme in a small voice, defeated.

Mrs Bee's answer came out in a sob that was muffled by her tissue.

'This afternoon,' said Sophia, stepping in and looking at her watch. 'Soon. Come on Es, let's go and pack.'

Esme spent the rest of the morning getting ready. She went to collect some clean clothes from the laundry room, where some of her mother's nightdresses hung on a rack, suspended from the ceiling. They had been washed but when Esme pressed her nose to them, they still smelled faintly of smoke.

She was relieved that Mrs Bee only packed a few things for her; just enough for a weekend. The last item to go in her suitcase was a smart dress.

'You never know,' said Mrs Bee, smiling.

As she was closing the lid, Sophia came into the room.

'How're you doing? All ready?'

'Yes, we are,' replied Mrs Bee. 'Lots of fresh, clean clothes for your sister. We can't have her turning up at the castle with dirty linen.' She picked up the suitcase by its hard plastic handle. 'I'll take this downstairs. Don't be too long – Jimmy has a little surprise for you.'

Sophia sat on the bed and pulled Esme to her. 'How are you feeling, Es?'

'Worried,' said Esme, quietly.

'I'm not surprised. I am too. But Mummy *has* to get better this time. She's going to the best hospital in the world. And we need to give her time to recover.' She fished a bit of paper from her pocket. 'I've written Grania's telephone number on here. You can call me any time until I go to Switzerland. I'll send you a postcard every day and I'll try to call you at the castle.'

'What if no one answers the phone?' said Esme, her eyes welling up.

'Then call Jimmy. He's your knight in shining armour.'

'A very ugly one,' said Esme, giggling through her tears.

'Come on, let's go downstairs,' said Sophia, taking her sister's hand.

Jimmy was standing in the hallway wearing his hacking jacket and riding boots. She ran over and gave him a hug, which he returned.

'What's going to happen to Mummy, Jimmy?' she asked, hoping that he might know something Mrs Bee and Sophia didn't.

'Don't you worry about that – your mother's stronger than everyone thinks. She's going to get better very soon.'

'Why can't I stay with you? I don't want to go to the castle.'

'Come on, Esme! You love going up there and getting into mischief with Lexi. You'd starve if you stayed with me – I'm a terrible cook,' he said, smiling. 'Anyway, I'm not far away.'

Esme looked down at her feet, disappointed.

'It's only for a few days,' Mrs Bee added.

'Quite right,' said Jimmy. 'Now, go and grab your boots and hat, Homer's waiting for us outside and we'll ride up there together. Better to arrive in style than in Mrs Bumble's bloody rust bucket,' he laughed.

'Run and quickly say goodbye to your sister, love,' said Mrs Bee. 'I'm going to drive your suitcase up and give it to Nanny Patch, so I'll see you there.'

'I need to say goodbye to Digger, too,' said Esme.

'And Digger.' Mrs Bee smiled.

Esme knew that as soon as she was riding Homer she would feel better. She resolved to be as brave as possible and make her mummy proud, even all the way from London.

Chapter Eight

'Give him a kick!' shouted Jimmy over his shoulder.

Homer was barely moving. Esme gave him a sharp whack with her stick. Reluctantly, the pony quickened his pace and caught up with Jimmy, who was now dismounting at the castle entrance. He took Homer's reins from her as Esme climbed down and went to pull the doorbell.

As if she had been listening at the door Lexi flew out, followed by Mrs Bee and Mr Cribben.

'Esme!' shrieked Lexi. 'I can't believe it! You came by pony! How *thrilling*!' Her words tumbled out with joy. 'We've got your suitcase, haven't we, Mrs Bee?'

'Ay, that you have. Mr Cribben is going to kindly take it to your room.'

Lexi skipped over to the horses and patted Homer.

'Hi Jimmy,' she said. 'Thank you for bringing Esme.'

'Afternoon, missy,' said Jimmy in response, before hoisting himself back onto his horse and into the saddle and giving Homer's reins a tug. 'Right, I'd better be off. It's going to take forever pulling this lump behind me.' He looked down at Esme and took her hand. 'Call me if you need anything, Esme.'

Mrs Bee came over and put her arms around Esme's shoulders.

Esme waved Jimmy off then turned to face Mrs Bumble.

'I'd better get home too. Be a good girl, love. And have fun. Try not to worry about your mother; she's in the best place and will be better in a whisker's blink.'

'I'll miss you, Mrs Bee. Look after Digger and tell him every day how much I love him.'

'I will, love. Every night and every morning.' She turned away as her eyes welled.

'Bye, Mrs Bee,' said Esme one last time.

'It's going to be lovely having you here, Esme, isn't it Lady Lexi?' said Cribben.

'Isn't it just!' she said. 'When Papa told me you were coming to stay here I thought I might explode! This is the best and most exciting thing ever. We're going to have so much fun. Mama has given you a room in the tower – the one where we play hide-and-seek, with the huge bed and dustsheets. Nanny Patch has put a heater in there to make it toasty and a hottie to take the damp out of the sheets. I put a tin of biscuits out for you and some horsey books. Come on, let's go and find the others.' Lexi grabbed her friend by the elbow and dragged her into the castle.

Although Culcairn was immense and had more than 200 rooms, the part where the family lived was relatively small. It had only four reception rooms, a bedroom each for the children and the Earl and Contessa, and just a few guest bedrooms. Esme had never before worried about its enormity but this afternoon was different; she felt at once small and claustrophobic, like she was going to get trapped by high walls and faraway ceilings. Even the pictures and furniture seemed enormous.

When they arrived at the nursery, Lexi's brother and sister were sat at a table laden with food. The familiar battered sofas and threadbare pink carpet cast the walls in a rosy hue. Esme had always liked looking at the faded hunting prints, old family portraits and photos that lined the mantelpiece; picnics in the Spring Garden, Lexi at a gymkhana, Rollo catching his first trout on a fly rod.

'Look who's here!' said Lexi.

'Hi, Es,' greeted Bella, through a mouthful of crumpet.

'Esme's coming to stay for a while,' said Lexi to Bella and Rollo. 'It will be just like having another sister!'

It was the first time Esme had joined Lexi and her siblings for what they referred to as 'high tea'. She looked at the groaning table, weighed down by food fit for a king. Her spirits rose. Food always cheered her up and she hadn't often been privy to such a feast. Everything was beautifully laid out on an embroidered linen tablecloth, darns to its apple-blossom pattern revealing its age. There were plates of baked beans, crumpets, drop scones, anchovy toasts, Welsh rarebit and delicate cucumber sandwiches.

'Oi, Bella!' exclaimed Lexi. 'Don't eat all the crumpies. Save one for us!'

'Lexi,' said Cherry, walking into the room at that very moment, 'it doesn't matter; there're plenty more. It'll take me two ticks to toast another couple. Now, welcome Esme.

It's lovely to have you here. Sit down the two of you and have some cheese on toast whilst it's still hot.'

Cherry was the children's nursery maid and old Nanny Patch's assistant. Esme adored her. She knew exactly what the children loved to eat and made lovely simple things – unlike Seamus, the castle's chef, who her father said churned out food 'dressed like Madame Pompidou but inspired by the potato famine'.

'Bella, you need to put your arms on for a bit. Practice makes perfect,' said Cherry, bringing over a plastic waistcoat, complete with lifelike arms.

'Here we go. This is where I change into a robot,' said Bella, grimacing.

Esme watched Cherry place the contraption over her shoulders like a coat and buckled it up at the front. She felt embarrassed, as if she was seeing Bella naked. It looked like torture. Rollo and Lexi helped their sister put her sweater back on over the top. Esme was touched by how patient and gentle they were with her.

'Pass the Bovril, will you,' said Lexi.

'God, I don't know how you can eat that stuff! *You* pass it, Bella – let's see if your new hand can do it,' said Rollo.

Bella still wasn't used to her prosthetic arms. They were pretty basic – a bit like those long poles with metal claws on the end they used in supermarkets to get things off the top shelf, Esme thought.

The replica hand tried and failed. The Bovril tumbled off the table and on to the floor. Bella kicked the jar, sending it flying under the sofa.

'Ugh, it's so annoying. I *hate* these stupid things!'

Esme jumped down and picked up the jar. It was the first time Esme had seen her use the false arms. Her mother had told her that when the Contessa was pregnant she had felt very sick so the doctor had given her a pill, but it had turned out to be bad for the baby and had meant Bella's arms didn't develop properly. Apparently there were about 500 babies born the same way because their mothers had taken that pill.

Bella was funny and brave, managing so well that often Esme forgot she was different, but sometimes her frustration and pain would make her explode in a fit of uncharacteristic bad temper. She had once told Esme that she had no need for artificial arms, as she was able to 'do everything except wipe my arse with my toes', but her mother had insisted she be fitted with them, so that she would look more 'normal'. Esme could see now how painful it was for her to use them and how cumbersome they made things.

'Just take them off. You've done enough practice today,' said Lexi.

Bella looked expectantly at Cherry.

'Not so fast, young lady. You need to get used to getting dressed on your own. You won't always have your brother and sister to help you. Let's get it over and done with and then you can go out and play.'

'See you later, Bella,' said Lexi, as her sister got up to leave. 'Es, did you know that Princess Margaret is staying tonight? Let's spy on her in the bath later. Come with us after, Bella.'

'No thanks! But I'll give you 10p if you can steal her pants.'

'I'll pretend I didn't hear that, children. Come on, Bella,' said Cherry, leading the way.

Without a complaint, Bella followed the nursery maid

out the room, hotly pursued by Rollo, who had to 'make a telephone call'. Esme smiled, hoping Sophia was still at The Lodge.

'We can steal them easily, can't we Es?' said Lexi.

But Esme felt suddenly tired and sad, as if it had only just dawned on her again that she would be there still at bedtime. She nodded.

'May I quickly call Mrs Bee to make sure Digger's all right? He came running after me when I left. I just want to make sure Mrs Bee got him OK.' Although truthfully, she just wanted to know if there was any news on her mother.

'Oh, Es, he'll be fine. She would have phoned if there was anything wrong. Come on, we haven't got time for that. I've got a surprise for you!'

'OK.' As was often the case, Esme allowed herself to be overruled by Lexi.

As they made their way along the corridor, Lexi carried on. 'Guess *what*? I managed to pinch some ciggies off Mama. Let's go to the mausoleum — we definitely won't get caught there!' Excited, she tore off and, without a second to think about it, Esme ran after her friend.

Culcairn Castle had a seemingly endless warren of corridors that tunnelled through its guts and beyond, even to other properties on the estate.

The mausoleum was at the top of a hill overlooking the castle. Reaching the end of the corridor the girls dashed outside and away from Culcairn, taking a shortcut through the rose garden, the fountain covered in sheets to protect it from the frost and the surrounding rosebushes looking naked and cold. Lofty trees soared into the sky, their branches thatched in thick layers of snow. A gust of wind blew clumps of icy blossom, which Esme tried to catch, squealing with delight when one landed on her face, rapidly melting and dripping down her cheeks.

Scrambling up a steep bank, they finally arrived at the vaults where all Lexi's ancestors were buried. Out of breath and giggling, they flumped down on one of the tombstones outside.

'Is this where you'll be buried?' asked Esme.

'S'pose so. But you'll have to be next to me.' Lexi put her arm around her friend.

'Are you OK, Es?' she asked, her voice soft. 'Papa told me not to say anything but you must have been really scared when your mama was rushed to hospital. What happened? How is she now?'

'I don't know,' said Esme, relieved to have the opportunity to talk about her mother at last. 'Her bed was on fire from a candle she'd lit to make the room smell nice and the smoke made her fall into a very deep sleep. But I heard one of the ambulance men say she'd have to have her stomach pumped and that all the pills she'd taken would "cause trouble". And the drugs they gave her turned her into this horrible monster in hospital so I couldn't say goodbye and now she's miles away in London. I'm scared she'll die, Lexi, and that I'll be here.' Esme bowed her head to hide her tears.

'But she won't die,' said Lexi. 'I mean, she's not very old and she is so pretty. The doctors and nurses will make her better.'

'I suppose so...' said Esme.

'Trust me, Es, you're going to have so much fun while

you're here at the castle that you won't even have time to miss her. I promise. We can ask Papa when we get back if he has any news and if he doesn't we can take the car to Jimmy's tomorrow to ask him instead.'

'Yes, you're right,' said Esme, buoyed by her friend's optimism. 'You know, it was Digger who saved her. He barked to wake me up. He was outside Mummy's door trying to rescue her.'

'Really? I wish I had a Digger. He is possibly the cleverest dog in the world. Mama's dog is useless.'

Esme smiled at the thought of the Contessa's Brian, proud to be the owner of the cleverest dog in the world.

'Now, let's have a ciggie,' said Lexi, changing the subject and passing her friend the packet she'd hidden in her coat pocket.

The girls had smoked their first cigarettes in the nursery bathroom the previous Christmas. A year on, the smell of freshly lit tobacco and paper was even more intoxicating. Lexi struck a match then held the flame under Esme's expectant cigarette.

Puff, blow. Puff, blow. Cough.

'My turn!' Lexi took the cigarette from her friend's mouth, careful not to pull too hard, Esme's lips having stuck to the filtered tip. The girls had both learnt their lesson the hard way on that score.

'I'm so happy you're here, Esme,' said Lexi, puffing at the cigarette before hugging her friend. 'We really will be sisters now.'

'And Princess Margaret is here!' said Esme, excitedly. None of her friends at school believed she knew the Queen's sister.

'Yes, she arrived this morning! Papa does *so* love her. She makes him laugh more than anyone. She's so naughty for a princess.'

'If we were princesses we'd be naughty too.'

'She only gets away with it because she's the Queen's sister. I'd love to be a real-life princess. Imagine all those beautiful jewels, the dresses, the people curtseying all the time.'

'The last time I saw her she gave me a book: *The House at Pooh Corner*. It was hers when she was a little girl. She read it to me and every time she said Pooh's name she made a farting sound!' Esme laughed.

'I've got that book! Let's get her to read it to us,' said Lexi, clapping her hands.

'No, I've got a better idea,' said Esme, knowing how much Princess Margaret liked pranks. 'Let's make her an apple-pie bed!'

'Brilliant idea! She's in the Queen Anne Room, as usual. There's a really high window in the bathroom so if we get onto the roof, we can look in. Come on, let's do it. We need to hurry because she's already taking her bath before dinner. We can do the bed quickly, then climb up on to the roof. See, I told you it would be lots of fun staying here, Es!'

'Oh, we're just going to have the *best* time until Mummy is better.'

The girls crept quietly into the Queen Anne Room, peering around the door first to check that Princess Margaret was still in the bathroom. It was very grand, just like Esme imagined the Princess was used to back at her palaces. The four-poster bed was so tall it almost touched the ceiling and because the mattress was so high a footstool had been placed alongside it, to help the Princess climb into bed. Esme had heard her father say that the gigantic bed was one of the most famous things in the castle as it had been made especially for Queen Anne's one-night visit, or so the Contessa liked to tell everyone.

The Princess's suitcase had been unpacked and lay open on a chaise-longue at the end of the bed. A lace-trimmed nightdress hung from a pretty coat hanger and a pair of tiny satin slippers rested under the footstool. The room already smelled of the Princess, a heady mix of flowers and wood.

Lexi picked up the long, silky evening dress that was draped over a chair. 'I'm a Princess!' she whispered, twirling the bright-blue gown around the room in great leaps and bounds like it was her dance partner.

Esme ran her fingers down the Princess's nightdress. 'Oh, it's so soft,' she said, 'and the colour is so pretty – like the inside of a shell.' She let it fall back, doing her best to leave it smooth and unwrinkled.

'Let's make the apple-pie bed,' said Lexi, mischievously, carefully placing the evening dress back on the chair.

'Gosh, we need a ladder to get onto it,' said Esme.

The two girls set to work, folding the top sheet into a linen envelope into which the Princess would only be able to slide so far before her feet hit an unexpected barrier. Stifling their giggles, they then covered the sheets with the blanket.

'Do you think she's tall enough to get stuck? You don't think we should pull the bottom up a bit more?' asked Lexi.

'Let's try it out,' Esme said, sliding between the sheets

and finding that she was only able to squeeze in up to her tummy button.

'Perfect!' Lexi laughed. 'Quick, Es, help me pull the bedspread over.'

With great effort, they heaved the heavy, quilted silk over the pillows and patted it down flat.

'Look, here are her knickers!' Esme said, throwing them at her friend. 'Let's take them.'

Lexi shoved the cotton knickers down the front of her trousers.

'Good, now let's get up on the roof to watch.'

The roof of Culcairn Castle was a vast expanse of lead on which Esme had spent hours playing with Lexi and Bella. It had been in a state of disrepair for decades; just after Rollo's birth, a dead pigeon had got stuck in one of the rooftop drains, causing a terrible flood in the library beneath and damaging a vast collection of highly valuable ancient tomes.

Lexi pushed open the window and climbed out. Although it was dark outside now, the girls knew the layout of the roof like the backs of their hands. Esme followed her friend, and the pair made their way over the crumbling parapets and buttresses.

Feeling like Randell and Hopkirk, the private detectives on that new TV programme she and Lexi loved, they crouched down and crawled up to a window that looked into the Princess's bathroom. Esme pulled her sleeve over her hand and gently rubbed away just enough dirt to create a peephole through which they could spy.

And there was Her Royal Highness, soaking in the bath. A cigarette dangled in one hand and she clutched her whisky in the other, her face fully made-up. Other than her arms only her head, covered in a baby-blue bath hat trimmed with lace, protruded from the soapy water, the rest of her body hidden beneath the surface. The soft humming of a popular tune could just be heard floating up out of a side-window.

'She looks like a marble statue,' said Lexi, sighing. 'Like a Grecian Goddess.'

'Bathing in only the freshest milk and honey,' said Esme.

'Lexi and Esme,' called a velvety voice from below, 'I know you're up there. Once you two Peeping Toms have finished spying, will one of you ask Cribben to organize an extra heater? It's absolutely freezing in my room. I don't want to leave this godforsaken place with a chill.'

'How did she know we were here?' whispered Lexi, her eyes wide.

'I can see the reflection of your grubby faces in the mirror,' laughed the Princess. She took a sip from her crystal tumbler and stubbed her cigarette out in the soap dish.

'And Lexi, can you tell your naughty Papa that I'm running late? It's all his fault. I had to walk up the last part of the drive because the Bentley couldn't make it. Next time the weather is as awful as this, I'll bring my own bag of salt to grit the road. Not *all* of us travel in a Land Rover.' She turned and looked up at window with a twinkle in her eyes.

The girls grinned back, their cover blown. 'Will do!' shouted Lexi.

'Esme, darling, I'm so sorry to hear about your darling mama. You need to be a brave little girl.' She paused. 'Now, I can't wallow in this water all evening and I'd rather you didn't watch me get out of the tub, so, scoot! Why don't you come and join us for pre-dinner drinks after your baths? Lexi, I'll make sure your mother doesn't cause a fuss. It will be heavenly to see you both.'

❄

Esme whipped her clothes off and kicked them under the bed. She knew that Nanny Patch would tell her off if she left her new bedroom in a mess, but she didn't want to be late for the Princess. She covered her nakedness with an enormous towel and dashed into the corridor to meet Lexi in the nursery bathroom. Half-dragging the towel behind her, she struggled to keep her modesty before falling in a great puddle of material on the floor.

'Oh, bloody hell!' she said.

'Are you all right, Esme?' She looked up and saw the Earl smiling down at her. 'Here, let me help you,' he said, laughing. He tugged the towel away from her face and helped her secure it around herself. She wiggled her arms, delighted that her new dress stayed on.

'There we go. You look like a bride now. Shall I be your pageboy and carry your train? I presume you're heading to join my daughter in the bathroom?'

'Yes,' giggled Esme, she could hear splashing noises and Lexi's laughter from the end of the corridor.

The bride and her pageboy started to walk down the long carpet, Esme clutching at the towel to make sure it stayed in place. They passed a framed landscape of Culcairn Castle that looked like the artist had climbed all the way to the top of a mountain in order to paint it. She wondered which one – there were so many mountains in Scotland. Esme had never seen the castle look so small.

'Where did the artist go to paint this picture?' she asked, pointing to it. 'Oh, it must have been Ben Nevis!' she exclaimed. 'It's not too far from here, is it? And Sophia said that it's the biggest mountain in Britain.' The towel slipped a bit and she quickly pulled it back in place.

'Yes, it is,' the Earl said, kindly. 'But don't you think his fingers would have frozen before he'd finished? It's very cold at the top of a mountain, Esme. I think he probably used his imagination instead.'

'Maybe he made smaller sketches as he walked, then put them together in his head and created one gigantic picture?'

'I hadn't thought of that. It's probably exactly what he did. You are clever.'

'I love the paintings here. I could look at them forever. Although it must make it much easier for artists now to be able to use a camera instead.'

The Earl laughed. 'I wish my children showed as much interest as you, Esme.'

She smiled, turning with a great flourish so her bridal train flowed out behind her.

'Wait one second – I just need to fetch what I came up for,' he said, dropping the towel and slipping through a nearby door.

A few moments later he appeared again, clutching a card in his hands. 'It's for your mother, telling her to get well soon. I'll add some kisses from you, shall I?'

'Yes please! Three – that's her lucky number.'

'Here, you do it,' he said, passing her a pen. He bent down

and Esme added three kisses to the crosses and numbers already written.

'Are you going to give this to her? May I come too?' she asked.

'I'll leave it to the postman, as it needs to go all the way to London. We wouldn't want to put poor Mr Drabble out of a job now, would we?'

'Mmm,' Esme mused, knowing how long it took them to drive up to Scotland. 'Do you think I will see Mummy soon?'

'I'm afraid, my dear, that it's really up to those taking care of her, but I'm sure it won't be too long,' said the Earl. 'Come on, we'd better get you into the bath before Lexi manages to splash out all the water in the tub. You don't want to be late – Princess Margaret is a stickler for punctuality.'

Esme slithered into the bath alongside Lexi, causing the steaming water to slop over the side.

'Do we need to dress up like the grown-ups?' she asked.

'I don't know. I've never been allowed to go before. Well, actually, I've always been too scared to ask Mama.'

'Maybe we shouldn't go?' said Esme, her enthusiasm flagging.

'Esme! Her Royal Highness *commanded* it. We have to go, it's by royal appointment,' said Lexi, standing to wash herself. 'And I think we should dress up all fancy. We can steal some of Mama's lipstick and curl our hair. We could even stuff one of her bras each with loo paper, then we'll look *really* grown up.'

'I'll need lots of padding,' said Esme, pressing her nipples. 'I don't even have a little lump. Sophia's felt like cherry stones when they started growing and she said they were painful when she touched them.'

Lexi's hands prodded at her own chest. 'Oh my God!' she shrieked. 'Es, feel mine! I've got two pips!'

Esme did as instructed and, sure enough, there were two tiny lumps. 'Wow! Oh, Lexi, you are *so* lucky. Just think, you'll have to wear a bra *for real* soon. Mine are *never* going to grow. It's not fair!'

'You should ask God when you say your prayers tonight. Come on, Es, let's get out and steal that stuff from Mama's room.'

A few minutes later, still wrapped in their towels, they entered the Earl and Contessa's bedroom. It was a surprisingly pretty room, painted in a soft sky blue. The large four-poster bed had a fleur-de-lys cornet above it from which fell blue silk curtains.

'I'm just going to find the curlers. Don't move a muscle!' said Lexi.

Esme went to the Contessa's dressing table and picked up a cut-glass scent bottle, running her finger over the crystal. A silver-framed photograph showed the Contessa holding a large trophy and standing next to a racehorse. She was smiling but her eyes stared out at Esme, dark and cold. The Contessa was so different to her own mother, who loved everyone – on her good days, at least. Esme couldn't remember a time when Lexi's mother had asked her a question or shown the least bit of interest in her. She was sure that even if she jumped up and down right in front of her nose, shouting swear words, the Contessa would barely blink. It was as if she was invisible.

Opening one of the drawers she discovered a neat pile of lace handkerchiefs lying under a tiny bag filled with lavender. Strings of pearls hung from the mirror, along with a faded rosette. *Champion Broodmare.* That was nice, she thought. Esme kept her own winning rosette from Bonnyton Gymkhana on her mirror too. Maybe she could tell the Contessa about it, now she knew they had something in common.

After plugging in the electric curlers, Lexi opened a mirrored wall cabinet and took out a gold tube. 'Lipstick,' she said. 'What shade shall we choose?'

'Pink?' Esme said, thinking of her mother's favourite colour.

Lexi pulled out a box of curlers from inside a drawer and plugged them into the socket.

'Found them! Look, you see that dot?' she said, pointing at the side of the box. 'When that turns red it means they're hot.'

Esme stared at the little bulb, waiting for it to come on. The red light flickered a few times, then beamed steadily from the plastic.

'I think they're ready enough. Unplug them, Es.'

Esme pulled the plug from the wall.

'Now sit down and brush your hair. Get rid of all those knots.' Lexi took the hairbrush from Esme and separated a chunk of hair. 'I watched Mama do this once, I have to sort of curl your hair around it. Like this.' Lexi's tongue poked out of her lips in concentration as she wound the hair around the hot tube.

'Ow! That's hot!' Esme cried, as the curler bumped against her scalp.

'Sorry, Es.' Lexi pulled it a little further away from Esme's head and fixed the curler in place with a blue-tipped hairpin. 'The blue ones are for the fat curlers and the pink ones for the thin ones.'

When she had finished, Esme looked at herself in the dressing-table mirror. She laughed at her reflection. The curlers hung around her face like spaniel ears. 'How long do they have to stay in for?'

'Not long. Here, put on some lipstick.' Lexi handed her the tube, which she had twisted up to reveal a livid pink. 'It looks like Brian's willy!' she said.

'Yuck! I don't want to put it on, now,' said Esme.

'Go *on*! Stretch your mouth wide like this.' Lexi pulled her lips over her teeth and smiled to demonstrate. Esme did the same and smeared her lips with pink.

'Now smack them together.'

She did as she was told, clamping them shut to even out the colour.

'Perfect!' said Lexi. 'Now let's take the curlers out.'

Working together, Esme's hair was soon loose again, falling down around her in a cloud of clumsy curls.

'Beautiful. My turn now,' said Lexi, pushing her friend from the stool. 'We have to reheat the curlers but it won't take long. What shall we wear?'

'We could put on our nighties with some necklaces, then they'll look like long dresses,' suggested Esme.

'That's such a good idea. Mama keeps some of her jewellery in there,' said Lexi, pointing to a large leather trunk in the corner of the room.

Esme lifted the lid, ornately studded with brass tacks. 'I've never seen a box like this before, Lexi. It's amazing. Is it old? Looks like it came from a pirate ship.'

'It did. Papa said it was once filled with rubies and gold bullion. Can you imagine?'

'Will these do?' said Esme, holding up long strings of pearls and amber.

'Yes! And there should be some ostrich boas, too... There's a pale pink one. Oh, and I know – see if you can find the fox collar.'

Esme carried on rummaging. 'Here we go. May I wear the feather boa? It's just like one Mummy has,' she said.

'Sure. It'll look lovely with the pearls.'

'And the amber necklace is the same colour as the fox's eyes,' said Esme, thrilled with her booty.

Esme had done a better job with Lexi's hair. Once the curlers were out, her dark tresses tumbled about her in wild abandon.

'Wow, Lexi – look at you! You're going to be the belle of the ball tonight.'

'And you look exactly like your mummy. Well, a blonde version of her. She'd be so proud of you, Es.'

Esme smiled. She was going to tell Mummy all about this when she was better.

'Are we ready, Lexi?' she asked.

'Yes,' said Lexi giving a little skip. 'We *shall* go to the ball!'

They stood outside the library, giggling nervously.

'Oh, look at you both!' exclaimed Princess Margaret, looking stunning in the long, bright-blue dress. Turquoise and diamond earrings hung from her ears to match her necklace.

The girls curtseyed and the Princess gave them both a kiss. She still wore her hair in a curled bob and she had perfectly manicured nails, brightly painted lips and lashes stiff with mascara.

Esme's father said that she had the ability to make 'hell freeze over' if she wished, but Esme had only seen her other side, her wicked sense of humour and mischievous tricks. She loved to sing and dance, to drink and to smoke, and Esme adored her. Just like she and Lexi, the Princess found immense pleasure in being naughty and stirring things up.

'Well, you look so grown up, I think you'd better stand in for my ladies-in-waiting, tonight,' she said. 'Shall we give you a name each?'

'Oh, yes!' said Lexi. 'I want to be Dolly Parton as my boobs are starting to grow.'

'Let's hope they grow more than your mother's ever did,' said the Princess, smiling. 'And you, Esme, darling?'

'Dusty Springfield,' she said, gleefully. 'She's Mummy's favourite singer.'

Esme wished her mother were here. She would have worn her beautiful lilac Norman Hartnell dress that made her look so pretty. Her father would have brought up her precious jewellery from the safe in the cellar and Esme would have helped her choose which pieces to wear.

'Wonderful. So, shall we go and face the rabble?' said the Princess, eyes glinting wickedly.

Flanked by the two girls, each looking the very image of their mother, she held both of their hands and began to walk towards the sound of chattering voices and clinking glasses.

Esme knew that Princess Margaret liked to make a grand entrance, sweeping into large rooms of people with her jewels sparkling in the light. She braced herself, being in the spotlight was new to her.

Entering the room, the Earl strode over to greet the Princess, running his hand through his immaculate hair. It reminded Esme of a soldier's – swept-back, slick and gleaming. He tugged his starched cuffs out from the sleeves of his smoking jacket.

'Ma'am. You look marvellous. How wonderful to have you here,' he said, kissing her on each cheek then bowing his head to look at Esme and Lexi. He smiled. 'And who are these two beauties? I don't believe we've met before.'

'May I introduce to you my new ladies-in-waiting: Lady Dusty Springfield and Lady Dolly Parton?' She turned to the girls, 'And this is His Lordship, The Earl of Culcairn,' said the Princess.

'How do you do, Your Lordship?' giggled Lexi.

'It's a pleasure to meet you, ladies,' said the Earl.

'Oh no, the pleasure is all theirs, Henry – isn't it, ladies?' she said.

Lexi and Esme proudly smiled up at the Earl.

Princess Margaret opened her bag to retrieve a cigarette and placed it in a jewelled holder with the grace of a prima ballerina.

'I must introduce them to your wife, Henry,' she said, taking their hands again and leading the girls over to the Contessa, sitting on a large scarlet sofa.

'Lucia, I'd like you to meet my most loyal servants, Lady Dusty and Lady Dolly.'

'You look very pretty, Alexa,' said the Contessa, looking up and patting her daughter's curls with a white-gloved hand.

'Mama, don't you think Esme looks lovely, too – just like her mummy?' asked Lexi.

The Contessa took off a diamond earring and rubbed at her earlobe. She wore a dark velvet gown that matched her ink-black hair that was backcombed high on her crown, making her appear even more severe. An enormous diamond hanging from a necklace of pea-sized gems, emphasizing her long neck. Even sitting down she was nearly as tall as the pint-sized Princess.

'My goodness, Lexi,' gasped Princess Margaret. 'You are absolutely right. Esme, you look just like your mother. Did you know that every man in the world was in love with her before I introduced her to your father? I think there are still a few who hold a candle for her, but she is devoted to only one man. Isn't that right, Lucia?'

Esme waited for the Contessa's response but she said nothing, instead staring silently back at the Princess, until turning to call out to the butler, raising her glass. 'Cribben, more wine, please.' She reached for a book of matches, striking the sandpaper and lighting her cigarette from the flame as it hissed alight. Princess Margaret leant down to light her own cigarette from the match, looking deep into the Contessa's eyes, her own sparkling with amusement. Inhaling, she then slowly blew smoke out into Lexi's mother's face and led the girls to a large sofa at the other end of the room.

Esme couldn't believe what Princess Margaret had just done; she wished she could be just as brave in front of the Contessa.

'Come sit, my darlings,' said the Princess, patting the cushion next to her.

Dutifully the girls perched at the edge of the sofa, hands in their laps and on best behaviour. The room smelled of wine and cigars but fresh, rather than fermenting – the post-soiree aroma familiar to Esme from after her parents hosted friends. Mr Cribben buzzed around, refilling empty glasses.

'Who shall we get to come and join us for a chat?' said the Princess.

'Who would you like to talk to, ma'am?' asked Esme.

'Let's see.' She swirled her cigarette holder around, pointing from person to person before stopping at Lord Findlay. 'William!' she said. 'Run over and fetch his Lordship, Esme.'

Esme hopped off the sofa and wobbled over to Lord Findlay, feeling a little bit nervous when she saw that he was now talking to Lexi's mother. She tugged at his sleeve, 'Ma'am wants to talk to you,' she interrupted.

'Goodness, Esme, for a moment I thought you were your mother! How *is* dear Diana? Frightful shock for us all.'

The Contessa rolled her eyes. 'Amateur dramatics, William,' she said.

'Lucia, I hardly think…'

The Contessa's words crushed Esme, but she couldn't think of what to say. Lord Findlay took her hand. 'Will you excuse me, Lucia? When the Princess says jump, one *jumps*.' He turned to Esme, 'I must say, Mary-Rose and I were deeply upset to hear about your mother, Esme. We have sent flowers to wish her a speedy recovery.'

'Do you know how she is?' asked Esme, very quietly. 'I haven't heard from her and no one will tell me anything. Is she *dead*?'

For a moment Lord Findlay looked as though he didn't know what to say. He then bent down slightly, so that they were at the same level. 'Goodness me, Esme. Your mother is most definitely still alive,' he told her. 'She is going to get much better and when she is feeling stronger, you will see her. I'm sure of it.'

Esme breathed a sigh of relief and they started to walk back towards Princess Margaret. Lexi was cackling loudly at something the Princess had said. It was very kind of Lord Findlay to send her mother some flowers, Esme thought, and she remembered that the Earl would be sending his card too.

'Alexa!' called the shrill voice of the Contessa. 'I think we have had enough entertainment. It's time for bed.'

Lexi sighed, raising her eyebrows at Esme.

'You'd better do as Lucia says, my darlings,' said the Princess. 'Thank you for bringing William over to talk to me, dear Esme. You've both been most excellent ladies-in-waiting. Give me a kiss goodnight and I'll see you both in the morning.'

Lexi and Esme leant forward to plant a tentative peck on Princess Margaret's cheeks. The Earl walked over from the fireplace and greeted Lord Findlay before leaning down to ruffle the girls' hair.

'Goodnight, Lady Dusty, Lady Dolly.'

Esme knew that the Earl was pretending, but it still made her feel a little bit braver that he was speaking to her like a grown-up. She finally plucked up the courage to ask the Earl a question. 'Do you think we could call Mrs Bee tomorrow to ask about Mummy?

'Of course, we can, darling,' he replied. 'Now off to bed, I'm sure your mother is already fast asleep and dreaming all about her youngest daughter. So, the quicker you get to sleep, the quicker you can dream about her, too.'

Esme smiled up at Lexi's papa. Yes, she thought. She would meet her mother in her dreams and give her a big get-better-soon squeeze.

Chapter Nine

Esme stood in front of her enormous bed wishing that she was sleeping in the same room as Lexi. It was freezing. A feeble light revealed the haze of floating dust that made her feel as if she had drowned and now lay forgotten at the bottom of an ocean. A vast faded tapestry hung behind the bed. Everything was huge; the mirror, the paintings, even the door seemed fit for a giant. Esme suddenly felt very small.

The door creaked open behind her, making her jump.

'Hello, my love,' a kind voice said. It was Nanny Patch. 'Now, I've unpacked all your things. Your knickers and vests are in this drawer, socks and tights here, shirt and sweater in this one.' She pointed towards the different compartments of the huge mahogany wardrobe. 'Jodhpurs are in here and your dress and coat are hanging up so they don't crease. I've put your wellingtons in the gunroom and your hacking jacket, hat and jodhpur boots are in the boot room.' She paused for breath. 'Toothbrush and toothpaste are in the nursery bathroom with your bath hat. Nightie under your pillow. Dressing gown on the back of the door and slippers by your bed.'

Nanny Patch had a habit of speaking about everything as quickly as possible, like she was scared a sentence might get stuck if it wasn't pushed out by the next one. She wore her snow-white hair in a topknot, kept in place by a cobweb-like hairnet that was secured with two tortoiseshell combs. Esme didn't think she had ever seen her without her white pinny, which protected a tidy, pale-blue blouse and skirt.

'You need to get to bed yourself now, missy. You're going to the cinema tomorrow afternoon, lucky girl that you are. After riding, of course.'

'The cinema!' Esme gasped. 'That's so exciting. I've only been once before, with Mummy.'

'Yes, well, you'll need to wash your hair and polish your shoes first, after your hack. Do you have gloves? Not riding ones – white ones.'

'White gloves?' asked Esme. 'No, I don't have any.' She wondered why she would need these for the cinema.

'You, Lexi and Bella are going with the Earl's mother, the Dowager Countess, and we all know she's a stickler for etiquette. We'll need to lend you some gloves.' Nanny Patch shuffled over to the bed and turned the sheets down.

'All right, Esme. Be a good girl. Straight to sleep. No sneaking down to Lexi's room.' She walked briskly to the door, as if she had a thousand other things to do before the day was done. 'Night night.'

'Good night, Nanny Patch.' Esme was beginning to feel sad again. She wished she could speak to Mrs Bee before she went to bed. 'Nanny Patch, has anyone called for me? I know Mummy can't, but maybe Daddy has? Or Sophia?' Her voice felt small and wobbly.

Nanny Patch stopped still. 'Oh Esme, my dear. I'm not sure. Her Ladyship answers the phone most of the time. Ask her tomorrow. You go to sleep now and the morning will come soon enough.' She closed the door and left Esme alone in the bedroom.

The darkness seemed to creep in from the outside and she wanted to shut it out. She walked over to the window, unsure whether to pull down the parchment blinds or attempt to close the dusty curtains, whose embroidered silk was thread-bare in places. She tugged on the tasselled cord as carefully as she could manage and the central blind shot down to the window sill.

Esme shrieked and leapt back, suddenly surrounded by a swarm of dopey flies. Most dropped to the floor, where they either buzzed around in circles like a sea of swollen currants or lay motionless, dying. The buzzing became very loud, close to her ears, and she realized that some were caught in her hair. She screamed, shaking her head around and whipping her hands at her hair then stopped and listened, heart pumping, eyes wide.

'*Argh!*' There was one stuck at her neck. She smacked it away and watched as an obese bluebottle glided to the ground like a fighter plane, hit by the enemy. Brushing herself down, she took a deep, trembling breath.

She decided against pulling down the other blinds and instead climbed into bed. Despite a valiant effort by the hot-water bottle, the sheets were damp and it was so cold in the room that Esme felt the tip of her nose begin to tingle.

Leaving the bedside lamp on, she closed her eyes, put the palms of her hands together and said her prayers.

'God bless Mummy, Daddy, Sophia, Mrs Bee, Homer, Mr Quince and Elvis. Please make Esme a good and happy girl.

Amen. Oh, and please make my bosoms grow. Amen. And help Mummy to get better soon. Thanks. Amen.'

As the tide of sleep took over, an image she had managed to push away all day but which was seared on her memory, seeped back into focus. It was her mother, hissing and spitting, retching and straining, her words tumbling out so fast that they made no sense. Inflamed terror in her eyes, not knowing who Esme was, her body empty of her soul. Her mother gone.

Esme woke up with a start, not sure where she was. Someone or something was in her room. Her mind refused to regain full consciousness. Her beating heart thumped in her chest. She squeezed her eyes shut and pulled the sheets up to her chin.

'Don't for one minute think you are welcome here,' a voice hissed.

She felt an invisible finger poke her shoulder.

'You are unwanted at home and you are only here because he is weak. He believes the squalid lies your mother has been telling him. And now he feels guilty because she tried but failed to do the decent thing in killing herself. And now I have to look at you every day; a constant reminder of your insane mother.'

Esme kept her eyes firmly shut, powerless to escape. It was cold, so cold, but the heat of the horrible words burnt her face. She was unable to move, unable to scream. A floorboard creaked. She thought she was going to be sick. A rush of wind ruffled her bedcovers. The door opened and closed. She lay there, frozen. Was the voice real? A nightmare? Or was it a ghost? Why would a ghost say that her mother had tried to kill herself? Could it be *true*? The world suddenly seemed even more terrifying. It was even scarier than seeing her mother in flames. And this time she was alone. No Mrs Bee. No Sophia. Panic and fear unravelled within her, paralyzing her thoughts and catapulting her into darkness.

'Esme, wake up. It's a beautiful day!'

Esme could hear Lexi but couldn't seem to open her eyes. She was so tired.

'Come *on* – wake up, Es! We need to have breakfast then we can take Jalopy down to Jimmy. Come *on*, sleepy head!' Lexi shook her friend and then wound up the blind.

Esme opened her eyes. Lexi didn't even notice the flies, which crunched like gravel under her boots.

Esme sat up and stretched. She felt as if it were still the middle of the night. 'Lexi? Do you know if this room is haunted?'

'No Es, it's just a myth that castles are haunted. It just seems creepy because no one's slept in here for a bit. It'll be better tonight and if it's not then sleep in with me. Now get a move on, you lazy slug. Breakfast. It's about to be cleared away as everyone's eaten – *including* me.' She pulled Esme's jodhpurs from the drawers and threw them on the bed. 'Chop, chop.'

'Ugh, Lexi, stop it, I'm coming.'

She pulled on her knickers, layering them with a vest, long johns, shirt and Fair Isle sweater.

'How many pairs of socks have you got on?' she asked Lexi.

'Two. The snow hasn't melted at all. Now come on, let's go.'

'I'll meet you down there. I won't be long. What's for breakfast?'

'Kippers.'

'Yum,' said Esme, suddenly hungry. 'I'll see you downstairs in a min.'

After Lexi had gone, she set about making her bed. Lexi must be right. It had all been a nightmare. But as she went to turn her lamp off, she realized it was out. She felt the bulb; the stone coldness of glass that hadn't felt any electricity for many hours. She didn't remember ever switching it off. Grabbing a sheepskin waistcoat, she tied her hair back in a ponytail and went onto the landing. It must have been a dream, she thought.

The delicious smell of smoked fish made Esme's tummy rumble. She flew down the tower's spiral staircase, forcing herself to stick to the outer edges, where the steps were at their widest. The triangular stairs reminded her of big wedges of cheese as she sped round and round at such speed that she felt dizzy when she reached the bottom.

Passing through the pantry to reach the dining room beyond, she saw overflowing ashtrays and wine-stained crystal from the night before, littering Mr Cribben's benchtop.

On a small table lay two breakfast trays, each set with tiny glass pots of honey and marmalade, a dish of curled butter shavings, a silver toast rack, side plate and a delicate china cup on a saucer.

Esme opened the door to the dining room and sat down at the far end of the long table used to entertaining dozens. One place was laid with the same paraphernalia used for breakfast in bed.

Cribben sashayed into the room. 'Good morning, Esme. I'm afraid the gluttons have polished off all the kippers. Would you like a boiled egg?'

'Thank you, Mr Cribben. I'd love one.'

Cribben dropped a freshly boiled egg into her egg cup. 'Lady Lexi took her plate to His Lordship's study. She got the last kipper so I assume she's eating it in there. The whole place will stink of fish. Now, I must go and see to Her Royal Highness; she's been ringing her bell for fifteen minutes. Bloody woman seems to think I'm running a hotel! I've already been up and down four times. Coffee, not tea. Raspberry jam, not honey. Next she'll be wanting her nose picked.'

Esme wrinkled her own nose. 'Oh, but Mr Cribben, she *is* a princess!' she said. 'Please may I go up and say good morning?'

'I don't see why not,' said Mr Cribben. 'Go and see what she wants. Although she might be a little tired. As am I, you might know. I was sent to remake her bed in the middle of the night. It appears two scoundrels had made her an apple-pie bed.' He winked.

'Did Lexi tell you?'

'No. I was informed by Her Royal Highness. She found it highly amusing.'

Esme laughed. Scooping out the last of her egg, she turned the shell upside down so it looked like she had never even started it.

'Finished, Mr Cribben. I do so want to see Princess Margaret before she goes. She might have some news about Mummy.'

The butler's eyes twinkled. 'Off you trot, then. Go via the Armoury, it's quicker.'

Esme loved walking through the Armoury, it was one of the most magnificent rooms at Culcairn Castle. The vast collection of armour dated back to the sixteenth century and it always amazed Esme that just one castle could have so many swords. They were displayed in giant wheels like spokes on a bicycle. Two suits of armour stood sentry either side of an immense baronial fireplace and giant ceremonial flags embroidered with the Culcairn crest hung over the sweeping imperial staircase that divided the room. As Esme climbed the stairs, she felt as tiny as a flea. She tried to spot the ornate plasterwork roses from which hung two enormous chandeliers. Definitely fit for a Princess, she thought, as she knocked on the door to the Queen Anne Room.

'Come in.'

She poked her head around the door.

'Esme, darling,' came a regal voice from the bed. 'Come and give me a kiss.'

Princess Margaret was wearing a pale-blue bed jacket trimmed with white fur over her nightdress. Her lips were already painted and her skin glowed. She lifted her cigarette to her lips, tilting her head back as she inhaled. No one smoked as elegantly as she did; it was an effortless motion, the cigarette held lightly between her index and middle fingers whilst the rest of her hand fanned away gracefully.

Esme clambered up onto the bed and pecked the Princess on her soft cheek. She tried to curtsey, but it didn't work very well when she was balanced on the lumpy mattress.

'Mr Cribben said you might want something.'

'Lord, no! I just do it to annoy the lazy old bugger. The exercise is good for him.' She smiled, taking another puff. 'Come and sit with me, darling, and talk to me. Are you worried about your mother?'

Esme flopped down next to the Princess. She was surprised to find tears pricking at the corner of her eyes when she spoke.

'I miss her so much. Everyone says she is very ill and I don't know how long she will have to stay in London, away from me.'

'Well, darling, you haven't even been here for twenty-four hours yet. I'm sure she will be on the mend soon. She's tougher than she looks, although your father has never been able to see it. Henry, on the other hand... Well, he is marvellously understanding and patient. It must be terribly hard for you but you know what, Esme? It will make you strong. An easy childhood doesn't prepare you for life's future surprises.'

Esme didn't really understand. Surprises were meant to be nice things.

'Now, wipe away your tears and let's think of something else to annoy Cribben. I woke him last night because my bed had been made in an *extraordinary* way.' She paused and looked at Esme, who stifled a giggle. 'Oh, but he looked so funny. Just like Wee Willy Winkie in his nightshirt and slippers. So, what can we do next?'

'What was wrong with your bed?' asked Esme, trying not to laugh.

'Esme, darling. It's not the first time I have been made an apple-pie bed. I have children, too. But, it was amusing to call and have it sorted out for me. Now, back to Cribben – any ideas?'

'Why don't I tell him your loo is blocked?'

The Princess flung her arms in the air, like a swimmer preparing to dive. 'Marvellous idea. Tell him my morning constitution won't go down and he needs to bring a knife to chop it up so it will fit through the pipes.' She clapped her hands together, gleefully, her diamond ring flashing. 'He'll be hopping mad! Oh, well *done*, Esme.'

Esme giggled, looking up at the impish Princess. 'I'd better hurry – I'm going riding with Lexi. Just wanted to say good morning. I'll tell Mr Cribben.'

'Good. Now off you pop, I'm leaving in an hour. It's very lucky that Culcairn is so close to Balmoral. I can *always* find an excuse to see dear Henry. And you, of course, my darling. What a treat!'

Esme blushed.

'Give my love to your parents and don't let dreadful Lucia get to you. You mustn't show any weakness in front of her or she'll go for your throat like a pitbull. Even when you get nervous, show strength. Think of it as a game. She can be a frightful bully, especially to those prettier or cleverer than her. That's why she can't stand *me*!'

At the mention of Lexi's mother, a shadow crept across Esme. Did the voice in the darkness belong to the Contessa?

Lexi was waiting outside, next to a small green car, blowing into her hands and stamping her feet. She held a riding hat in each hand. Esme looked cautiously at the ground. It looked safe to ride out, just so long as they only walked and were careful not to let their ponies slip on the icy ground.

'Did your father say anything about Mummy?' asked Esme, as she climbed into the car's passenger seat, Lexi hopping in at the wheel.

'No, he didn't. But don't worry, Es, she'll be fine.'

Esme was getting fed up of everyone telling her that her mummy was *fine*. She needed someone to tell her what was happening. If Jimmy didn't know, maybe he would let her call Mrs Bee or Sophia. Somehow, in being beyond the confines of the castle she felt hopeful; she could find things out for herself.

'Which way shall we go?'

'Across the fields. It will be such fun driving the jalopy in the snow.'

Both girls were wrapped up against the cold day. Lexi had taken the roof off the Triumph and turned the ignition, the car's small engine stuttering as it tried to keep turning. Sweet papers and old crisp packets were strewn across the floor amongst loose pony nuts and straw. Lexi put her hand under the seat and shunted it closer to the pedals, her legs only just able to reach. She smoothly lifted the clutch whilst simultaneously putting gentle pressure on the accelerator. The little car bounced forward joyously, its passengers squealing with delight.

'*Yeeeee-haaa!*' shouted Esme, suddenly filled with a sense of certainty that Jimmy would tell her what was going on. She loved being in the car with Lexi. It made her feel grown up and free. They whooped and cheered as they rolled over the bumpy ground, their riding hats doubling up as crash helmets. The freezing air whipped around their ears and their eyes watered. Esme put her hands in her pockets to keep warm and found some Refreshers.

'Look, Lexi! Mummy must have left them for me. Open wide,' she said, dropping a pink one into Lexi's mouth.

At the end of the drive they turned left and pulled to a halt in front of the gates. Esme stepped out to push it open but it was stuck in the frozen snow. She lifted the gate up and over the mini mountain range and jumped back in the car.

'We don't need to close it, do we?' she asked, once they had driven through. 'All the sheep are in the barn during the snow.'

'No, we're fine. Now, are you ready for the *ride of your life*?' asked Lexi, as if she was a circus ringmaster announcing something spectacular. 'One, two, three… *Go!*'

Lexi pressed her foot on the gas and they shot forward down the steep hill. Esme clung to the top of the windscreen for dear life, whilst Lexi gripped the steering wheel with grim determination. Once enough momentum had been gained, she moved the gears to neutral, took both feet off the pedals and yanked up the handbrake, switching the car from motor to toboggan. It felt as if the world had turned upside down and they were flying over billowing clouds with a crystal-clear Caribbean Sea above their heads. The wind whipped through the car sending flecks of hay, empty Tootie Frootie packets and their favourite red-and-gold Caramac wrappers swirling up and out, blazing a trail of colour against the whiteness. Faster and faster they flew towards the most precipitous point of the run; a ridge that, given enough speed, would turn the Triumph into Chitty Chitty Bang Bang, making it soar off the ground for a few brief seconds.

'Here we go – hold on tight, Es!' shouted Lexi.

Esme clutched her seat with both hands, bracing herself for the crash landing.

Both girls screamed at the top of their lungs as the car took off. They leant forward, as if jumping a fence on their ponies, their backs slapping back against their seats on landing.

'Well done, Jalopy. That was *amazing*,' panted Lexi. 'I wish Rollo and Bella had seen us.'

The old banger creaked and squeaked upon impact and came to an abrupt stop as its front wheels dug deep into the snow.

'Uh-oh – we're stuck,' said Lexi, sighing, but with the composure of someone who knew exactly how to rectify the problem.

Reaching over to the back seat she dragged a horse rug over, got out of the car and positioned it on the snowy ground before the front wheels.

'Es, help me tuck this under the tyres.'

Kneeling in the snow they pulled the rug taut and pushed its edge under the rubber tyres as far as they could, hoping it would provide enough grip for the wheels.

'That should do it. We'll pick the rug up on the way back.'

The girls jumped back in the car and eased the vehicle out of its grave. Esme cheered. Lexi sped the car across the final field before Shere Farm, then braked sharply as they entered the stable yard.

The snow had been swept off the concrete and lay in dirty mounds alongside the stable walls, stained by various dogs and flecked with stray clumps of horse manure. A large barrow of steaming straw stood in front of an open stable door. A large shovelful of dung flew from the stable into the barrow and Jimmy appeared from inside. Dirt was stuck to his sweat-peppered lip and brow whilst the tweed of his flat cap was hidden beneath a thick layer of dust and wood shavings.

'Morning ladies.' He took off his hat and wiped a sleeve across his forehead, smearing grime into his sweaty hair.

'There'll be no riding until you've cleaned all the crap your horrid ponies have dumped. Dirty little toerags.'

'Have you exercised all the horses yet, Jimmy?' asked Lexi.

'Of course I have! Go on; don't stand there gormless – get a spade and start shovelling.'

'Oh, Jimmy,' said Lexi. 'Can't we do it when we get back from our ride?'

'What do you think this place is? Some fancy-pants livery? And do I have "slave" tattooed on my forehead? Get your miserable arses into gear. Pick up the shit, brush those hairy brutes and *then* you can saddle up. Hurry up! I haven't got all effing day. Lady Mucks you ain't. Not down here.'

'Gosh, you *are* in a mood this morning. Did you wake up on the wrong side of the bed?' asked Lexi.

'I'll show you the wrong side of my hand if you aren't

careful. And yes, I am in no mood to wait around for you two brats all day. I have to leave at twelve so *hop to it.*'

'All right Jimmy, keep your knickers on,' said Lexi. She picked up the wheelbarrow and pushed it across the yard to Jupiter's stable.

'Follow your friend, Esme,' said Jimmy.

'Jimmy?' she asked, tentatively.

'What *now*?'

Collecting all her questions on the tip of her tongue, Esme took in a deep breath before speaking. 'Do you know exactly where Mummy is? What's wrong with her? And when—'

'Steady, Esme! Too many questions, too fast. Let's start with where she is—'

'Did she do suicide? Is it my—'

'*Esme!* Let me answer, for God's sake.'

Another deep breath. She wanted the truth and right now Jimmy was her only hope.

'Now listen here. You know your mother loves you. She has a condition that means her brain doesn't get the chemicals it needs to remain stable. She's gone to a special hospital where the doctors will give her the chemicals she's missing. She will live. And you don't *do* suicide, you *commit* suicide. Although that's beside the point,' he said, sighing. 'Your mother is in the right place and will be home again soon.'

'What is suicide?' asked Esme. 'Did Mummy *want* to hurt herself?'

'It's what people who are very sad do.'

'Why is she so sad?' she asked, quietly.

'Like I say, she has happy chemicals missing. A bit like a car having no petrol.'

'Oh?' muttered Esme. 'Can't I be her petrol?'

'Well, you can help just by loving her. That's what the Earl does.'

'What? Lexi's papa? Is he her petrol?'

Jimmy looked as if he was about to say something but then took his hat off and smoothed his hair. 'Esme, I've given you the answers to your endless questions and mooning around won't make things any better. Go and sort your bleeding pony out.'

Tears threatened to run down Esme's cheeks as she picked up a spade and opened her pony's stable door.

'Oh, Homer. I don't know where Mummy is. I've lost her.' She pressed her face into the animal's neck, tears sliding down his shiny mane.

Sometimes it felt as if Homer was the only one who really understood how she was feeling. She buried into his warmth as he nuzzled her pockets, smelling the packet of sweets.

'I miss her so much.'

The pony butted her as if to repeat Jimmy's request.

'OK, OK, I'll clean your bed. Good boy.'

Esme clipped a rope to his head collar and tied it to a ring as she set about cleaning his bedding. First she shovelled his droppings into a pile, then she forked out the soaked straw, the strong smell of ammonia making her eyes smart and adding to her tears.

Once the dirty straw had been removed, she shook out a fresh half bale, banking it up the stable partitions so the pony wouldn't get cast when he rolled, which he always did as soon as he got back from a hack. Esme had to be quick as a whip untacking him, as he would try to lie down while still wearing both saddle and bridle. She took great pride in keeping his stable clean enough even for her to sleep in; there had been many a time when she had lain for hours talking to him. Now that his stable was in order she felt better and a familiar joy at the thought of riding again helped erase some of her anxiety.

'Es, are you going to fill Homer's hay net now or when we get back?' said Lexi, indicating the empty bag and interrupting Esme's thoughts.

'After we ride,' she answered.

Running her hand down Homer's fetlock, the pony automatically lifted his hoof for Esme to pick out a compact mixture of gravel, mud and manure. It was satisfying, scraping the pick along the grooves; like cleaning dirt from under her nail.

'Look at him,' said Lexi. 'I wish Jupiter was as helpful. I have to use both hands to pull his leg up. He's so stubborn. But I suppose he got that from his mummy.'

Esme laughed. 'He's as bolshie as you are!'

Jimmy appeared in the door, legs wide apart with the broom in his hand.

'Listen to you two. Just like a couple of old fish wives, gossiping away as though you had all ruddy day. Well, I don't and I am now asking politely if you would get your skaggy ponies saddled up and ridden so that I can go and get on with my life before the next sodding century.'

Newly motivated, Esme pulled Homer up to the mounting

block, put her left foot in the stirrup and swung her right one over his back, her bottom landing lightly in the saddle. She gathered the reins to push him forward so that Lexi could do the same. Homer wouldn't move. On routine hacking days, her pony was a lazy sloth and completely oblivious to his mistress's commands. Esme kicked hard and tapped his bottom with her whip. He moved a couple of paces. Her mouth twisted in apology at Lexi for her pony's insolence.

'It's OK. I've got just enough room to get on. I'll go first, then Homer will follow.' Lexi stood up in her stirrups and turned around.

'Which way shall we go?' Esme asked.

'Let's go down the back lane. We can walk on the verge – it'll be less slippery.'

The morning was bright but bitterly cold. Frost clung to branches like an old man's stubble. A herd of cattle huddled together, their freezing breath clouding above them.

'It looks like they're smoking,' said Esme.

'I am, too – look!' Lexi let out a great gush of air from her lungs.

'Me too!' laughed Esme, her sadness evaporating like her breath. She was with Lexi, doing what she loved doing most. It could have been any normal day. The only difference was that she wouldn't be going home in the evening.

'Shall we trot?' said Lexi.

'OK, and we can trot carefully back. Homer won't be so lazy on the way home.'

Esme knew that her pony usually found another gear when he knew he was headed back to a bucket of feed. Jupiter broke into a trot and Homer reluctantly followed, tripping over his hooves, too lazy to pick them up properly. He soon got into a rhythm of sorts, though, and Esme managed to pull up alongside her friend.

'I'm so excited about this afternoon. I haven't been to the cinema for ages,' said Lexi.

'Me neither. Mummy and I saw *Barefoot in the Park*. I l-o-v-e Robert Redford. So does Mummy. He is gorg—'

Both ponies shot forward, terrified by a pheasant that burst out from the hedgerow.

Esme quickly gathered her reins and sat tight as Lexi and Jupiter bolted down the icy road. She watched in horror as Jupiter slipped and came crashing down onto the snow-compacted tarmac. Legs, tail, arms and more legs tangled into a mess of indistinguishable body parts.

'Oh my God! Lexi!' she shouted.

Homer, revved up by the drama, danced forward on the ice, while Esme did her best to stop him from breaking into a gallop.

'Steady, boy. Steady! *LEXI!*'

Jupiter had scrambled to his feet again and was standing still with shock. Lexi lay immobile on the ground, groaning.

'Lexi, are you OK?' asked Esme, riding up beside her.

'It's my leg.'

'Can you move? Wriggle your toes. Can you do that?'

'Yes. I don't think I've broken anything. It was just that stupid bloody pheasant. Is Jupiter all right?'

'I think he just got a fright. I can't see any blood or any-thing...' said Esme, dismounting and walking around the pony to check. 'Hold on to Homer and I'll trot Jupiter up to make sure he's not lame,' she added, giving Lexi the reins.

Skittish and jumpy after falling, the girls could see his movement was fluid.

'He looks fine,' said Lexi.

'I really thought you were a goner then, Lexi. Are you sure your leg's OK?'

'It's fine. At least Jupiter was careful not to step on me. I knew we were going to slip. It's always a nasty spot even when it's not icy. Thank goodness we were just trotting.'

'Let's get back to the yard. Do you want to walk or get back on?' asked Esme, biting her lip to stop herself from laughing now she knew her friend wasn't hurt.

'Esme! It's not funny.'

'I know,' she said, giggling. 'I shouldn't laugh but it did look funny. Like a cartoon crash.'

Lexi started laughing, too. 'We have the best adventures together. Let's not tell Jimmy. He'll just swear at us and say we're *silly idjits*.'

'That's a *baaaaad* swear word but a good accent, Lexi!' said Esme, laughing.

Back at Shere Farm's stables, Esme heaved her saddle off Homer and hung the bridle up, quickly rinsing off the bit.

'Do you think Jimmy will mind if I use his loo? It's too cold to use the outside one and anyway I bet the water's frozen.'

'No,' said Lexi. 'He won't see you go in. I can hear him clipping Badger. I'll keep a look out.'

Esme dumped the rest of her tack and left the stable,

walking towards the house. Once inside, despite knowing the coast was clear, she tiptoed upstairs; she had never ventured to the first floor before. The carpet was the same as the one in the pub: loud and red. The floorboards creaked underfoot. She turned round to check that no one was following her. It was dark upstairs; the daylight struggled to get through the grease-smeared windows and the gaps between the falling-down curtains.

Wandering down the corridor, she saw one of Jimmy's shoes lying abandoned in an open doorway. She went inside. It was very messy. Used teacups, an empty bottle of whisky and a plate with curling bacon rind sat on the bedside table. Next to them was a photograph of two people. She picked it up. It was a picture of Jimmy, her mother and the Earl in Jimmy's sitting room. They were laughing and the Earl and her mother had their arms around each other. She wondered if they often met here. Maybe that was how the Earl knew where her mummy was on Christmas Day?

'Esme! What are you doing?' Jimmy asked, making Esme jump.

'Um, nothing. I was looking for the loo,' she said, dropping the photograph. 'Jimmy... does Lexi's papa come and see you a lot?'

'Stop asking questions and get downstairs. I don't want you coming up here again. Do you hear? This is my house. My bedroom. And who I invite here is none of your business. Do you understand? I don't know how your mother copes with a nosey little runt like you snooping around. Now, *out!*'

Esme's face crumpled. 'I'm sorry, Jimmy.'

'If you were sorry, you wouldn't have come up here in the first place. Take a piss in your pony's stable. *Go!*'

Esme stumbled out of the room, shocked by Jimmy's reaction. She knew he had a foul temper but he'd never shouted at her like that before.

'Esme!' Jimmy called after her.

She stopped on the landing and turned. Calmer now, Jimmy took her hands and looked into her tear-stained face.

'I'm sorry I got angry. I'm upset about your mother too. It's a shock what happened and I feel so helpless; if she was a horse she'd have been sent here for me to fix. But she's in good hands. The doctors will mend her and when she gets back home we can all look after her so it doesn't happen again. You and me. We can do that.' He gathered her in his arms and hugged her tight. 'Everything will work out. You'll see.'

Esme clung to him, relieved that he was still there for her.

Chapter Ten

Jimmy waved the girls off and told them to drive back to the castle using the road, as Jalopy would struggle going uphill cross-country; it would take longer but they would get back in one piece.

Esme drove as Lexi's leg was aching. Distracted and not quite as competent as Lexi, her gear changes were clunky and the gearbox screeched in protest, making for a bumpy ride.

Lexi could see that her friend was upset and squeezed Esme's arm, supportively.

'I was thinking just now,' said Lexi. 'We can't change what's happened with your mummy so let's try not to worry about it. If we worry about it, we won't enjoy all the fun things we usually do.'

'You're right. But it's hard. I'm trying not to worry but I'll feel better when I've spoken to Daddy. I might try and call Sophia too.'

'That's it, chin up. Your mummy wouldn't want you to be sad, especially here. She loves the castle.'

Lexi had a good point. Esme resolved to enjoy herself to make her mother proud. Besides, she didn't want to make any other members of her family or Mrs Bee worry.

When they got home, Lexi plonked herself down on the hall bench and asked Esme to help with her boots. Not bothering to replace them with shoes, the girls entered the drawing room in their socks to find the Earl sitting on the sofa reading the paper, which he peered over as they walked in.

'Papa, look! I took a fall and Jupiter trod on my leg.' Lexi pulled down her jodhpurs to reveal her bruises.

'Good heavens, that looks painful!' said the Earl.

'Alexa! Pull your jodhpurs up. What will the staff think?' snapped the Contessa.

Lexi looked like her mother's words hurt more than her leg.

The Contessa was sitting in her usual chair by the fire. She wore a camel skirt, green cashmere twinset and silk scarf tied around her neck like a Boy Scout. Her fingers fidgeted with her wedding ring, her nails filed into pointy ovals. Esme remembered being poked sharply in the shoulder last night. Looking at the Contessa's face for a clue to her mood, it didn't look too unfriendly, just mildly bored. Esme's desire to hear news of her mother overcame her nervousness.

'Has anyone called about Mummy?' she asked.

The Contessa turned to her ashtray and addressed the wall. 'No,' she said, shifting her gaze not to Esme but out of the window.

'Esme, you weren't hurt too, were you?' asked the Earl.

'No, Papa – Esme was amazing. She rescued me and Jupiter,' said Lexi, jumping in.

'Did she now? How very brave, Esme,' the Contessa answered. 'Not so like your mother after all, then.'

'For goodness' sake, Lucia!' said the Earl.

The Contessa let out an exaggerated sigh, held up her hand and stared at her nails as though she had just filed them. She then blew on her enormous diamond ring and polished it with her scarf.

'Excuse me, Your Ladyship.' Cribben entered the room. 'One of Princess Margaret's staff has just called. Apparently she left behind her "*trousse de voyage*".'

'Her "*trousse de*" *what*?' said the Contessa.

'Her vanity case,' replied Mr Cribben.

'Why didn't you just say that, Cribben? Goodness, you're pretentious sometimes. What do you want me to do about it?'

'I was going to get Miller to drive it to Balmoral. The roads should be clear now as they've had the gritters out every morning. She's flying out to Mustique in the next few days and needs the case for her holiday.'

'I see; if it has all the woman's make-up inside, she will certainly be needing it. I will find it and give it to Miller, he can drive it up tomorrow.'

'Very good, Your Ladyship.'

'Why don't Lexi and Esme look for it?' asked the Earl.

'Because I know exactly where it is and, Henry, *I* am dealing with it. So please, allow me to do just that before we get another nuisance call from the palace.'

'Esme was with the Princess this morning. Did you see it, Es?'

'No, I didn't,' she replied, shaking her head.

'I'm sure Lexi and Esme will find it, dear. Run along now,

girls – or in your case Lexi, limp – and take it to Miller, please,' said the Earl, overruling his wife.

The two girls found the vanity case immediately, underneath the Princess's dressing table. Small and glossy, it had gold hinges and a tiny lock with a tasselled key.

'How could the Princess have left it behind? It's so beautiful.'

'Mummy has one too,' Esme replied. 'It's made of black crocodile skin and has lots of little pill bottles in it.'

Lexi's eyes widened. 'Mama keeps hers locked.'

'Do you think this one is too?' Esme asked, picking up the box cautiously and peering at the tiny keyhole.

'I don't know,' Lexi whispered. 'There's only one way to find out.'

Esme placed the box back on the floor and Lexi leant forwards to lift the lid, which opened easily. Resting delicately on the top tier of compartments lay a gold charm bracelet and a few pairs of glittering earrings.

'Maybe we shouldn't look through the rest,' Lexi suggested.

'You're right,' Esme said. She felt slightly guilty for opening something so private, especially after Jimmy had given her such a talking-to earlier.

'Although, if she really cared then she wouldn't have left it here…' Lexi smiled, mischievously.

Esme grinned back and lifted the next layer out of the box, revealing glittering cosmetics below. She tipped them onto the carpet and Lexi snatched at a shiny tube.

'Oh, look Esme, mascara!' she said, extracting the fine wand and dabbing its sticky contents on her own lashes.

Esme picked up a foundation bottle and poured a little of its contents into her hand. She started to rub the chalky mixture onto her face.

'Esme, you look like a clown! That stuff is almost white,' Lexi said, laughing.

'Just shows how pale Princess Margaret's skin is – she must never go out in the sun. Mummy always says it's better to be pale and interesting, but I'm always covered in freckles.'

'Not any more, you're not!'

Rummaging around in the box, a blue and white paisley-patterned tube caught Esme's eye. The label read *Yardley Slicker Lip Polish* and a small sticker on the base described the colour as Portobello Rose.

'Lipstick, Lexi!' she exclaimed. 'We have to try it – we'll look just like her.'

She twisted the small cylinder and a pink tip appeared. Esme applied it to her own mouth, then turned and pouted at Lexi.

'You look like a ghost!' Lexi said.

'It would look lovely on Mummy, though,' Esme said, wiping the colour off her lips with the back of her hand and dropping the lipstick back. It was then that she noticed something sparkling, caught in the velvet lining in the depths of the box. Sticking her hand into the case, her fingers touched something cold and hard. She tugged gently and gasped as her fingers pulled out a ring set with an oval gemstone.

'Oh wow, Lexi. This is beautiful,' she sighed.

'Let me see,' said Lexi, ripping it from Esme's hand. She held it up to the window. The stone was a vivid, intense blue with a white, six-pointed star that appeared to float across its surface as she tilted and rotated it in the light: an orb fenced by rose-cut diamonds.

'Gosh, this is the loveliest thing I've ever seen. It looks good enough to eat,' she said.

'It does. Like a delicious boiled sweet covered in sugar. Might turn your tongue blue.'

'Like sucking the end of a fountain pen,' she giggled.

'We'd better put it back. Looks awfully precious. Do you think we should tell Mr Cribben? Or your mother? Take it down to them?'

'No! We can't take it down to them, if anyone knows we've been trying on Princess Margaret's make-up we'll get into such trouble. We'd better leave it in the case, like we found it, and take it to Miller.'

'OK. Do you think I've got time to call Mrs Bee before we go to the film?'

'Definitely, but don't be too long. I'm going to change and you need to wash all that stuff off your face. Nanny will be chasing us with her rolling pin soon.'

'Which phone shall I use?'

'The one in Papa's study or the pantry.'

Esme ran downstairs to the Earl's study. Sat at his desk, he was bent over some important-looking papers but he looked up as Esme knocked on the open door.

'Esme, come in darling,' he smiled, his eyes flicking over her face. 'It looks as if you've found Princess Margaret's case.'

Esme licked her fingers then rubbed at the make-up still smeared across her face, nervously looking up at the Earl.

'It will be our little secret,' he winked.

Esme beamed back at him. 'Lexi's just taking it to Miller now. I wondered if I could use your phone to call Mrs Bee, if that's OK?'

'Of course it is.' He stood up and a few papers drifted down to the floor beside him. 'Thank you for looking after Lexi this morning. You are a good friend to her. Just like your mother is to me. Do you know, one time she drove me all the way back here from London because I'd lost my car keys? I could have taken the train, of course, but she insisted. And that's just one of many, many nice things she's done.'

'That must have been a long time ago. Daddy doesn't let her drive any more.'

'I bet she would if you were ever in trouble. You're so precious to her.'

Esme looked up at him and smiled, then frowned. 'But I'm not precious enough to make her happy.'

'Esme, none of this is your fault. If anything...' He stopped. 'Come on, let's call Mrs Bee otherwise Lexi will be fretting about time.' He dialled the number for The Lodge and handed the receiver to her.

'Munroe residence, may I take a message?'

Esme loved hearing the sound of Mrs Bee's voice. She wished she could just nestle into her arms and stay there forever.

'Mrs Bee, it's me!'

'Oh Esme, I've missed you, love. Is everything all right?'

'Yes, thank you. I just wanted to know if you've heard from Mummy?

'No news just yet, but Sophia has tried to call you a few times, love. Did you get her messages?'

'No, I didn't,' Esme said, surprised. 'Maybe someone forgot to tell me. Do you know if Mummy is getting better, Mrs Bee?'

'Och, I'm sure she is. You're not to worry about a thing – your mother will be back as soon as possible. She'll be missing you.'

Esme hoped so. She caught sight of the Earl, who was smiling but tapping his watch.

'I've got to go and get ready, Mrs Bee. Give Digger a kiss and tell him I miss him.'

'I will, darling. Have a lovely time.'

Back in the nursery bathroom, Esme looked at her reflection in the mirror. The glass was cloudy with age, looking like it had raindrops dribbling down it. She rubbed her face with a flannel, splashed herself clean with water from a jug, then tentatively reopened her eyes and patted her face dry. Her skin had regained its rosy glow, but remnants of mascara still clung to her lashes. It made her eyes look even bigger.

Her hair was stuck flat against her head because of her riding hat. It felt greasy and damp. 'Helmet hair', Sophia called it. She sighed; she would need to wash it and realized she would have to do so in cold water; the water at the castle was only heated in the evenings.

With no time to trek to the nursery wing, she filled the basin in the bedroom adjoining hers. The water was icy cold, but it felt good and added to her excitement. She'd adored the time she had gone to the cinema with her mother and was looking forward to seeing a film with Lexi and Bella, although it wouldn't quite be the same.

Kneeling down in front of a blow heater, she flipped her wet hair over her face and ruffled the sodden strands in an attempt to dry her locks. The lukewarm air had little impact. She started shivering and reached for her towel, tenting it over her to keep her warm in the cold bedroom. Time was not on her side. She needed to hurry to finish drying her hair and get dressed.

Esme had never met Lexi's paternal grandmother before, though she had heard all about her. Like the film star Elizabeth Taylor, she had been married five times, which was nearly as many as Henry VIII. Esme wondered if she'd felt lonely whenever a husband died, and that was why she always found another. Lexi had told her that her grandmother had wanted to be an actress in the time of silent films but she hadn't been allowed to work because her parents didn't think girls of her status should do anything except get married. Well at least she'd been a success in that area, thought Esme, and they'd be pleased she'd been married five times.

There was a knock on the door before it opened.

'Esme, what on earth are you doing?' It was Nanny Patch, her chest puffed up like a pigeon, bristling and twitching its feathers. 'Everyone is waiting for you. Quick, put your dress on. Don't worry about your hair – it'll be dry by the time you reach the cinema.'

Pulling on her underwear, Esme then stepped into her Liberty print, smock-fronted dress. Thank goodness Mrs Bee had had the forethought to pack it; she didn't want to look like an urchin in front of the Dowager Countess. The dress had a princess collar and a line of pearlized buttons down its back, which Nanny Patch swiftly fastened.

'Where are your shoes? Ah, here they are. Very smart. New idlers. I like them in navy. Quick, slip them on. Now, let's give your hair the once-over.'

She took the hairbrush, combed through the damp tresses, and handed Esme her velvet hairband. Esme plonked it on top of her head.

'No, no Esme – like this.' She swept back the unruly wisps that covered Esme's face with the hairband. 'There we go. Pretty as a picture. Now skedaddle. Lexi has gloves and your coat is on the hall bench. Run! Have fun. And don't forget she likes to be addressed as "Your Ladyship"!'

'Thanks, Nanny Patch. See you later.'

Esme tore out of her bedroom and onto the landing, her new leather-soled shoes slipping on the sisal matting. Flying down the closely placed steps, eyes focused on her feet, she leapt off just before reaching the bottom to land heavily – and smack into a wall of fur. The wall stood firm.

'Ah, so you must be the famous Esme?' came a rich voice.

Esme looked up, following the seam of stitched-together mink pelts until she reached a face that reminded her of a wrinkled Snow White. The old lady's eyes sparkled.

'Oh, golly! I'm sorry to bump into you... er... Your Ladyship.' She noticed Lexi and Bella standing beside her.

'You may call me Granny Daphne, as by all accounts you are almost a member of the family anyway. Now children, are we ready to leave? Esme, where are your gloves?'

'I've got them, Granny. Here Es, take these,' piped Lexi.

Esme took the gloves from her friend. It was the first time she had worn gloves off the hunting field. She knew the Queen wore them to make her hand more visible when she waved. But to go to the local cinema? In gloves? She didn't understand why she had to wear them and the white was going to get dirty so quickly.

'Etiquette and hygiene,' quipped Granny Daphne, reading Esme's mind. 'It is vital that we aristocrats set ourselves apart from the riffraff. We must maintain our standards, especially in these times of foreign infiltration, and cinemas are notoriously grubby establishments. Filled with germs and bacteria, like all public places. You don't want to get some horrid disease, do you, Esme?'

'Er... no... but I've been to the pictures before with Mummy. I didn't wear gloves then and I didn't get poorly, Granny... um...'

'Granny Daphne. And we don't say "pictures", we say "film" and you don't "get poorly", you "become ill".'

'"Film" and "ill", Granny Daphne,' repeated Esme.

If the Dowager Countess thought cinemas were such horrid places, Esme wondered why she was taking them. Cinema outings were a rare occurrence for all the children. Lexi had told Esme that the Dowager Countess thought that it would be good for her grandchildren to 'mix with the commoners', little knowing that Lexi spent much of her time with Jimmy and Esme and other children who lived on the Culcairn estate.

The three children settled into their seats in the Land Rover, aware that Granny Daphne was looking at them through the mirror of her powder compact. Like the Contessa, she wore lots of lipstick, her preferred colour making her lips look like they were painted on; it was blood-red and bled into the lines around her mouth. Her face was powdered to perfection and set against the coal-black of her curls, she did indeed resemble an aged Snow White. The fine black hairnet, patterned with velvet polka dots, covering her hair seemed more for effect than necessity, her locks lacquered into place – immoveable and sculptural. It looked like a nest of eels on her head. Her pearl earrings were so large the two gleaming half-moons could be seen from behind, clipped to her lobes. Around her long elegant neck sat three strands of more pearls, held together by a diamond clasp. She looked as expensive from the back as she did, greedy and overdone, from the front.

At the bottom of the drive they swapped cars. Granny Daphne's powder-blue Rolls-Royce was waiting with her chauffeur as she herself was far too grand to ride into town in a Land Rover. Its engine purred softly, marking the car's sophistication. The children scrambled into the leather-and-walnut interior after the Dowager Countess.

'Ah, that's better. Who wants a travel sweet?' Granny

Daphne passed a metal tin of brightly coloured boiled sweets to the children, each one dusted in icing sugar.

'Thank you, Granny.'

After a few minutes' quiet, Lexi spoke again. 'Are we there yet?' she asked, shoving four of the sweets in her mouth.

'I hope I didn't hear you asking that horrible childish question. However, if I did, the answer is: we will be there when we arrive.'

The car pulled up outside the Odeon. Above the entrance *HELLO, DOLLY!* was spelled out in large black-plastic letters, some slightly wonky, with the various showtimes written underneath. There was a long queue of people in flared jeans, platform shoes and leather jackets leading up to the box office.

Everyone looks the same as they did in London, Esme thought. It was hard to tell the difference between the men and the women, apart from those wearing ponchos and gypsy skirts; they all had long hair and appeared to be wearing each other's clothes. Now, they turned in unison to look at the Rolls-Royce and its occupants. If there was ever a moment to wave like Her Majesty, this was it, but both girls instinctively kept their hands firmly on their laps.

The chauffeur pulled on the handbrake and got out of the car to open the door for the Dowager Countess, before doing the same for Esme, Bella and Lexi. Granny Daphne stood for what seemed an age, cigarette holder in hand, to ensure that the onlookers had no doubt that someone of great importance was about to mingle with them. A hush came over the queue of people. Esme half-expected Granny Daphne to make some form of announcement, but her appearance and stance were enough to maintain a brief silence. She then walked past her audience and into the foyer of the building, followed by the three children, each with their head bowed and eyes downcast.

'God, that was embarrassing,' whispered Bella.

'Children, I have the tickets. We will go straight in. Choose an ice cream and say thank you to the nice lady.'

An usherette, holding a tray of ice creams and brandishing a torch, took them to their seats, slap bang in the middle of the stalls. Filmgoers already seated stood up to let the small, privileged army through. Granny Daphne made no effort to slide in sideways, instead huffing and tutting, her body grazing each person she passed. The girls tried harder, pressing their bodies against the row in front to avoid upsetting their neighbours or their cups of Kia-Ora.

Flipping down the seat between Lexi and Bella, Esme felt the prickle of velvet through her dress.

Dim lighting captured the faded glory of the auditorium's pseudo-baroque décor. Plush curtains covered the screen. No one talked. Instead, some were whispering in excited anticipation of the film, others doing so behind their hands and looking in the Dowager Countess's direction.

Esme knew Granny Daphne was famous and had been in the newspapers because she had fought some robbers who tried to steal from her. She had supposedly hit one with an iron but Bella said this was highly unlikely as her granny had probably 'never set foot in a laundry room and wouldn't know an iron from an anvil'. She was often being photographed alongside movie stars and royalty.

It was so quiet that Esme could hear the rustle of sweet papers and fidgety bottoms making their chairs squeak in protest. Suddenly, the still-drawn curtains sprang to life with *Pearl and Dean* appearing on the fabric, the words showing through from the screen behind. *HELLO, DOLLY!* followed. The foggy image crystallized into a tunnel of racing rectangular shapes, like a space ship flying through asteroids. A musical jingle bellowed in stereo around the theatre, choppy voices punching the silence like gunshot. As the final 'Yeah!' rang out, Lulu appeared, singing and jiving in a snazzy selection of 'Happy Shoes', followed by a series of advertisements for shops and restaurants.

'Yuck, that looks revolting,' concluded Lexi at the sight of a plate of something that was on offer at a local restaurant.

'It looks a damn sight better than anything we get sicked up at home!' retorted Bella.

A drawn-out '*Shhhhhhhh*' departed Granny Daphne's lips, along with a stream of smoke and 'The film is about to start.'

With that, the lights went out and their eager faces were illuminated by the opening credits on the screen.

Esme sat spellbound. Her small trowel-like ice-cream spoon suspended between the tub and her mouth, which fell open in wonderment. On screen, people in old-fashioned dress hustled and bustled through the street, like marching ants, each with a destination in mind. No one dawdled and everyone was cheerful. All of life in an American city was held in this one scene: the postman delivering letters; dustbin men collecting the rubbish; doormen opening doors for smart ladies and gentlemen; flower sellers; newspaper vendors; passengers hopping on and off the tram. All set against the glorious backdrop of a bright blue sky and sun-dappled streets. The camera panned out and suddenly the most beautiful hat that Esme had ever seen filled the screen: feathers in the colours of autumn, encircled by finely woven straw and topped with a velvet crown. The hat turned around and there she was: Dolly. Dolly Gallagher Levi, in all her golden glory. Esme wished a giant wish that her mother was with her and promised herself to bring her to see this film when she came home.

'Oh,' sighed Esme. 'She is so beautiful. So perfect – her smile.'

Slowly she put her spoon in her mouth but the ice cream had melted and dribbled down the front of her red coat. She didn't notice, didn't bother to scoop up more and her orange juice stayed untouched. She sat, mesmerized. Dolly had such a voice – so acrobatic; it jumped all over the place. High. Low. Shaky. Esme could tell how strong and determined she was just by her singing. Dolly was a person who made the best of life. She had cast a spell over Esme and made her want to love life too.

Emerging from the darkness of the cinema all three children blinked in the harsh strip-lighting of the foyer. Esme didn't want to speak, didn't want to break the spell.

'How I wish we still dressed like that. All those hats and feathers and tiny waists,' said Lexi.

'Oh, Lexi, don't be such an idiot,' said Bella. 'She would've been wearing a corset to winch in the flab. Granny, is that what you had to do in those days?'

Esme chuckled. She was happy because she felt part of the family and that was fun. She liked being part of a gang that shared inside jokes and laughed at the same things. Of course, she and Sophia shared their sibling bond, but she was a teenager now and too old to want to play with her little sister.

'Dear Bella, you know perfectly well I wasn't alive then and believe me, if I had been, there would have been no need for such sartorial trickery.'

The Dowager Countess shooed the children into the car like chickens. They sat quietly, still lost in the magic of the film.

Esme wished she had a Dolly in her life. Someone who could fix things and make her mother happy. She looked out of the car window. The sky was stained with the bright, dense colour of the sinking sun and the first few stars began to appear. She wondered how her mother was – whether she was seeing the same stars right now. She often said that her stars were Esme's too – that they shared them and that they belonged in a sky only the two of them could see. She said that even when she was away, they would be looking at the same stars at the same time. Would the nurses allow her to look at the stars? Would she have a window, even, in her new hospital in London? She felt a familiar coldness take root in her belly. Gazing up at the sky, she tried to sense her mother, find some form of connection – but none came.

Lexi was already halfway up the stairs, Bella chasing behind her. Esme held back when she saw Mr Cribben arrive out of nowhere and wordlessly help the Dowager Countess with her coat.

'Hi, Mr Cribben,' she said. 'Have Mummy or Daddy called?'

'Not that I know of, Esme, but I will check with the rest of the staff. How was the film?'

'Marvellous, Cribben. Camp as Christmas – like one long drag act,' replied Granny Daphne. 'I am going to take a nap before dinner, now. Have my suitcases been unpacked?'

'Yes, Your Ladyship. Rose has seen to that. You are in the Romney Room, as usual.'

'Any guests tonight?'

'I believe not, Your Ladyship. Just you and His Lordship and Ladyship.'

'How dull.'

'Indeed, Your Ladyship, but nothing a little champagne cocktail can't remedy.'

'I'll need extra brandy!' she said. 'Right-ho – I'm off for my nap. Can you ask Rose to lay out my black Dior dress in the dressing room and get her to knock on my door at six?'

'Certainly.'

'Esme, dear, are you going to join that naughty grand-daughter of mine?'

'Yes,' said Esme in a small voice. 'Thank you for taking us today, Granny Daphne. It was lovely.'

'You sweet, polite child. Unlike my bloody ungrateful grandchildren. I'm glad you enjoyed it. Let's hope we can do it again next year.' She gave Esme a peck on her cheek. 'Come, let's go upstairs together. You can be my walking stick.' She took Esme's hand and when they reached the top of the stairs, gave her a gentle push towards the shrieks of laughter already coming from the nursery.

Bella and Lexi were having a cushion fight that had got a little out of hand and Cherry the nursery maid was trying to separate them.

'Stop it – both of you. One of you will get hurt!' she said, pulling a laughing Lexi off her sister. 'Look, here's Esme.'

'Hi, Cherry,' she said.

'Now, what are you all going to do until supper?'

'I've got to write thank-you letters,' moaned Bella.

Esme wondered how she managed.

'What shall *we* do, Es?' asked Lexi.

'Let's go on a ghost hunt!' said Esme.

'Ooh yes – we can go up the servants' tower. You know the one where our old teacher Mr Footit lived. It'll be empty now and really scary.'

'Maybe he didn't even leave. Maybe he *died* up there. Or was murdered,' said Esme, stretching her eyes wide with her fingers for dramatic effect.

'Oh, I'm *scared*,' said Lexi, laughing.

Up in the tower, the grandeur of the castle evaporated into dowdiness. Discoloured prints tarnished by patches of damp replaced old masters, and cobwebs swayed eerily in the omnipresent draught, seeping from high-up, narrow windows. Dusty lampshades hung far above from the lofty ceiling, any light they emitted engulfed in shadows.

It was strange to feel a sense of claustrophobia in such a huge space but in the gloom the walls seemed to close in around them. They were definitely in the old servants' quarters.

'I can feel a presence – can't you, Es? Like someone's watching us,' whispered Lexi.

'It's like Mr Footit was banished up here or something,' agreed Esme.

'Locked away like a prisoner, miles from the gilded staterooms and sealed in a coffin.' Lexi added.

'Maybe he's a vampire and only waking up now?' said Esme, her heart thumping in excited fear.

'Shh!' Lexi stood stock-still.

Esme grabbed and clung to her friend, trying to hear what Lexi had heard.

A door near to where they stood rattled. Both girls squealed.

There's someone in there, trying to get out!' breathed Lexi.

'Run!' whispered Esme, ready to take flight.

Lexi stopped her. 'No – we have to go in. Maybe Mr Footit needs saving?'

What had started out as a ghost hunt, in seconds became a rescue mission. Emboldened by the thought of being hailed a heroine, Esme turned the key. The lock was sticky and the door heavy.

'It feels like something's blocking it,' she said, shoving at the peeling wood.

Finally, the door opened and they tiptoed through before a mighty gust of wind slammed it shut behind them. They screamed. The darkness was suffocating and it was freezing cold.

'Turn the light on, Lexi!'

Esme's hand traced the roughness of the woodchip wall until she found it. With a flick of the switch everything changed; they were plunged into a scene of disappointing normality.

They had walked straight into a multi-purpose living space, smelling of fresh paint and Ajax. A kitchenette with pinewood table and chairs and a plastic fern in a painted flowerpot shared space with a moth-eaten sofa and an old trunk that served as a coffee table. The huge fireplace was ready-laid with newspaper and kindling. A pair of flimsy, washed-out-looking curtains hung around an open sash window, gently moving in the breeze. There were two closed doors on the far side.

'It smells like an old people's home,' said Lexi.

'It must have been painted for the next person.'

'To cover up the blood-splattered walls...' Lexi's voice had lost its urgency.

What an anticlimax, thought Esme. 'We might as well have a snoop now we're here,' she said.

She went into the first bedroom. There was a big mahogany bed with a thick patterned eiderdown. On the bedside table stood a brass lamp and crystal water jug. On the floor lay a sheepskin rug. A solid chest of drawers was topped with a small vase of dead flowers and freestanding mirror. Esme glanced at her reflection and pushed a strand of hair behind her ear, then went to look out of the window. Pressing her face up close to the glass, she cupped her hands around her eyes to block out the light from inside. All that was visible outside were the lights of Bonnyton village, way off in the distant blackness.

The second bedroom was cheerier. A single bed jutted out from an alcove. Lightweight material hung down from either side of a button-backed headrest; it looked feminine and fresh.

'This is really pretty. I wouldn't mind sleeping in here,' Esme said as Lexi joined her, sitting on the bed.

'What about the ghost?'

'How d'you know it's haunted?'

'Mr Footit said he saw a lady in olden-day clothes.'

Esme thought about telling her friend what had happened last night. The ghost, if it was true, might have wandered into her bedroom.

'No ghosts or hidden bodies today, though,' said Lexi. 'Let's go back down.'

As Esme followed her friend out of the bedroom, a telephone caught her eye. Lexi had gone on ahead, so Esme picked up the receiver and fished out the bit of paper Sophia had given her when she'd left for the castle.

Just a quick call, she thought.

The numbers clicked down the line but were met with a continuous flat tone. She tried again. Same thing. Sophia must have given her the wrong number. Mrs Bee would have it. She started dialling home.

'Esme!' echoed Lexi's voice from the tower. 'What are you doing? Come on! It's nearly bedtime.' And there she was, back at her side, out of breath and beaming.

'What have you been doing?' she asked her friend.

'Nothing,' Esme lied.

'That's not true; the receiver isn't on the telephone properly. Were you calling Mrs Bee?'

'No – Sophia. Doesn't matter. I'll try another time.'

Now she knew she could call any time from Mr Footit's old rooms, everything felt better. She would find the number of the hospital her mother was staying at and call the nurses and ask to speak to her. No one could stop her and no one would know she was all the way up here.

'I'll race you to the bottom,' said Lexi, sprinting away into the gloom.

The girls flew down the tower's spiral steps. They never walked anywhere inside the castle as it took so long to get anywhere. Screeching to a halt in the nursery, faces aglow with merriment and joy at being in each other's company, they forced themselves to compose their faces before going in to see Nanny Patch, who was waiting with two nightdresses draped over her arm.

Chapter Eleven

Bedtime at the castle was something Esme found strange, so different from being at home. If it was one of her mother's good days she would come into Esme's room as she was getting ready for bed and talk to her, give her a cuddle and kiss her goodnight. Sometimes, if her father was at home, he would give her what they called 'The Bumps', bouncing her up and down on her bed, which she loved. But here, at the castle, when there weren't guests for drinks or dinner, the children had to present themselves to their mother washed, brushed and in their pyjamas. They would file down, like the von Trapp children in *The Sound of Music*, and kiss the Contessa goodnight, except they didn't break into song. Rollo first, Bella, then Lexi. Tonight, the line-up included Esme.

Esme had never been in the Contessa's study properly before, only having used it as a thoroughfare to get to the drawing room. As she waited her turn to say goodnight now, she looked around. It was a pretty room with pale-green silk walls adorned by paintings of dogs and horses. The matching silk curtains were drawn. Esme was standing by an ornate desk, crammed with photographs of horses with rosettes pinned to their collars. The Contessa was in all of them, holding the leading rein, standing in profile or smiling as she was presented with a trophy.

'Rollo, darling, I swear you have become even more grown up since last night! Look at you, so tall and handsome. Come and give me a kiss.'

He looked embarrassed under the spotlight of his mother's attention. 'Night, Mama.' He gave her a light kiss and left as he had entered, shoulders stooped and hands dangling at his sides.

Bella was next up. 'Night, Mama.'

'Aren't you going to give me a hug, Arabella?' she said.

Esme's eyes widened. She was shocked that the Contessa would ask this of her, knowing it was an impossible task.

Bella pressed her body to her mother's, in a sort of clasp. It was a struggle for her and painful to watch.

As she held her daughter, Esme heard the Contessa whisper in her ear.

It was the same whisper Esme had heard in her dream. She froze. Bella pulled away, visibly crushed by her mother's malicious words.

'Mama, look!' Lexi opened her mouth and wobbled a molar. 'My tooth's about to fall out. I'm going to tie a bit of cotton round it, attach it to an open door and slam it shut. The tooth fairy will give me sixpence for it, then I can buy more sweets so more teeth fall out and I can get more money. Isn't that clever?'

'I really *don't* want to see the inside of your mouth,' snapped the Contessa. 'Goodnight, Alexa. And don't forget that you are spending the day with the Findlay family tomorrow. Lady Mary-Rose invited you weeks ago.'

It was now Esme's turn. The urge to run away overwhelmed her. She turned to Lexi for support but her friend had already gone – to comfort Bella, Esme supposed. She pulled the sleeves of her nightdress over her hands and balled them into fists to protect herself. The Contessa wasn't looking at her but Esme could see tension building in her body. She could hear nothing and everything; the clarity of her breathing, the clicking of the Contessa's jaw as she ground her teeth. Butterflies swarmed her stomach – thousands of them, fluttering away and scrambling her nerves. And there was that smell, the tart stench of bitterness and decay. It coated the back of her throat as she tried to speak.

'Goodnight,' she said, hearing her heart pounding in her ears. She hesitated, then, her voice trembling, 'I haven't heard from Daddy or Mummy... Do you know if anyone has called for me?'

The Contessa stiffened, then turned to look at her. The whites of her eyes were yellow and mapped by small red veins. 'No,' she breathed, icily. 'They've probably forgotten about you.' Still glowering at Esme, she extinguished her cigarette in a crystal ashtray then stood up and walked out of the room without uttering another word.

Esme let go of her cuffs and flexed her fingers, looking at the marks her nails had made on her palms. She rubbed them away. Her parents would never forget her and the Contessa was stupid to say such a thing. She wasn't going to let it upset her.

Feeling a little braver she looked at the telephone on the Contessa's desk. It was nearly eight o'clock. Mrs Bee would surely be home now. She reached for the receiver then stopped, her hand clutching the cold moulded plastic. On the blotter was a handwritten note to the Contessa.

Sophia rang for Esme. Please tell her to call her sister back.

Her heart lurched. She picked up the piece of paper. The writing was neat and evenly spaced, clear and easy to read. She looked up again. Her eyes darted back and forth across the room, seeking something – anything – to resolve her confusion. She rubbed her face and read the note again. There was no room for misinterpretation: the Contessa had lied.

Esme wondered why she hadn't been told? If someone leaves you a note, you pass the message on. It's just what you do. That's why people leave messages.

Her eyes swept the desk to see if any other notes lay amongst the documents and letters, and as she did so the telephone rang. Esme pulled her hand away, jolted by the vibrating bell. She darted out into the darkened passage, straight into the Earl.

'Hello, Esme. Why are you in such a rush?'

'Er… I was just catching up with the others,' said Esme, though she knew she didn't have to lie to the Earl.

'Ah, I see. And how is everything? Are you and Lexi having fun? How was the film?'

'It was lovely. I'm going to tell Mummy all about it, even if I have to write her a letter. I was going to ring Mrs Bee to say goodnight just now but the telephone rang and I saw a note. In there,' she added, pointing to the Contessa's study. 'It said Sophia called.'

'And have you? Called home?'

'Well, no. Sophia's gone skiing now.'

'Ah yes. Switzerland I gather. Perhaps we can find a number

for her tomorrow. And maybe we can nip down to see Mrs Bee for a cuppa.'

'Oh, yes please!'

The Earl smiled. 'By the way, your mother loved the card – she has it by her bed.'

'Have you been to see her?' Esme asked, full of hope.

'No... I mean... No, of course I haven't. I'm just imagining how happy it will have made her,' he said, looking strangely flustered. 'Right now, young lady, it's your bedtime.'

Esme put her arms around the Earl's neck and hugged him hard. Over his shoulder she saw a shadow pass across the wall of the study.

❄

Esme found Lexi in her bedroom being a read a story by Nanny Patch.

'Hello, Es. Come on, get into my bed and snuggle up. Nanny Patch, can Esme sleep here tonight?'

'Well, I don't see why not, seeing as there's nothing much on tomorrow, apart from going to Findlay House for lunch. I assume you'll be going down to the yard, though? What time does Jimmy want you there?'

'Not 'til 10.30. So can she? *Please?*'

Esme held her breath and willed Nanny to let her; she didn't want to be alone in her own bedroom again.

'Only if you both promise to go straight to sleep,' she agreed. 'And we won't tell your mother. It'll be our little secret.'

'Our secret, Nanny Patch!' Lexi and Esme chimed in

unison. They clasped each other's hands in excitement and giggled.

'Well, I'm sure you two have lots to talk about. We'll continue reading tomorrow night. Ten minutes then lights out, please. Esme, be sure to sleep in the other bed.' Nanny Patch stood up and walked across the room. 'Night–night, girls, sleep well,' she said, leaving the door slightly ajar as she left.

'Night, Nanny Patch,' they called.

'Does your mama ever kiss you goodnight when you're in bed?' asked Esme.

'No. She never comes in here. Does yours?'

'Always. Well, nearly always,' said Esme.

'Except when she's in hospital. It must be horrid for you, Es. Sometimes I think you have two mummies: one that's happy and one that's sad. I heard Mama tell Papa that your mother is deranged.'

'What do you think that is?' It didn't sound very nice.

'I don't know. Let's look it up.'

Lexi switched her light back on, got out of bed and pulled a book from a shelf. *The Oxford English Dictionary*. Hopping back in, she told Esme to join her. She flicked through the pages.

'Here we are. Deranged. It says: *mad, crazy, insane, lunatic.* That can't be right.'

Esme picked at a hangnail. 'No, it can't,' she said. 'Mummy isn't mad. She's the best mummy in the world. Sometimes when she's crying she hugs me even though *she's* the one who's sad! And once she got in the bath with me, with all her clothes on. We laughed so much.'

'With her clothes on?' said Lexi.

'Yes! And another time she washed my hair with tomato ketchup, pretending it was shampoo. She can be so funny.'

'Mama has never done anything like that with me,' said Lexi, sounding a bit sad now. 'I've never even seen her cry. But washing your hair with ketchup... Isn't that a bit *loopy*?'

'No – it was funny!' But as she said these words, the snowball in Esme's stomach froze hard and fast, chilling her blood. Her mother had followed the ketchup with mayonnaise. 'Conditioner,' she called it. Was that funny or mad?

'What are you two witchlets brewing?' It was Bella in her blue and white striped nightie, the sleeves shortened, toothbrush poised at the ready. Toothpaste bubbled around her mouth, foaming and making her look like a friendly rabid dog.

'Hi, Bels. Nanny Patch said me and Es can sleep together tonight.'

Esme got out of Lexi's bed and into the other one. She wanted to know that her mother wasn't deranged and so blurted out, 'My mummy isn't mad, is she Bella?'

'No, Es, of course she isn't,' Bella said, quickly. 'I don't think she'll be in hospital for long. Anyway, I think it's good for her to have a rest.'

She spat her toothpaste into the basin in the corner of the room, before gulping water straight from the tap for a final slosh.

She sighed. 'People get ill all the time, Es. That's why they have hospitals. And sometimes illness isn't obvious, like a broken leg or something. Sometimes people get a sick kidney, heart – stuff you can't see. Unlike me. It's obvious I'm not normal. In some ways that's easier 'cause I get an instant reaction – pity or horror. If it's an invisible illness, you don't get sympathy. Maybe your mummy's organs need a rest. I don't know.' She sat down next to Esme. 'If I had a mother like yours, I'd run away and find her.'

'Why would Es want to do that? She has us,' said Lexi.

'It's easier when you can picture where someone is,' said Bella.

Esme thought about the Earl imagining their get-well card.

'I mean, you don't have to run away and never come back, just *disappear* for a few days. Get the train down and a taxi to the hospital.'

'But I don't know where her hospital is. And how would I get to the station, it's a half hour drive from here?'

'I could drive you!' said Lexi, clearly excited by the possibility of an adventure. 'To the bus stop at least.'

Esme was warming to the idea, even though she'd never travelled so far on her own before. Imagine how surprised her mother would be!

Turning the light out so Nanny Patch wouldn't come down from her room to tell them off, the three girls whispered for hours, plotting how they would find train times and get the address of the hospital until, exhausted by it all, Lexi and Bella were unable to keep their eyes open any longer.

Esme, though, couldn't sleep; her tummy was filled with nervous fleas and her mind was racing. Downstairs, the grandfather clock gently chimed midnight. She turned and looked at Lexi in the darkness. Her eyes were closed – but fluttering.

'Lexi?' she whispered. No response.

She nudged Bella but she was dead to the world.

A door slammed. A high-pitched cry came from the hall-way.

'Lexi, are you awake?' she asked. 'Did you hear that?' She slowed her breath to better hear the silence that might hold a clue as to who or what had slammed the door. Nothing but the thump of her heart, knocking at her ribcage, her blood hissing in her ears. A fox barked outside. What a strange sound it was – like a cat being strangled. Esme often heard them from her own bedroom at The Lodge.

Sliding her arm out from beneath Bella, Esme left the warmth of her bed and opened the door to the hall. It was in almost total darkness, with just a sliver of light coming from the entrance to the Long Gallery. She headed towards it, tiptoeing, her small feet barely touching the ground. She glanced up at a portrait. The subject, a woman, looked out with a blank stare, her face luminous and white, her eyes black. The ermine that edged her velvet gown and the lace that gathered gracefully around her elbows looked almost real, giving the portrait an eerie quality. There was something about her that made Esme feel the woman was alive; she could almost feel the warmth of her breath, see the rise and fall of her décolleté. She was a comforting presence, despite her sad eyes. The plaque at the bottom of the frame was too high up to read, so she made up a name for the model: Katherine. An ugly woman in a beautiful dress.

Entering the Long Gallery, Esme realized the light she had

seen escaping from the door was that of the moon. It shone through windows tall enough to do justice to a cathedral and which, just like those in a place of God, were crafted from stained glass, their green tint responsible for the peculiar hue that washed over the old masters.

It felt like she was underwater; everything was translucent. She imagined the entire castle resting at the bottom of an ocean, perfectly preserved by seawater, dust motes glistening in the air like orbs of plankton.

She continued down the gallery, its icy flagstones stinging her bare feet. The cold air smelled damp and clung to her hair and nightdress, making her shiver. No noise. Total quiet. Was that a movement she saw ahead? There it was again.

Inching forwards she heard a sob, followed by quiet weeping. She peered around a pillar.

The Contessa was sitting in a beautiful antique chair that Esme recognized; it was usually roped off with a sign saying *No sitting*. The moonlight shone upon its elaborate carved arms and the folds of satin draped around the Contessa fell in a puddle at her feet. Like the tail of a mermaid, thought Esme. The Contessa's head was bowed and her body trembled as she brought a handkerchief to her eyes.

The Contessa was crying. Why? wondered Esme. Daring to move closer, she tripped over the pedestal of the column. The Contessa looked up. Esme had no choice but to reveal herself.

'Hello, Your...' said Esme, trailing off. Then, 'Are you all right?'

The sadness in the Contessa's eyes caught Esme unawares; without her make-up she looked very different – pale and younger. She held her hand out, tears running down her face, and Esme let the Contessa draw her into her arms. Her hold was strong. She pressed her lips to her ear.

'Spying on me? Scurrying around like a sewer rat? You are a curse. A curse on your mother. A curse on this family. Here to inflict misery. The truth will come out and you will be sent away whether your deranged mother survives or not.' She released her grip. 'Get out of my sight. You sicken me.'

Scrabbling up, Esme fled, horrified.

Reaching her own bedroom, she leant against her door, drinking in great gulps of air to push away the bile that had risen at the Contessa's words. She looked back towards the gallery where the woman had been and shivered.

Esme wanted to creep back to Lexi's room but was too scared of getting caught, even though Nanny Patch had said it was OK. She had also said to keep it a secret.

She opened and closed her bedroom door silently. Her heart was racing. Facing the enormity of her room, engulfed in darkness, she felt her way to her bed. She groped for the light switch and when the bulb sprang to life, quickly took in her surroundings: the curtains were drawn, her bed sheets turned down and a now-cold hot-water bottle was lying on her mattress.

Shocked and frightened, she willed her imagination to take her home. She missed The Lodge, Mrs Bee and Sophia. But more than anything, she longed for her mother. Uninvited tears welled in her eyes. She didn't make a sound as big fat tears rolled down her face, collecting in her ears and running down her throat. She thought again about returning to Lexi's room but was now too disturbed to move. She had never felt so alone. She wanted to be braver but felt dread at an impending doom. She tried to rationalize that she was just being silly. But tonight, as with last night, she felt loneliness take hold, as if she had fallen into a black hole. She was cold but also felt an unbearable heat. She tossed and turned, trying to settle, but it was useless. Her current surroundings consumed her; it was just too far to travel back home on the wave of a dream.

Tomorrow, instead, she would run away to find her mother.

Chapter Twelve

The following morning, Esme ran down to Lexi's room to explain why she had left in the night. The beds had been made and the room tidied. Esme looked at her watch. She had overslept and missed breakfast. She wondered where to begin looking for her friend.

'Ah, Esme, there you are,' said Nanny Patch, coming in. 'I was just coming to wake you. Thought I'd let you lie in, given the Contessa has sent Lexi and Bella to Findlay House today.'

'I thought I was going, too?'

'Yes, I know. It was a last-minute thing. Their mother arranged for them to go earlier than planned this morning and will be meeting them again for lunch.'

'But I thought we were going riding?'

'Be that as may, they've gone. Lexi was none too happy and told me you could play with these until she gets back.' Nanny Patch tipped a cardboard box of toy horses onto the floor. 'If you get hungry, there's some bread and cheese in the nursery kitchen. You'll be all right? It's only for a few hours and I'll pop in to check on you.'

Esme sat on the floor and rifled through the mound of toys.

'Right,' said Nanny Patch with a big sigh. 'I'd better get on.'

And with that, Esme was alone. She half-heartedly picked up a pony. And then it came to her: this was her opportunity to run away! Jalopy was parked by the back door and Mr Cribben would know where the key was kept. Assuming he would be in the butler's pantry, she set off to find him.

'I thought I told Nanny Patch to keep you in Alexa's room?'

Esme jumped. It was the Contessa's voice but she couldn't see her because of the sunlight shining in her eyes, just a mere black shape before her.

'Go back – now. I don't trust you not to steal something that doesn't belong to you. Like your thieving mother.'

Esme tried to say something but her voice wouldn't work. Instead, she pushed past Lexi's mother and fled down the stairs, past a surprised Mr Cribben, who said something she didn't hear, and on until she reached the back door. Without closing it behind her, she bolted down the drive, not looking back until she reached a small gate into the field that would take her home. No one had followed her. She drank in the clean, cold air.

Horrible, hateful woman, Esme thought. There was only one place she wanted to be and that was with Mrs Bee.

She waited a few minutes and then made a dash for it across the fields.

As she arrived at The Lodge, Esme was reassured to see it looking exactly the same as usual. She had half-expected the house to have crumbled to ruin, broken like her mother when she visited her in hospital.

'Esme!' exclaimed Mrs Bee, opening the front door. 'What are you doing here?'

'I've come to see you, Mrs Bee. All by myself. I walked here,' said Esme, grinning with pride.

Mrs Bee seemed surprised.

'Aren't you happy to see me?' asked Esme.

'Of course I am, love, but… Well, I just wasn't expecting you,' she replied.

There was a flurry of activity and barking.

'Digger. Oh Digger!' cried Esme.

The dog leapt into her arms and licked Esme's face in a frenzy of excitement, his ears now flat against his head and his tail wagging furiously. He squeaked with delight. Esme covered his head in kisses. She had missed him so much and it felt wonderful to feel the warmth of him against her, the warmth from someone who really loved her.

'Hello?' came a man's voice from inside.

Esme looked at the housekeeper and ran into the kitchen.

The Earl was standing by the sink.

'Esme!'

Why was everyone so surprised to see her? Why was the *Earl* here? This was her home.

The Earl hesitated, just for a fraction of a second, then, 'Oh Esme – I'm so glad to see you. Mr Cribben said you were upset and last seen running across the field. I came to see if Mrs Bumble knew where you were.' He looked at Mrs Bee, who scooped Esme into her arms and hugged her.

'It's lovely to see you, darling.' Her voiced had returned

to its usual warmth. She released her grip and examined her, as if inspecting her for injury; touching her face, her arms. She pinched her chin and searched her eyes.

'Yes, Mrs Bee – it's me! It's really me!' Esme hugged her, pressing her cheek into the housekeeper's bosom. 'And now I'm in your kitchen, I'm hungry.'

Mrs Bee laughed. 'No surprise there,' she said. 'And you're cold, too. Sit down and use your wee dog as a hot-water bottle.'

Taking the chair opposite the Earl, Esme beckoned Digger to jump up onto her lap.

Mrs Bumble swilled boiling water round a blue and white teapot. 'Gets it nice and warm so the leaves brew properly,' she explained. She put a large slice of cake in front of the Earl, who was now sitting at the kitchen table, his tweed jacket slung over the back of the chair.

'Would you like a fork, Your Lordship? The icing is a wee bit sticky.'

The wedge of sponge had a soft butter icing, decorated with crystalized nuggets of ginger.

'Thank you, Mrs Bumble. It looks delicious. You *are* clever.'

Mrs Bee smiled, then asked, 'How has my wee lady been doing?'

'I think you've been doing splendidly, don't you, Esme?' said the Earl.

'Yes, but I've missed you *so* much, Mrs Bee. But guess what? We saw *Hello, Dolly!* yesterday. At the cinema. With Lexi's granny, the Dowager Countess.'

'Well I never. Look at you, living the high life. That's

much better than doing the housework with me,' said Mrs Bee, smoothing down her pinny.

'Do you know how Mummy is?' asked Esme. 'Will she be home soon?'

She saw the Earl and Mrs Bee exchange glances.

'Your mother is doing fine, Esme.'

Again, they shared a look.

'Esme, love, why don't you take Digger outside? He's missed his walks with you.'

'OK.'

'Go on, be off with you – the poor lamb looks like he might pop with excitement!'

Esme knew they wanted her out of the way and played along with it. 'Come on, Digs – walkies, then you can help me choose some more clothes,' she said, leaving the room with her dog. But she wanted to hear the truth about her mother so she locked Digger in the cloakroom, promising she would be back very soon, and went back to the kitchen, standing behind the door to listen.

'She was very low,' she heard the Earl say. 'Frail. It was difficult for me to get her to talk.'

'It's not right that such a beautiful, kind lady should have done such a wicked thing,' Mrs Bee's voice was stifled with emotion. Esme heard her blow her nose. 'And for Esme to have seen her mother like that! No child should have to drag her mammy from a burning bed. We've lived on a knife-edge for years, waiting for something like this to happen.' She blew her nose again.

'It's a dreadful thing. Terribly distressing for all of us. But she's in the best place and the doctors seem to be on top of things,' the Earl continued. 'Esme can stay at Culcairn for as long as necessary. It's actually been wonderful having her, especially for Lexi. She's a breath of fresh air, like her mother. It breaks my heart that she is the victim in all this.'

'The thing she loves best after her mother is that wee dog,' said Mrs Bee. 'Perhaps he could go back to the castle with her so she feels a bit closer to home?'

Esme's heart skipped a beat. She wanted to burst through the door but if she did that Mrs Bee and the Earl would know she had been eavesdropping on their conversation. She counted ten hippopotamuses then, as casually as she could, entered the kitchen.

'Digger's already done a piddle outside,' she lied.

The Earl and Mrs Bee crossed glances.

'That was quick,' said Mrs Bee.

'I know,' said Esme. 'He was bursting.'

'Esme, I've suggested to Mrs Bumble that perhaps Digger comes back to the castle with us. What do you think?' asked the Earl.

'Oh, yes! Yes, please! Can he, Mrs Bee?'

'Och, of course. That's marvellous, Your Lordship. Esme, go and collect his basket and a few more clothes for yourself.'

The house was shiny and clean. It felt as though no one had lived there for a long time. All evidence of Christmas had been tidied away, even the Christmas tree. No scattered newspapers. No coats flung on chairs. No mother. No father. No Sophia. Esme felt like she was snooping in someone else's home.

She climbed the stairs and walked along the corridor, passing her mother's room. Mrs Bee had been busy. The door was sticky with fresh paint and inside the room bore no sign of there having been a fire. A dustsheet covered her mother's bed and the windows were missing their curtains, giving the sense of a place no one would be coming back to. Her feelings were reinforced by the sight of picture frames, lying face-down on the floor. Esme's stomach churned.

It was with relief that she found everything remained the same in her bedroom. Lying on her bed, it felt like she had never been away. Her bedside clock ticked loudly, Mrs Spider was still in residence in a corner above her head. She closed her eyes and sighed the long sigh of someone at peace.

'Darling,' said Mrs Bee, coming in, 'what are you doing? The Earl is waiting for you.' She gathered some clothes from Esme's chest of drawers. 'I expect you need some more trousers and a couple of sweaters. This wee blouse is lovely,' she said, holding up a floral print. 'Your mother loves you in this.'

'I don't want to go. I want to stay here.'

'Come on with you, love. You have to. Digger is all a dither. He knows something exciting is happening.'

It was pointless trying to change things. She felt like everyone close to her was doing their own thing. Moving on and leaving her behind. Even her home had adjusted to the changes. Nothing was as it had been.

Digger stood on Esme's knees with his front paws on the dashboard, his wagging tail brushing her chest.

'He seems happy, doesn't he?' said the Earl.

'Oh, he is. Perhaps I won't miss home so much now. Or Mummy and Daddy and Sophia.'

'Yes, well, I'm not sure how Lucia will take it, having another dog in the house, so we'll have to keep it a secret from her.'

'Will she be very cross?' asked Esme.

'Only if she finds out. You'll have to be on your best behaviour and so will Digger. Then she won't notice a new guest.'

'You're very kind. Mummy is lucky to have a friend like you. I don't know, but—'

'Well, I'm very fond of your mother, so of course I am concerned for her welfare.'

'Is that why you were in the room off your library together on Christmas Day? Why did she run out crying? Were you looking after her welfare then?'

The Earl hesitated, leaning forwards over the steering wheel as if he was looking for something. 'Yes, in a manner of speaking.'

'And after that she tried to do suicide.'

He cleared his throat. 'Esme, your mother isn't very well and regrettably the illness she has isn't like a cold that can be cured with a Disprin. It's a bit like Homer getting a splint. You can't get rid of it but you have to manage it forever to make sure he doesn't become irreparably lame.'

'So if we look after her she won't have to be put down?' asked Esme.

'Exactly.' He laughed. 'That's exactly right. We must keep her safe. You would do the same if Lexi was ill.'

'Oh, I would! I would nurse her back to health. Bring her homemade soup and a feather pillow. Mop her brow until the fever broke.'

'Of course you would. And your mother would do the same for us both should, God forbid, we end up in hospital,' said the Earl. 'You really are so like her, my dear. So kind and compassionate and understanding and gentle.'

'Do you love her very much?' asked Esme, knowing now that he did. Properly, with all his heart.

'Of course I do,' said the Earl, softly. 'I remember when we met.'

'Really? Do you remember what she was wearing?'

'No, but I do remember how pretty she was. She still is. There are many things I adore about your mother. She is very modest and a little shy but her face is so expressive that she doesn't have to say what she's thinking. She could never tell a lie without being caught out.'

Esme looked at him. She had never heard her father talk about her mother in this way. 'Were we living here already? When you met.'

'Your parents had just arrived. Sophia was a baby and you were still a twinkle in your mother's eye. It was when there was petrol rationing. The car had broken down and she was in the car with Jimmy, stranded in the middle of the road. I gave them a can of petrol. That evening, she and your father were guests at Lord and Lady Findlay's home. I sat next to her at dinner. I didn't know they'd rented The Lodge. Your mother teased me for not knowing what was happening on the estate. "Is it *so* large that you can't keep a handle on it?" she said.' He smiled at the memory.

'And that's when you became friends?'

'Yes, I suppose it was. And we always will be, dear Esme.'

'That's good. Everyone needs friends.'

He looked at her with all the love he had for her mother still in his eyes. 'Esme, I…' But he stopped and squeezed her hand. 'I will take you to see your mama as soon as she is strong enough. I promise.'

She felt a comforting warmth towards the Earl. Everything was getting brighter. She couldn't run away now that Digger was to be staying with her secretly at the castle.

'May I call Sophia when we get back?'

'Absolutely,' said the Earl. 'Mrs Bee has given me the number of the hotel where she's staying.'

It was Digger's first visit to the castle. He ran through the entrance hall then stopped suddenly and took in his surroundings. He looked skywards, his comma-shaped nostrils inhaling new smells. Esme wondered whether dogs got shy like she did.

'We'd better go the back way; we don't want to get caught red-handed, smuggling in a dog. He might get put in quarantine,' said the Earl.

Esme was enjoying their mission to sneak Digger past the Contessa. Sharing a secret with an adult made her feel important and grown up.

'Come on, Digger,' she urged, patting her thigh for him to follow the Earl down the corridor, brightened by sun streaming through an arched window at its end.

Digger scurried along, nose down, sniffing his way along the skirting. Every so often he would stop to better smell a spot that interested him.

All of a sudden, an elongated shadow appeared before them; approaching was the tall silhouette of a woman. The Earl curled his arm behind him, pulling Esme into his back. She held her breath.

'Henry, what on earth is that dog doing here?'

The Earl gave Esme a little tickle. She put her hands over her face, not daring to move.

'I found him on the drive. He doesn't have a collar. Rather sweet, don't you think?'

'Well, it can't stay here. Poor Brian will have his nose put out of joint.'

Esme thought her voice sounded almost good-natured.

'I'll give Trent a call. He may know who it belongs to.'

'No need, Lucia. I have a meeting with him anyway, regarding the shoot. I'll take the dog,' said the Earl.

Esme heard feet running up behind her. Turning around, she put her finger to her lips but it was too late.

'Esme! What are you doing hiding behind Papa?' It was Lexi. 'And why have you been *so* long? I've been waiting for *ever* for you to come back.'

Next appeared Bella. She had clumps of snow in her hair and appeared to be eating something chewy.

'Digger!' she shouted when she saw the dog.

Delighted to be recognized, Digger's ears pricked to attention before flattening as he crouched and slowly wagged his way towards the girl.

Esme stepped out from behind the Earl.

'Oh, I see. That filthy thing belongs to *her*. Get it out – *now!*' ordered the Contessa in a raised voice, her finger pointing at Esme.

'Calm down, Lucia – it's only a dog!' said the Earl.

'It looks diseased. Brian will catch some frightful virus off it. I want it to go. Immediately.' The Contessa's coal-black eyes glinted like volcanic glass, her stature growing with her suppressed rage.

'Mrs Bumble said Digger had been pining for his mistress, poor thing. He'd gone on hunger strike in protest and refused to leave her bed. We thought it would be best for his welfare to come and stay here,' said the Earl, as if talking to a child.

'Is this some sort of joke? It's a mongrel, not a bloody refugee!'

Esme slipped her hand into the Earl's. Bella came to stand the other side of her and Lexi picked up Digger. The four stood together in mutual defiance, united in their silent resolve to oppose the Contessa's wishes. Esme felt as though she were at the top of a roller-coaster, scared and excited at the same time.

For a second the Contessa looked defeated but quickly regained control. She stared just above their heads for a few seconds then projected her gaze towards her daughter.

'Alexa, will you take that mongrel and put it in the kennel on the terrace until Miller has time to take it back down to The Lodge?'

'Mama, you can't be so mean! Look how happy he is to be with Esme. He'll die if he's kept apart from her a single day longer,' declared Bella.

'This is deliberate, isn't it, Henry?' said the Contessa.

'The dog will stay,' said the Earl. 'Esme, his basket is in the hall. Go and put it in your room. Digger can sleep with you. He will keep you company. God knows why you were put in that tower room in the first place.' He turned to his wife, accusingly.

'So now we have two mongrels in the house, do we Henry?'

'Don't you have something to do, Lucia?'

She raised an eyebrow. 'And what would that be? A stroll through the Rose Garden with my beloved husband?'

'You know exactly what I mean,' said the Earl, firmly.

'Indeed I do. I'll leave the children to you, then. And if you insist on that creature staying, I don't want the servants feeding it. It's *not* their responsibility. Do you understand?' She turned on her heels and left. Esme breathed normally again.

'Woohoo! Fifteen-love to Papa!' cried Bella.

The Earl smiled.

'Come on, Es, I'll help you get Digger settled. He can become part of the gang!' Lexi said, then went up and hugged her father. 'You are so kind, Papa. It's going to be so much fun having Digger here. Do you think I can sleep with Esme and him tonight?'

'You'll have to check with Nanny Patch, darling, but I can't see why not,' he said. 'Now, I need to write some letters. I'll try and see you later, but we have the shoot tomorrow, so I might be a bit tied up.

'Who's coming, Papa?' asked Lexi.

'Just the locals, darling.'

'May I pick up with Taxi, Papa? Mr Trent says he's a natural,' said Bella.

'What's Taxi?' asked Esme.

'He's my gun dog – a ginger pointer.'

'And he's a stunner!' said the Earl. 'Of course you must go out with him, darling, and Digger has to join us too.'

Esme gave a little skip. 'Digs, did you hear that? You're coming on your first shoot!'

'Right, I must get started. You and Esme go and show Digger where his bedroom is.' The Earl turned to leave. A hand rested on his arm.

'Thank you. For everything,' said Esme.

'It's my pleasure, Esme. One thing before you go.' He bent down to her level and took her hands.

'Yes?'

'There's something I want to tell you,' he said in a whisper. 'If it hadn't been for you, your mother might have died – suffocated in the fire. But you saved her and we'll tell her all about it when she's well again. She will be so proud of you. I know it can't be easy for you staying here but think of yourself as Lexi's sister. You're part of the family.'

'Lexi and I *are* sisters,' said Esme.

The Earl's eyes widened, his grip becoming stronger. 'Well, there you go,' he said, not letting go of Esme. 'She is lucky to have you.'

'And Digger,' smiled Esme.

'Yes, and Digger.'

'And me and Mummy are lucky to have you,' she added, giving the Earl a brief hug.

'Where shall we put the basket? By your bed or in the corner over there?' asked Lexi, pointing to the other side of the room.

'By my bed, under the table. Then he can jump up if he has a bad dream. Look, here's his food.' Esme took out from her coat pocket a freezer bag that held four enormous turkey legs.

'Is that what he has? Blimey, Brian only gets Pal and a Bonio on special occasions. Well, that's what he's *meant* to get. I think Seamus gives him all the leftovers too.'

'Mrs Bee says turkey legs are cheaper and much better for dogs. I give him a Good Boy when he's been clever, which he always is. Watch this.' Esme started saying Digger's name over and over again in a high-pitched singsong voice.

'Diigggeer… Diigggeer… Diigggeer…'

The dog pointed his nose upwards and howled.

'He's singing too! What a clever boy. You are lucky having a dog. Mama won't let me. She has Brian and Bella was given Taxi by Papa, but he's not really a pet. He can't come into the house or anything. He lives with Mr Trent.' Then, 'Shall we give Digger some food so he feels more at home?'

'That's a good idea. I need to borrow a bowl – and one for water too.'

'I'm sure we can find something in here,' said Lexi, walking over to the mantelpiece. 'Here we go, this'll do.' She took down a small red porcelain cup decorated with green and blue flowers. 'Looks Chinese. There'll be a bigger one in the bathroom. Or maybe even a potty.' Lexi sniggered.

'Eww! He can't drink out of a potty.'

'Don't be silly, Es. No one *uses* them any more. They're just for decoration.' She disappeared through the bathroom door and shouted, 'Bingo!'

She reappeared in the bedroom. 'This is perfect. I've given it a quick rinse and put the water in.'

Lexi placed the potty next to Digger's basket. He gave it a sniff and continued on his exploration of the room.

'Girls?'

'Oh, you made me jump, Nanny Patch!'

'Sorry, Lexi. Oh, who is this?' Nanny Patch bent down stiffly to stroke Digger.

'Digger. He's my dog. Lexi's father said I could bring him,' said Esme proudly.

'Well, there you are. You won't be alone, which is good because your mother doesn't want you two sleeping together, Lexi. You're to stay in your own rooms, she said.'

'What?' said Lexi, hands on her hips. 'No way. That's ridiculous. What's the point of having Esme here if we can't sleep together?'

'It's what Her Ladyship wants,' said Nanny Patch, which seemed to close the subject. 'Now, don't forget you're shooting tomorrow. Lexi, I've laid your plus twos and your shooting socks out on the chair. Esme? Do you have plus twos? I couldn't find any in your clothes, just the socks. Very nice, too. Did Mrs Bumble knit them for you?'

'Um, I'm not sure. Probably. They used to be Sophia's but they shrank, so she gave them to me.'

'Most unlike Mrs Bumble to shrink anything. Tell her to use Lux; best soap flakes for wool.' Nanny Patch looked at her watch and disappeared from the room, leaving behind her a smell of witch hazel.

'Can you believe it? I *hate* Mama. How can she do this? It's a stupid, *stupid* idea and I won't obey her. I'll pretend. I'll put pillows down my bed and come and sleep in here with you.'

There was a sudden crash as the door flew open; unable to do so with her hands, Bella just kicked it hard with her foot. The strength she might have had in her arms and hands had doubled the power in her legs.

'Oh, Bella – Mama won't let me and Es sleep together. Can you believe it? Why would she say such a stupid thing?'

'Because, Lexi, she's trying to put a wedge between you. It's so obvious, it's sad. She'll expect you to make a fuss, so don't; that'll really please her.'

'Why would she do that? Put a wedge between me and Es?'

'She wants to make Esme's life hell because Mrs Munroe's so much nicer than she is. Grown-ups are such children sometimes. I wouldn't worry about it. Just sneak out and sleep here anyway.'

'That's what I just said to Es.' Lexi turned to her friend. 'It could be fun. Bit like escaping the baddies in a film. Esme and Digger can hide me from the evil monsters.'

'Exactly! We can come and rescue you, 'cause Digger can find his way anywhere, even in the dark. He'd make a brilliant dog for the blind. Let's show him the route now, whilst it's still a bit light and then he can sniff his way tonight. Then I need to cook a leg of turkey. Will Seamus mind?'

'I'm sure he'll do it for you,' said Bella.

'I'll do it,' said Esme, remembering the Contessa's order

that none of the servants were to look after Digger. 'I just need a big pot.'

The castle kitchen was huge and functional. It held none of the warmth of Mrs Bee's, with its Aga and shelves lined with exotic ingredients.

Seamus was tall and lanky, with long hair that he tied back in a ponytail. He was busy defrosting prawns in the sink under cold running water. Three empty tins of canned mushrooms sat next to an ancient Kenwood mixer, which was doing its best to pulp the fungi.

'Hello there, ladies,' he said cheerfully. 'What brings you down here?'

'Esme needs to cook Digger's turkey leg.'

'Does she indeed? Will you be roasting or boiling that? Because if it's the oven you need, my Beef Wellington will be stopping you. No room in there for... Is it your *dog*, Esme?'

She nodded.

'For your dog's dinner,' he finished.

'I need a giant saucepan and some water. It takes about an hour to cook. Is that OK, Seamus?'

'Of course it is, my treasure. It can go in with the potatoes – give them extra flavour. Is it defrosted? You don't want to be poisoning Digger now, do you?'

Esme prodded the meat. It was soft, if still chilled. 'It's fine. May I do it now? He'll be hungry and I want to feed him as soon as possible, otherwise he might want to poo in the night. He's sleeping in my room. He's not allowed at home. He has to sleep in the cloakroom there. Mrs Bee thinks he's a fleabag. But she loves him too, just not as much as me.'

'Well, isn't that lovely for you both. It'll be like a holiday for him. I tell you what, I'll cook it up now and you girls come back at – let's say five?'

'That's really kind, Seamus. Are you sure you don't mind?'

'Not at all. See you in a bit.'

An hour later Esme put the porcelain bowl on the floor of her bedroom.

'Din-dins, Dig.'

The dog gave his meal a sniff, then sat down and looked up at his mistress as if to say *I'm not hungry.*

'Come on, Digger, you must eat to get your strength up.'

He didn't move, just continued staring up at Esme with sad eyes.

'Why do you think he's not eating, Es?' wondered Lexi out loud.

'I don't know. He's normally such a pig.'

'Maybe he wants company? Why don't we eat with him? We can put our supper in bowls and eat it on the floor. You wait here and I'll run and get our food.'

Esme sat on her bed and looked at her dog. He was normally so boisterous and full of life.

'What's wrong, boy? I'm here; it's all OK now. You're lucky because, unlike me, you're with your mummy. If you don't eat your coat might fall out. Now be a good boy; eat up.'

Digger seemed to take advantage of the word 'up' and jumped onto Esme's knee. He was shivering.

'Are you cold? Is that it? Here, let me put my dressing gown over you. Good boy. No need to be scared or sad. I'll look after you. I always do, don't I?'

He gave a low growl.

'Hey, don't be rude. That's just Lexi.'

Lexi emerged from the gloom, out of breath and carrying two plates.

'Cherry wouldn't let me bring our supper. Said it would make a mess, so I grated some cheese.' She put the food on the floor next to Digger's turkey.

'He might have liked the smell of our dinner better than his! Let's eat it like him, straight from the plate with our mouths, like we're dogs too.'

The two girls went down on their knees, hands behind their backs and scooped up the cheddar with their tongues.

'Mmm, yummy. Come on, Digger, eat with us,' said Esme.

But the mongrel didn't budge. He laid there, his paws and head hanging over the edge of the dog bed.

'I don't know what's wrong with him,' said Esme.

'Maybe it's just because he's in a new place. I remember when Jupiter came over from Ireland – he didn't eat anything for two days! Jimmy said it was normal. He wouldn't even eat oats and molasses. Then suddenly he was fine. Just needed to settle in to his new home.'

'You're probably right. Let's leave it. I'll leave it here and try later on when we go to bed. Or should I bring it down with me? Do you think Cherry will mind if I bring him down to the nursery?'

'She loves dogs, so I'm sure she won't, and Nanny's always saying we should be allowed a dog.'

'Digger! Come on. Let's go downstairs,' said Esme, encouraged.

Digger flew off the bed and followed his mistress out of the door, tail wagging.

'Good boy. That's more like it.' Esme turned to her friend. 'Maybe he just thinks it's bad manners to eat in the bedroom? He seems happy now.'

'Perhaps he'd like a toy for his basket? He could borrow one of Brian's. Mama gave him a squeaky lamb chop, but he just turned his nose up at it. Probably cross it wasn't real. Last time I saw it was under the piano in the drawing room,' said Lexi.

Peering around the door to the drawing room, Esme was relieved to see it empty. Just as Lexi had said, the rubber bone lay beneath the grand piano. She crawled under to retrieve it and squeezed it a few times. It let out a high-pitched 'peep'. Digger sat behind Esme, ears pricked, waiting for the toy to be thrown for him.

'No time for games now, boy. Not in here, anyway. We can play catch in our room,' she said.

Thinking of a happier night ahead, with her dog for company, she heard voices approaching.

'Esme, Esme, Esme. Bloody *Esme*,' the Contessa was saying. 'Why didn't you just leave her there with the housekeeper? What is it with you and that damned child? You're obsessed with her.'

At the sound of her name and approaching footsteps, Esme shrank back under the piano, making herself as small as possible. Praying they couldn't see her as well as she could see them, she crouched, motionless. They stood by the fireplace. The Earl swept his hair back with his hand.

'For goodness' sake, Lucia, her mother is in hospital. Has it ever occurred to you to show even a modicum of kindness? To anyone?'

'I allowed that dog to stay, didn't I?' said the Contessa, looking over her shoulder as she walked over to the drinks cabinet to pour herself a glass of wine.

'Only because I put my foot down.'

The Contessa tossed the wine into her mouth and moved to stand by the piano. Terrified, Esme squeezed her eyes shut, folded herself over Digger to keep him still and put her arms over her head like a fallen jockey in the Grand National.

'And *I* haven't got myself locked away in the madhouse. Even *I'm* not that selfish. "Oh but poor Diana can't help it. Poor Diana isn't selfish. Poor Diana is unwell." Well, poor fucking Diana was selfish enough to pour vodka down her throat and torch herself in a laughable attempt to get attention. Is *that* how a loving mother behaves?' The Contessa laughed.

She was now so close to where Esme was hiding that she could see a tiny ladder in her tights and although her upper body was blocked by the piano, she could see her fingers twitch at her sides. Hypnotized, Esme watched their frenzied movement, her fear diverted for a moment.

'You ought to try it. Just be sure to succeed,' muttered the Earl.

'And rid you of the one person that makes your life hell? You're right, Henry; I'm not that kind.'

'Indeed. But understand that Esme is going nowhere until her mother recovers. She will stay and that is final. Do yourself a favour and accept it. I'm going to bed. We have the shoot tomorrow and our guests arrive at 8.45 to make the most of the light. I suggest you get an early night too. Your vitriol must be exhausting.'

The Earl walked to the door.

'Henry?'

'What now, Lucia?' he said in a tired and resigned voice, turning to face her.

'Why did you marry me?' asked the Contessa, her voice suddenly trembling.

'What do you mean?'

'Why did you marry me when I'm clearly not good enough for you?'

'I really don't want to have this conversation now.'

'Our marriage could have been different had you allowed it to be, Henry. I am redundant here – and not just in the workings of the castle. In our marriage also.'

'We've been together for nearly twenty years. All marriages tire after that long,' said the Earl, with a hint of kindness in his voice.

'There have been three people in this marriage for twelve years,' said the Contessa sadly. 'I will never be able to understand your weakness for that child and her psychotic mother.'

The Earl seemed to have nothing more to say. He went over to his wife. Esme could almost see her reflection in his highly polished shoes. He must be kissing her goodnight, she thought. Her heart hammered in her chest and her breath stopped until he left the room and the Contessa walked back to the fireplace. Taking residence in her usual chair, she chucked her cigarette into the hearth and stared at the flames. She began to cry, like she was trying to get rid of her unhappiness.

Her brightly painted nails tapped out her thoughts in a lonely Morse code against her skirt. The rhythm became faster then stopped. She lifted her hand up and looked at her wedding finger. She let out a snarl of anger. Esme clamped her own hand around Digger's muzzle to stop him growling. She watched, hypnotized, as the Contessa pulled the diamond ring from her finger and stormed across the room to the bay window where the piano stood.

She opened the glass door and flung the ring out into the darkness. The curtains snapped angrily as the cold air rushed in, blowing the Contessa's hair out behind her. The fire of the Contessa's wrath raged back to life, its flames leaping dangerously high. Esme heard more things crash and splinter in protest, the photo frames on the piano falling backwards on their stands. Seeming not to notice the storm she had invited in, the Contessa turned on her heel and left the room.

Shivering, Esme let go of Digger and with great effort closed the window. Instantly, the room returned to calm but the wind had caused mayhem. A porcelain lamp lay smashed on the stone hearth, cigarette butts scattered the carpet. She put the fireguard in front of the fire but left everything else untouched before turning off the lights and leaving the room.

Lying on her bed, Esme realized she must hide from her friend her shock at what she'd just seen, otherwise Lexi would know immediately that something was wrong and Esme knew instinctively that what she had heard must be kept to herself. She needed time for her speeding thoughts to slow down. She had learned a lot today – about the Earl's affection for her mummy, about the Contessa not liking that, and that the Earl also cared for Esme. There were things she couldn't understand; she was stuck on how there could be three people in a marriage. There was only one Earl and Contessa of Culcairn.

Without bothering to change into her nightdress and with Digger already asleep alongside her, Esme carefully got under the covers and tried to do the same. Lexi would wake her if she wanted to sleep with her. And if not, she would make up an excuse for her absence in the morning. Tomorrow was the shoot and they would have an early start.

Chapter Thirteen

The bitter cold woke her. Tucking the covers around herself to trap what little heat was left in her body, she looked at her watch. It was already eight o'clock but the gloom of a winter's dawn clung to the morning.

'Damn. We'd better get up, Digger, or we'll be too late for the shoot.'

It was Esme's first time going shooting without her father. Normally, she loved it because it was one of the things they did together. He liked having her with him to help load his gun. Her small hands were fast and nimble putting in the new cartridges so he could quickly shoot the next brace of pheasants. Everyone had a purpose, be it to flush out the birds or pick them up with their dogs once they had been shot. Esme always kept a keen eye on where her father's birds landed so she could collect them herself. She much preferred eating pheasant to chicken now, knowing that pheasants had such a good life before ending up in the pot. She wondered whose gun she would load today.

Esme was surprised that Lexi hadn't joined her in the night or at the very least come to wake her this morning. She then remembered that she had sneaked off to bed without a word; Lexi was probably cross with her.

Dressing quickly, she called for her dog. 'Where are you Digger?' She noticed her bedroom door was open. He must have gone exploring.

She found Lexi in her bedroom and saw she was indeed upset.

'You've missed breakfast,' she said accusingly. 'Why did you go to bed without me?'

'Well, I went upstairs and just passed out. I'm sorry, Lexi. Did you sleep well?' Esme asked, hopefully.

'No,' Lexi said. 'I wanted to do our thing of putting pillows in my bed but you obviously had better things to do.'

'It's not my fault I conked out. Anyway, I can't find Digger. Has he been in here?'

As quickly as she had fallen into her bad mood, Lexi snapped out of it. Esme loved that about her friend and gave her a big hug.

'Did he sleep in your room?' she asked.

'Yes, but when I woke up the door was open and he had gone. I must not have shut it properly last night. I'm sure he's fine. But if I can't find him, I'll have to leave him behind. He'll be sad to miss his first shoot.'

'Hurry up, Alexa!' The Contessa's voice carried down the passage.

'We're going to have to leave him, Es. We can't be late.'

'*Alexa!*'

With Esme in tow, Lexi hurtled down the corridor and stopped at the entrance of the Contessa's bedroom, Esme slightly to the side and out of sight. Lexi knew better than to go in.

'What are you still doing here?' snapped the Contessa. 'The

guns will be leaving and your father will be furious if we're late. Now run along and make sure you have everything. Wellington boots, coat...'

'We want to take Digger but we can't find him and Esme—'

'For goodness' sake, Alexa! That mongrel isn't fit to be in the castle let alone to come shooting.'

'You are so mean, Mama. Papa said we could bring him.'

'Why are you children so disobedient? This is typical of your father. He has spoilt you. No dog. And get a move on.' She turned back and the girls left her to finish getting ready.

Esme stalled. 'Lexi, I'm just going to have another quick look and tell Mr Cribben. If he's not about I'll leave a note in the pantry.'

'Good idea; he'll look after Digger. But be quick otherwise Mama will leave you behind too.'

Of course she will, thought Esme. But the Contessa probably wouldn't notice whether Esme was around or not.

She shouted for her dog but to no avail. He could be anywhere. But he was a resourceful creature and boundlessly loyal; wherever he was, she knew he would wait for her. She grabbed a pencil and wrote a quick note telling Mr Cribben to put Digger in her room if he found him.

❄

The boot room was like a shop. Row upon row of tweed, wax and fur jackets hung from large iron hooks. Boots, brogues and shoes were lined up on racks below. A couple of reindeer skins covered the rush matting, which was prickly beneath Esme's feet. She jumped from one foot to the other.

'Any joy?' Lexi asked.

'No. It's OK, but shooting would be much more fun with Digs,' said Esme.

'Bet he can sense Mama hates him.'

'He's clever that way. He's probably hiding,' laughed Esme, taking her quilted jacket off a peg.

'I think you should wear this. Here!' Lexi threw a light-weight jacket at Esme. 'This won't keep you warm, but at least your Husky won't rip on the brambles. Put it on over the top.'

Esme tugged it on. It was tight. 'I feel like a sausage. Have you seen my boots?'

Lexi held up a pair of black go-go rain boots.

'Not those – they're granny shoes!' She laughed.

'Alexa! We're leaving.'

It was the Contessa. Esme hurriedly pulled on her boots and followed Lexi out to the car.

'Poor Miller has been waiting for you both for ages,' the Contessa said, as Esme climbed into the back seat.

'It's all right, your Ladyship,' said Miller, starting the car. 'We've still got plenty of time.'

Air hissed out from between the Contessa's teeth. She looked supremely elegant, wearing a tweed skirt and jacket cut to accentuate her small waist. She turned and looked at the girls, her eyes widening as she noticed on what Esme was sitting. Too late, Esme realized it was the Contessa's coat.

'You stupid child!' she shrieked, leaning over and yanking the material out from underneath the little girl, then spread-ing it over her legs like a blanket. Esme shrank back into her seat, terrified.

'Will you be warm enough, Mama?' said Lexi, trying to distract her mother. 'Esme and I are wearing two coats each.'

'You're right, Alexa. I forgot how mind-numbingly long these drives are. Go and fetch my sealskin jacket. Standing still for hours on end is boring enough – I don't want to be cold, too.'

Lexi gave a theatrical sigh and got out of the car.

Alone on the back seat, Esme caught the Contessa looking at her through the rear-view mirror. She didn't need to see her whole face to know that it glared with undiluted hatred. Esme felt herself tremble and looked away, grateful to see Lexi reappear carrying the jacket.

She got back in the car and slammed the door. 'This is the one, right?' she asked, chucking the sealskin over the headrest.

'Yes, thank you Alexa. It's not the most attractive thing but it will keep the wind out,' she huffed.

The jacket looked old. The fur had worn thin to expose the leather on the collar and cuffs, and a buttonhole had ripped. It appeared extremely heavy and smelt of stale perfume.

Esme was very glad when Miller put his foot on the accelerator and they sped out of the gates towards the shoot.

❄

As they pulled up alongside the other vehicles, the Contessa touched up her make-up, brushing her lashes with a fingertip and adding another layer of lipstick.

'Look at them,' she said. 'A silly sport for silly people.'

What a funny thing to say, thought Esme. The Culcairn shoot was a source of great pride for the Earl. It was the same with the hunt. Although maybe the Contessa thought that was stupid, too.

Up ahead Esme saw the men, all dressed in shades of green, talking and laughing beneath a small cloud of smoke and frozen breath. She wished her father were among them. At the sight of their car, Mr Trent and his dogs, glued to his heels, came over and opened the door for the Contessa.

'Good morning, Trent.'

'Morning, Your Ladyship.'

'I think I'll stay in the car with Miller until the drinks. It's awfully cold.'

'Very good, Your Ladyship. And what about you, Lady Lexi? Are you and Esme going to help pick up?'

So that was her job this morning, thought Esme: collecting the dead birds and putting them in the trailer for the local butcher to sell to eager customers for their Sunday roast.

'Of course we are, Mr Trent,' said Lexi, as they clambered down from the car.

The men positioned themselves by their pegs, spread apart at equal intervals down the track that divided the densely wooded escarpment. They stood alongside their empty weapons, waiting for the sound of the horn that would tell them it was safe to load them with ammunition. It was a familiar sight to Esme. Ever since she was tiny she had taken part in shoots, often walking with the beaters to flush the birds out by waving a plastic flag or popping cartridges into empty barrels. One day she would have her own small-calibre shotgun to shoot vermin.

The Christmas shoot was always one of the biggest. Birds flew fast and in great numbers. Esme anticipated that she would be kept busy picking up masses of pheasants, along with woodcock, snipe, pigeon and jays.

As usual, the guests were made up of an assortment of tried and tested local friends, who knew the correct form for one of the best shoots in the country. Despite the relaxed chat, Esme could see they were nervous and excited – like she was when she went hunting. Each man stood tall, balancing with one foot in front of the other as if they were at the start of a running race. Their dogs sat to heel, shivering in anticipation. The hunters wore their breeches in varying degrees of elegance. Rollo and the Earl were in three-piece tweed suits, three finely tailored pieces made especially for them. Esme's father's suit belonged to her grandfather and was too big for him, but he said wearing a hand-me-down indicated that his family had been shooting for generations. Everyone wore green cable-knit socks, held up by wool garters.

Esme knew all about the hard work and skill required to run and maintain a shoot of this importance. Mr Trent and his team kept the pheasant chicks safe by staying up all night to catch the stoats and weasels that saw baby pheasants as fast food. She eyed him now, standing with his four Labradors at the end of the line. He looked calm but inwardly he was probably praying that the day would reap the benefits of his hard work.

'Pigeon!' someone yelled, but no one raised their gun, aside from one guest who took aim and fired, even though the horn still hadn't been blown. Esme recognized him as Martin Smunt, an old school friend of the Earl who had fallen on hard times and now lived in a cottage on the estate. Esme didn't like him at all. She had always thought there was something creepy about him.

Esme and Lexi were standing next to Lord Findlay. 'Idiot,' he muttered, a cigar clamped between his teeth. He peered down the line. 'God, that man is a slimy individual.'

The girls followed his gaze. Mr Smunt grinned from underneath his tweed cap; he was wearing a tired-looking jacket with raggedy cuffs that looked as if they had been nibbled by mice. The back of his collar was darkened by grease from his thinning hair. Esme remembered that her father always said that a gentleman should wear his hair short at the back and sides, and that any man with hair below his earlobes was untrustworthy. So she immediately distrusted Mr Smunt.

The horn finally sounded, barrels were loaded and the shotguns were raised, erect and ready. Hundreds of pheasants suddenly took off in a cloud of wings high above the trees. Shots rang out into the cold and birds curled out of the sky, stopped mid-flight by a barrage of lead. Some landed with decisive thuds whilst others dropped a wing and glided on, before gently touching down in the brambles.

Esme didn't like to see the birds being wounded but she knew that everything shot would be eaten. It was a natural part of country living. Country folk lived off the land and ate pheasant and duck, just as they did cows and sheep.

'Over!' someone yelled at the Earl, to warn that two pheasants were flying over him.

Esme watched as the Earl aimed at a very high-flying bird, shot it with his left barrel and in a blink killed the other with his right. She spotted Bella standing close to him, her ginger pointer, Taxi, sat patiently beside her.

'Good shot!' shouted the same voice.

'Well done, Papa!' cried Lexi, clapping her hands. 'Wasn't that an amazing shot, Es? Such a shame your daddy isn't here. Dead-eyed-dick, Papa calls him.'

'I wish he was here too. Hopefully Mummy will get better soon and they'll be able to leave the hospital in London,' said Esme. 'Although, I don't know if I'd have been able to load Daddy's gun fast enough.' She stared up at the sky. 'Lexi, look!'

Birds rained down like hailstones. Dozens of them, tumbling and bouncing to earth. Esme saw the row of beaters down their sticks and flags, like policemen combing a piece of land for a missing person. The horn sounded, marking the end of the drive.

At the command of their owners, the waiting dogs sprang into action, leaping over dead bracken and twisted brambles in search of the lifeless birds. No fowl was left undiscovered. The wounded ones were chased and caught in gentle but effective jaws; a gundog was trained not to damage the flesh of their quarry and to answer to the order of a whistle. There was so much joy in the dogs' tails and eyes as they hunted through the vegetation to proudly deposit their catch at their masters' feet.

Lexi and Esme followed Lord Findlay, who strode over to the Earl with a huge smile on his face. Bella waved at them briefly, but she was focused on commanding Taxi to pick up the birds.

'By god, old boy, that *was* exciting. The *height* of those birds. I don't think I shot more than a dozen. Mind you, that bloody Smunt kept getting in my way. What a nuisance he is. I don't know how you put up with him. You are a more patient man than I, Henry.'

'Keep your friends close and your enemies closer, isn't that what they say? He's harmless, really, William. Just a bit of a lost drunk, but then who isn't?' said the Earl.

'That's very philosophical of you. I suppose it's not like he's sleeping in the guest room. A blessing that you hardly ever see him? Bit like my bloody dog. Now where is he?' He blew the whistle that was hanging around his neck. 'Buster! *Buster!* Bring it on, boy. Bring it on.'

A black and white springer came bounding over to his master with a cock pheasant still flapping in his mouth.

'Good boy. Drop. Drop it.'

Buster sat down and looked up, his docked tail still wagging furiously, sweeping dead leaves from side to side.

'Buster. *Drop.*'

The dog lowered his head and gently released the bird at the toe of the Lord's boot. It lay there, immobilized with shock.

'I'll kill it,' said Lexi.

She picked it up and swung it round and round to break its neck, adding it to the pile of other dead birds to be collected by one of the beaters.

Soon, Trent's son came over and picked them up by their necks, placing one between each finger, until he carried all eight animals like the stems of wine glasses.

'Good, good. Well, we'd better load up for the next drive.

Bloody cold. I'm in need of something to warm me up,' said the Earl.

Mr Miller drove the Land Rover further into the field, happy for it to be visible now that the first shoot was over. The Contessa slid out of the passenger seat and Esme and Lexi ran over to help her unload the boot. Bottles of whisky, ginger beer, sloe gin and white wine were stacked against the sides, along with two large thermoses that had rolled over during the journey. The Contessa undid the leather straps of the giant wicker picnic basket and took out a selection of chinaware, packed with sausages and pork pies.

'Mama, can we have a ginger beer?' asked Lexi.

'Help yourself,' she said, disinterestedly.

'Thank you,' said Lexi, grabbing two clinking bottles and handing one to Esme.

'Henry,' said the Contessa, her voice rising as if she were hailing a porter in a noisy railway station. 'If you don't get a move on, your guests will be drinking lukewarm bullshot and they will start to show the first signs of frostbite.'

'Morning, Lucia,' said Lord Findlay, walking over. He kissed the Contessa on both cheeks, although his eyes were focused on the thermos of steaming cocktail. 'Shall I pour?' he offered, filling a mug and passing it to the Earl as he approached, then pouring one for himself.

'Simply delicious. I must say, I've been looking forward to this all morning. Best part of the day, isn't it?' he smiled at the Contessa, Esme and Lexi, then reached for a cold sausage.

'Did you enjoy that, girls? It's a shame Colin isn't here,' said the Earl.

'And Digger!' replied Esme. 'He would have loved it.'

'Why didn't you bring him?'

'Esme couldn't find him this morning and Mama refused to wait for us to look for him.'

'Has he gone missing?' asked the Earl, looking at Esme with concern.

'I don't know... I hope not,' she said, in a quiet voice.

'Well, why don't we ask Miller to collect him from the castle and bring him here? I'm sure he's turned up by now. Is that OK with you, Miller?' he turned to the chauffeur.

'Very good, M'Lord.'

'Any idea where he might be?' the Earl asked Esme.

'No,' interjected Lexi. 'Mama was rush, rush, rushing,' she said, shaking her head frenziedly and running on the spot to illustrate her mother's impatience.

'Miller, just speak to Nanny Patch. She'll know where to find the dog,' said the Earl.

'Indeed I will, Your Lordship,' said Miller.

'Henry, I really don't think this is necessary,' said the Contessa. 'All this fuss over one little dog. You can't go disrupting the shoot and Arabella won't manage without you; she's a liability at the best of times but on a shoot she's downright dangerous.'

'Bella is more than capable,' said the Earl sharply.

Standing amongst the throng of guests, there was nothing more the Contessa could say. Instead she rolled her eyes and turned to Lord Findlay. 'How did you do this morning, William?' she asked, linking her arm through his. 'I couldn't really see from the car.'

'I had my two lucky charms with me, so better than expected. How did I do, girls?'

'Really well,' they replied, smiling.

'Not as well as your father would have done, though, Esme. Colin is quite the marksman. We've all missed him today. And your darling mama, of course.' He put his arm around Esme's shoulders and gave her a squeeze.

'Oh dear, William,' the Contessa said, smirking. 'I've just realized, what on earth are you going to do for New Year? Colin won't be able to host the annual party at The Lodge on his own.'

'I believe that Colin is hopeful that Diana will recover in time,' Lord Findlay replied. 'So, until we hear otherwise, we're assuming the party is going ahe—'

He was cut short by the Contessa's laughter.

'Well, that's not going to happen, is it? You can hardly see in 1970 with a mad woman. Although I suppose it would make for a very *novel* New Year.' She laughed again.

'Lucia, that's enough!' said the Earl, as Esme dropped her bottle of ginger beer, horrified. It fell in slow motion onto the grass, bouncing gently before rolling to a stop, its contents lazily spilling out.

The Contessa's face twitched, as if she had been slapped.

As Esme bent to pick up her bottle, the world swam before her eyes. Why had the Contessa said that? *Was* her mother *mad*? Everyone said she was just very upset. Black spots clouded her vision. She tried to blink them away but realized that she was crying. Quickly, she wiped her eyes then straightened up, pressing into Lexi's side. Her friend squeezed her hand and she felt a little bit better.

'Ah, here comes Bella!' said Lord Findlay, triumphantly. 'What a resilient little lady she is… Well done, Bella. Are those my birds that my useless Buster missed?'

Bella had five brace bound together in pairs with binder twine and slung across a stick, balanced over her left shoulder. They looked heavy.

'Taxi found them,' said Bella, looking up at Lord Findlay. 'He's got a nose like a radar.'

'He's a beauty, Bella. And you are an excellent picker-upper. Perhaps you can stand with me for the next drive? Buster's mind is not on the job today. I'd really appreciate your and Taxi's support.'

As Bella's godfather, Esme knew how much Lord Findlay adored her. It wasn't difficult to love Bella. Esme looked at her now. Her hands sprang directly from her shoulders and the few fingers she had resembled clumsily tied balloon figures with knotted skin tags instead of fingernails. But none of that was important. Bella was in every way exceptional. Her killer sense of humour was lethal and, as Esme had witnessed, cutting words wrapped in wit were just as effective as throwing a punch.

'Are you sure about that, William?' asked the Contessa, surprised. 'I wouldn't want your day ruined by Arabella and her unruly dog following you around. I suspect she will be more hindrance than help.'

'Bella, your mother's just joking,' said Lord Findlay, uneasily. 'Aren't you, Lucia?'

'No, she's not! She can't bear to see me be good at anything,' cried Bella. 'She's scared that if I'm good at something, people will notice me and that just embarrasses her, doesn't it, Mama?'

'The one thing you are excellent at, Arabella, is being insolent and bad-mannered. If Lord Findlay insists on having you with him, you'd better keep that dog on a lead. And you will have to answer to Mr Trent after you've wrecked the day.'

'Bella's so brave,' whispered Esme.

'She's not scared of anything,' said Lexi.

'Well, that's agreed then,' said Lord Findlay, putting an end to the conversation. 'Bella, you will come with me and *together* we'll try not to wreck the day. Esme and Lexi, I believe the beaters are in need of some extra hands on deck, if you're up for it?'

'Oh, yes!' Lexi cheered. 'We'll scare the pheasants into flying really fast, won't we, Es?'

Esme nodded, afraid that if she spoke the Contessa would try to stop her taking part, too.

'That's very kind of you, young lady. You'll have to share Bella's stick with Esme,' he said.

'Alexa should have it,' said the Contessa. She snatched the hazel stick from Bella's shoulder and passed it to Lexi, allowing the birds to slide onto the ground.

Brambles clawed at their faces as Lexi began to beat their way through the thick foliage, the spiky branches tearing their tights and gloves.

'I'm glad you gave me the Barbour,' said Esme, the thorns sliding off her waxed jacket.

'It's so tiring,' panted Lexi, swishing her stick. Esme

laughed as she watched her friend using her brute force to fight her way through the undergrowth.

'Don't laugh at me, Esme! It's *hard*!'

'Lift your legs up like me,' Esme suggested, raising her knees high and stamping down on the brambles.

'Urgh. It's like we're in the rainforest,' said Lexi.

'People who don't shoot would think we're mad!' giggled Esme.

'Two crazy girls who prefer everything to be old and dirty or outside in the mud. No wonder Mama hates it.'

'Oh no, my glove!' squealed Esme. Her wool mitten had been ripped off her hand and was being held hostage by a cluster of snow dusted thorns. Her hair fell into her eyes and stuck to her face, now beaded in sweat. She tore her glove free, leaving half of it behind in the blackberry bush. Birds were bursting into the air around them, the sound of their wings adding to the noise of gunfire. Her school friends in London asked her if the countryside was boring, but Esme was thrilled by it.

Busy checking her shredded glove whilst still moving forwards, Esme didn't notice that she was free from the undergrowth and back on clear land – and about to stand on Martin Smunt's toes.

'Watch out, Esme!' shouted Bella as a final swarm of wings that, with nowhere else to hide, detonated the air; the horn hadn't yet sounded and the drive was still in full swing.

Instinctively, Esme fell to the ground, crouched in a ball, face planted in a patch of muddy snow; she had forgotten her ear defenders so was rendered temporarily deaf by the noise.

'Es? Esme? Are you all right?'

The voice seemed to come from a long way off. It held concern and suppressed laughter.

Esme raised her head, eyes wide with alarm.

'Poor you, Esme – that was close.' Lexi helped her up as the horn sounded.

'I could have killed you!' said Martin Smunt, looking shocked. 'Here, let me give you a hand.' He brushed her down, like a garment that had been dropped in a pile of leaves.

'You stupid, *stupid* child. Someone could have been shot!' yelled the Contessa, running towards them. 'You should know better than to stand in front of the guns when the drive is still in progress. Didn't your parents teach you these things?'

'Whoa, Mama!' said Lexi. 'Esme didn't mean to fall over.'

The Earl rushed over, full of concern.

'Esme! Are you all right?'

'Yes, I'm fine. Just wasn't concentrating,' said Esme, trying to smile, aware that the Contessa was glaring at her. Flustered, she put her hand up to her face. It was slimy with wet mud.

'She nearly caused a terrible accident, Henry,' the Contessa said to her husband. 'The idiotic girl ploughed into Martin, mid-drive. Just as well that dog of hers isn't here to cause even more damage.'

'Lucia, I think Esme is frightened enough,' said the Earl, his tone threateningly low. 'Lexi, I'd like you both to go back to the castle. Miller can drive you up. He'll be here any minute.'

'With Digger, hopefully,' said Lexi.

'Ah, speak of the devil. Here's our man,' said the Earl.

Miller came towards them, his arms wide. 'I'm terribly

sorry, Your Lordship. Nanny Patch and I looked everywhere for Digger but we couldn't find him. Mr Cribben helped us too.'

'He's still missing?' Esme asked, fearfully.

'We need to send out a search party,' said Lexi. 'Maybe he's fallen down a rabbit hole?'

'The only way Digger could have fallen in a hole, Lexi, is if Mama pushed him,' Bella said, looking hard at her mother.

The tentative faith she had had that Digger was safe collapsed, guilt filling Esme's stomach. How could she have been so heartless, so selfish, to come out to the shoot today? She had abandoned him.

'Lexi, I'm sure there's no need for us to worry,' said the Earl. 'I suggest that all you children head back and continue looking for him. He's probably asleep somewhere warm and cozy.'

Esme prayed the Earl was right. It had started to snow again.

Chapter Fourteen

Esme emerged from the cloakroom clean again, her right hand puffed up and showed signs of a large bruise developing. She had used the clothes brush to tidy her hair into a rough ponytail.

'Better?' asked Lexi.

'Yes. But my ears are still ringing,' she said, shaking her head from side to side. 'That gun went off right above me.'

'I started looking for Digger while you were in the bathroom. I couldn't see him anywhere,' said Lexi.

'I'm so worried, Lexi. Where do you think he could have gone?' said Esme.

'He's clever. Do you remember the time he found you at the village shop?'

'But he's never stayed here before – maybe it confused him?'

'You've been here for a few days now – your smell will be all over the place.'

'Let's split up. I'll start in my bedroom.'

'Good idea,' Lexi agreed. 'I'll go down to the kitchen and work my way up. You work your way down and we'll meet in the drawing room.'

Mr Cribben's high-pitched voice rang down the corridor.

'Esme? *Esme?*'

She popped her head out of her bedroom. 'Hello! I'm here – in my room!' she shouted.

'I'm coming up. I found your dog!'

Puffed from walking up the stairs, Mr Cribben appeared before her with Digger in his arms. As soon as the dog saw his mistress he started to whine and wriggled to escape the butler's hold.

'Oh, Mr Cribben – thank goodness. Thank you so *so* much.' Relief swept through Esme as she took her beloved dog from him. The joy of being reunited with him overcame the ache in her fingers.

'Careful, boy,' said Mr Cribben. 'You've already soaked my waistcoat with all that melting snow.'

'Snow?' exclaimed Esme. 'Where was he? How come he's wet?'

'He was out on the first-floor terrace. Freezing cold, he was, the poor lamb. I was in the pantry and heard scratching on the glass. Gave me a terrible fright.'

'Oh, poor Digger! How did he get there, do you think?'

'Your guess is as good as mine, my dear. Her Ladyship wants him to sleep in the kennel out there, now he's been found.'

'But it's too cold!'

'Yes, but he's a little ruffian – he'll survive. The Contessa said that if she discovers him sleeping indoors she'll send him straight back to The Lodge, so best to do as you're told, don't you think? I've left some things to keep him warm and toasty. Remember, the fox hounds sleep on straw! Digger will have the advantage of Shetland wool and a hot-water bottle.'

'That's so kind of you, Mr Cribben,' said Esme, 'but he's never slept outside before.'

'Well, Esme,' said the butler, 'by the time you've used all the blankets I've left for him, he will be quite cozy. May I suggest you get his bed ready now? We don't want you know who realizing his kennel is being turned into a five-star hotel room, do we? And it will be tea soon.'

The sunlight was fading now and the temperature was dropping fast. Esme collected her quilted jacket and wellington boots, putting them on before heading out onto the terrace. She had seen the kennel before but she had assumed it was only used during the summer.

Looking inside it now, she was no longer concerned that Digger would be cold. He was a tough boy. And having a hot-water bottle would be a positive luxury – just as Mr Cribben said; like staying in a hotel. Tucking the plaid picnic blanket over a pillow, she knew her dog would be as snug as a bug.

'Here, boy, come and test your bed out. Come here,' she said, patting the padded interior.

Obediently, Digger ran inside and eagerly nestled down into the pile of blankets. He looked at her and thumped his tail.

'I could quite happily sleep with you in there, Digs,' Esme said, putting her head and shoulders inside the kennel. 'You'll be quite warm.'

She pulled her head back out. 'We must go and tell the others that you've been found. We've all been terribly worried about you. Come on, fella – now you know where your bedroom is.'

She stood and patted her thigh for the dog to follow, walking back to the house. Tugging on the door, she found that it was stuck. Damp and age had warped the frame over the years, so Esme was used to this happening on her adventures with Lexi. She pulled again. Nope. It was really stuck this time.

'Ugh, Digger, this is so annoying.'

She rattled the door and tried to prise it open, but it didn't move at all. She realized that someone must have locked it, not knowing she was outside.

Esme walked along the terrace, past the dining room and on to the drawing room, where she stopped to bang on the glass. Cupping her hands around her face she peered in. All the lights were off and the place was deserted except for the piano she had hidden beneath the night before.

Surely Lexi would come and find her? But Lexi wouldn't know where she was. Nobody knew where she was apart from Mr Cribben, but he wouldn't be down until teatime. Everyone would think her very rude if she didn't show up for tea. She didn't know how she was going to escape; the terrace was high on the first floor and enclosed by battlements. The only access was through the locked doors.

Esme banged on the door again and yelled. No response. 'Digger, I think we're going to be here for a while.'

She looked around, wondering if she could climb through an open window. The only one that appeared to have been left ajar was high up on the second floor. She knew from her adventures with Lexi that it was the Earl and Contessa's room. She wolf-whistled loudly. The sound pierced the air with glass-shattering clarity. She waited. Nothing.

'Oh well, Digs, we'll just have to wait. Let's get your blankets back out and we can snuggle together.'

✻

She knew that most children would be alarmed at the prospect of being stuck out on the cold balcony of an immense castle, but for Esme, solitude was often her saviour and as long as she had her dog, she never felt alone. It was nice to have a bit of peace without having to make an excuse to find it. It reminded her of being in her secret place and she felt a pang of longing to be back there amongst her things. Staying at the castle was exhausting.

She fished in the pockets of her jacket and found a KitKat in one and fruit gums in the other. Well, she might get a bit chilly but she wouldn't go hungry.

She looked at her watch: five o'clock. A sharp wind was starting to blow across the terrace. She looked up as a light came on in one of the upstairs windows.

'Heeelllooooooo?' Esme cried, her voice carried up by the wind.

'Esme? Is that you?' called Lexi, poking her head out from inside. 'Where have you been? Everyone's been looking for you!' She hung out of the window like Rapunzel with her fairy-tale curls dangling over the sill.

'I've been here the whole time. Someone locked the door so I couldn't get back in. Will you come and get me? I'm *freeeeezing*,' Esme shouted back.

Her friend's head vanished and soon reappeared at the terrace door. Lexi unclipped the lock and kicked the door open.

'Oh, Lexi, thank you. I'm so cold,' Esme said, shivering.

'Your lips are blue. How long have you been out here?'

'Since we separated to look for Digger. Mr Cribben found him. He told me that your mother said he has to sleep in the kennel, so I was making it nice and cozy for him. Then I tried to open the door and it was locked. Luckily I found some sweets in my pocket and I had Digger to keep me warm. Oh, I must put this back in his kennel,' she said, taking the blanket off her shoulders.

'Don't worry, I'll do that. As Mrs Bee would say, you need *a wee cup of hot tea*,' Lexi said in a Scottish accent.

'She would!' Esme laughed. 'Where's Bella?'

'Dunno, but weirdly I just saw Mama come out of the pantry. First time I've seen her in the servant quarters.'

'I knew you'd be the one to find me. Did you hear my whistle?'

'That was you? I didn't know you could do that! You have to teach me,' said Lexi, struggling with the large blanket.

'Here, let me help you,' said Esme, taking a corner to stop it dragging on the ground.

'Is that grass?' Lexi said, pointing to a spear of green piercing the frost and snow at their feet.

'Probably.'

'Maybe it's the first sign of a thaw?'

'I don't think so,' said Esme, looking up at the snowflakes that had begun to fall once more. 'I think it's only a sign that Digger has done a widdle on that spot.'

'Urgh, yes, you're right,' said Lexi, peering at the yellow snow around the grass.

Together, they stuffed the cover back into the kennel and wandered towards the edge of the terrace. Looking out across the view and the darkness stretching far below, there was nothing to indicate that a civilized world lay beyond.

'I'm cold, Es, I'm going in,' said Lexi.

Esme nodded, spotting something sparkling by the castle ramparts. 'I'll come inside in a sec.' She walked over and bent down to throw whatever it was into the void. Her eyes widened in surprise. It was the Contessa's diamond ring. She remembered her throwing it out the window the previous evening but wondered why she wouldn't have fetched it by now. Tucking it into her pocket to return it to her later, she put Digger back in his kennel and gave him a kiss.

'Be a good boy. I'll be back soon.'

On her way to the kitchens, Esme bumped into Lexi, carefully carrying a cup down the corridor. Most of its steaming contents seemed to be slopping over the side.

'See? I didn't forget your tea. Hot and sweet like I promised.'

Esme reached for the mug and as she did so the diamond ring fell onto the floor. She must not have pushed it into her pocket as far as she'd thought.

'What's that?' asked Lexi.

Esme was unsure whether to divulge last night's events.

'Promise you won't be upset?' she said, her voice dropping to a barely audible whisper.

'What?' Lexi whispered back.

'Well,' said Esme, choosing her words carefully, 'last night I got stuck in the drawing room – I was getting Brian's bone when your parents came in. They were talking – well, arguing. About me. So I hid under the piano. Your papa left the room and your mother threw the ring outside onto the terrace.'

'*What?* Why would she do that? Is she mad? It's her engagement ring. Granny Daphne gave it to Papa to give to her. It's a famous diamond. Even has its own name but I can't remember what it is… The White Star or something. Here, let me try.'

Esme handed it to Lexi.

'Your mama said that there are three people in her marriage. Does she have another husband?'

'No, silly,' laughed Lexi.

'I wonder what she meant then? She seemed… *sad.*'

'She probably got her sums wrong and meant to say five: Papa and us.'

Or perhaps she didn't account for her two youngest children, only Rollo, thought Esme.

'We'd better hang on to this 'til we see Papa. I think you should be the one to give it back to Mama as you found it.'

Tucking the ring into her pocket again, Esme made sure it wouldn't fall out this time and then followed Lexi back to the nursery, where they snuggled onto the sofa.

They were watching TV when the Earl came in.

'Hello, girls.'

'Hi, Papa,' said Lexi. 'Did you have a good afternoon?'

'Indeed we did. I must say I'm glad everyone has gone home now, though.'

'Is there any cake left?' asked Lexi.

'Funny you should say that. I was just coming to get you. I made sure to save two large slices – one each.'

'Oooh, yummy! Esme, you *have* to try Seamus's lemon drizzle cake. It's the best *ever*.'

'Come on then, let's go back to the dining room before your mama feeds them to Brian.'

The Contessa was still in the dining room when they walked in, sitting silent and erect. She lit a cigarette and drew hard on its filter.

'Hello, Mama,' said Lexi.

'Alexa,' she said.

The Earl brought two plates over to the girls. 'There we go. An enormous slice each to thank you for all your hard work this morning.'

'Henry, we don't want Alexa getting fat.'

'That's not very nice, Mama,' said Lexi, stuffing the sponge into her mouth as if she hadn't eaten for years. 'By the way, where's your engagement ring?' she went on, grinning at Esme with a mischievous glint in her eye.

The Contessa hesitated, looking at her naked finger. 'I took it off and put it in a safe place. Not that it's any of your business.'

'Well...'

Esme could see the excitement building in her friend.

'Well, what?' snapped the Contessa.

'You didn't put it in a safe place, Mama, but luckily Esme found it and I think you need to say a great big thank-you.'

Esme delved into her pocket and pulled out the ring. A flash of panic crossed the Contessa's otherwise impassive face. She then turned to look at Esme, her eyes narrowing.

'Um… I… I found it out on the terrace in the snow,' said Esme, feeling as though she had done something wrong. 'When I went to make Digger's bed. It was just sitting there.'

'You mean *this* terrace?' asked the Earl, looking confused.

'Yes,' said Esme. 'I got locked out and Lexi let me in. I told her I found it.'

'How odd,' said the Earl, turning to his wife. 'Lucia, you never venture outside except to get into the car. Esme, where exactly was it on the terrace?'

'I found it by the wall, where the flowerbed is,' said Esme.

'Were there any footprints leading up to it?' asked the Earl.

'No. It was like it had dropped from the sky,' she said, cautiously.

The Contessa jumped up. 'One minute, Henry,' she said, looking at Esme. 'Rings don't *fly* so someone must have stolen it, then accidentally dropped it. But isn't it rather coincidental that the only person who was out on the terrace was *Esme*?'

Esme stared back at her.

'It's actually rather ingenious. She throws the ring outside and then pretends to "find it", as if she's our very own little hero,' she sneered.

'But Mama, if Esme had stolen it, she wouldn't have told me she had found it,' said Lexi.

'Alexa, it is nice of you to stick up for your friend, but I think it's obvious what happened here.' The Contessa sucked in the last of her cigarette then threw it into the fire. 'We all know that the Munroe family have a tendency to take things that don't belong to them,' she looked at her husband.

Esme stood rooted to the ground, the sound of her heart thumping in her ears. She shook her head, feeling guilty for a crime she had not committed.

'Lucia! That's enough. She didn't take the ring. She hasn't got it in her to do anything of the sort,' said the Earl, drawing Esme close and encircling her protectively in his arms.

'Of course she didn't, Mama. Esme wouldn't do anything like that. She even takes back crisps that Digger steals from the village shop!' said Lexi.

'I don't know how the ring could have ended up on the terrace, Lucia,' said the Earl, 'but it is unforgiveable of you to accuse Esme. What are you thinking? Her mother is in hospital! The Munroes are friends of ours, for goodness' sake.'

'Henry, we all know that the apple does not fall far from the tree. The child cannot be trusted,' retorted the Contessa.

'Lucia!' said the Earl. 'Can't you see Esme is standing here?'

'Yes, Mama. Esme isn't invisible,' said Lexi.

'Ah... I see. So, in your view, Henry, stealing husbands is not considered theft?' said the Contessa.

Esme looked at the Earl and he appeared even more furious than he had been last night. The veins in his neck were straining and his face was turning a bright, burning red.

'Should I embrace your extra-curricular activity with open arms? Should I turn a blind eye? It wouldn't surprise me if that child isn't the only secret you're keeping!'

Esme froze, looking from the Contessa to the Earl.

'What on earth are you talking about?' he spluttered.

'Yes, Mama. What are you talking about?' said Lexi.

'Quiet, Alexa. This has nothing to do with you,' the Contessa snapped. 'Or maybe it does…' she continued. A hint of spiteful pleasure distorted her lips into a sadistic smile as she turned back to her husband. 'Perhaps you would like to explain things to your daughter, Henry?'

'Explain what, Papa?'

'I have simply no idea what your mother is talking about,' the Earl replied, more calmly. He turned to Esme. 'I am sorry about this, my dear. You don't deserve it.' He stroked her hair.

Esme kept looking at him. Lexi grabbed her hand and clung to it ferociously.

'Do you really not know?' A crackling laugh escaped from the Contessa's throat. 'Oh, that is simply too funny. You truly haven't been told. My, my, does that woman have a conscience after all?'

And with that the Contessa left the room before anyone could ask her anything more.

Sitting in her bedroom, Lexi patted Esme on the back. 'Don't worry, Es,' she said. 'Mama just said it because you were in the wrong place at the wrong time. It was most frightfully horrid of her to accuse you. I think she blamed you because she was scared Papa might think she'd been careless with her ring.'

Esme nodded, her body shuddering with dry sobs, inhaling small gulps of air between hiccups.

'Mm,' she mumbled. 'Do you think Digger's all right?'

'I went to let him in but Mama stopped me. It's snowing really hard. I mean *really* hard. A blizzard.'

Esme jerked her head up. 'What? A blizzard?'

'I think you should get him. The snow might trap him in his kennel. If it does he could suffocate.'

'How could she *do* that? I *hate* her,' said Esme, but immediately regretted it. 'Sorry, Lexi, I shouldn't say that about your mother.'

'It's OK. I hate her too for making Digger sleep outside.'

'I'm going to get him. He can't be out in weather like this, even with a hot-water bottle. It's cruel. How can she be so unkind? He's just an innocent dog who has never hurt a fly. He'll die if it's snowing that hard.'

'Just be careful Mama doesn't catch you,' said Lexi.

'I don't care if she does,' said Esme, feeling bolder than she had done for some time. 'She can be as cross as she likes. I will report her to the RSPCA.'

'Maybe you should get Mr Cribben to do it? Or I could come with you...'

Whilst she adored Lexi and knew her offer was genuine, instinct told Esme she was nervous about stepping out of line. In this moment of urgency, she thought, the only person she could rely on was herself.

'Don't worry. Digger is *my* dog and I have to take responsibility for him. That's what Mrs Bee would say.'

'OK – but I'll keep guard,' said Lexi.

Digger was standing with his front paws pressed against the French windows. Each had a halo of condensation from the warmth of his pads. At the sight of his mistress, he jumped up and down on his hind legs and wagged his tail furiously, tongue hanging out the side of his mouth. Esme opened the door and he jumped into her arms, licking her face and whining.

'What *is* going on?'

Esme jumped, swinging round to face the Contessa.

With the speed of a rattlesnake, her bony hand reached out and grabbed the scruff of Digger's neck, hoisting him high into the air. The dog struggled, his paws swimming strokes of helplessness. The Contessa looked at him with revulsion. A murmur of disgust came from her throat. Digger was trapped in a grasp of rage that went far beyond annoyance at his being outdoors. The Contessa opened the door again and flung him outside. He landed on his back and scrabbled to right himself, lunging at the door as it was slammed shut and locked in one swift move.

Stunned, Esme watched the Contessa stride out of the room with the key gripped in her hand. She looked back at the door. Snow was falling fast and relentlessly. She yanked at the door handle and then fell to her knees, pressing her hands and face against the glass. Digger sat, ears cocked and inquiring, his eyes looking into hers. Esme started to panic as the falling snow erased him into a vague form.

'It's all right, Digger darling. I'll get you. Don't worry.' She knew if she left, he would be clever enough to take refuge in the kennel – if he could still get in.

'Digger, go into the kennel,' she whispered, indicating at her dog through the glass. 'It's nice and warm and you have your cozy blanky in there. I'm going to find help.'

She walked along the windows and the dog followed her until he was next to the kennel.

'*Stay!*' she commanded, pointing her finger to reinforce the order.

Digger sat down immediately and she walked away, looking over her shoulder to see him go into the safety of his shelter.

Up until this moment, the castle had always felt safe and secure. A strong fortress built to keep the baddies out. But an evil witch lived inside and it suddenly felt like a prison with the Contessa its jailer. Esme would not allow Digger to become her latest victim.

Unsure whether Mr Cribben or the Earl would be her knight in shining armour, she set off to see who she could find first. Running blindly through the castle she looked into every room she passed. She wanted to shout for help but experience told her silence was more effective; it was vital to stay hidden from the Contessa. She saw a shadow pass up ahead and pressed herself into an alcove, breathing heavily. The footsteps approaching were measured and assured – not the sound of the Contessa's pointy heels, but leather soles slapping against stone. Esme leapt from her hiding place, blocking the Earl in his path.

'Esme! Are you all right? I was just coming to find you,' he said and smiled.

'Digger is locked outside. On the terrace,' she gasped. 'The Contessa did it and she took the key! We have to get him inside or he'll die. It's snowing like mad and he'll get buried and suffocate. He is going to die! You have to help me…' Her words tumbled over each other, getting trapped and then released by waves of panic.

'Esme! Slow down, everything is going to be OK.'

'But you don't understand,' she pleaded, worried his composure meant he didn't care.

'Listen to me: we'll get Digger out, I have another key. But I have some news for you…' He hesitated, waiting for Esme's breathing to return to normal.

'News about Mummy?' she asked, a flicker of excitement in her belly.

'I've just got off the telephone to your father and you are going home. Today. Now, in fact!'

'Now? What…? Mummy's already home?' Esme was confused.

'Your mother suffered little more than a few minor burns and smoke inhalation. She is on the mend and all concerned felt it was better for her to recuperate at home. No one can look after her better than you and Mrs Bee, don't you think?'

Esme stared at him, stunned. She thought back to the sight of her mother possessed by the monster and held prisoner by all the tubes. Could smoke do that to someone? The grown-ups smoked all the time.

'I know it's difficult to understand,' said the Earl, slowly. 'Your mother had a moment of madness in the fire that she could not control, but the doctors say she is doing very well. She's recovered much more quickly than anyone expected.'

'Really?' asked Esme, her lip trembling.

'Yes, really,' he smiled. 'You're going home.'

Esme felt her legs weakening beneath her. She had longed for this moment but hadn't dared hope that it would arrive so soon. She burst into tears.

The Earl looked at her in shock. 'There, there, Esme,' he said, rubbing her shoulders. 'I thought you'd be happy to be going home – it's all you've talked about since you arrived.'

'I am… It's just…'

'I know. It was a surprise for me, too. Your mother is very lucky to have a daughter who loves her so much. Come on, I'll go and fetch Digger and pop him in the pantry. Why don't you go and tell Lexi?'

Esme gripped the Earl's outstretched hand, warmth flooding through her body. She was going home.

Esme ran to the nursery to find her friend. Lexi was sat by the fire reading her new annual.

'I'm going home!' she shouted.

Lexi jumped, her book falling to the floor. 'Wh… what?' she asked.

'Mummy's coming out of hospital. Your papa just told me – I'm going home!'

'But we haven't had any time to do anything, yet!' cried Lexi, throwing herself down on the sofa. 'I get so bored when you're not here to play with me.'

'Lexi, that's selfish.'

Her friend lifted her head, guiltily. 'I'm sorry, Es. Of course, I'm happy your mama is coming home. I'm just going to miss you, that's all.'

'Oh Lexi,' said Esme. 'I'll miss you too. But you'll have Bella and I'm only down the road. Nothing is going to change. We can still go riding and on our adventures together. I just won't be sleeping here any more. You can come and stay at The Lodge whenever you want.'

Lexi smiled back at her. 'You're right.'

'I have to go and pack, but I'll come and say goodbye with Digger before I leave, I promise!'

'OK. I won't move a muscle until you return,' Lexi said, going stiff like a board.

Esme laughed. She really would miss Lexi, but she couldn't wait to get back to The Lodge and see her own family.

Half an hour later, with Nanny Patch's help, Esme had finished packing. She breathed a sigh of relief as she closed the door on the damp, fly-infested room that had been hers. Looking at her watch, she saw that it was nearly seven o'clock. Digger had clearly sensed there was change afoot and, no longer cautious, scampered ahead of her, sniffing at the cracks and crannies where Brian had left his mark. Stopping at a corner, he cocked his leg.

'Digger!'

Esme ran to scoop him up but he shot off, forcing her to chase after him, through the dining room, into the drawing room and finally into the Contessa's study, where his escape reached a dead end.

'Digger!' she whispered as loudly as possible from the doorway, her voice catching in her throat. She tiptoed into the darkened room. At first she thought it was empty, but then she saw the glowing tip of a cigarette. The moon emerged from behind the clouds and the room lit up as if struck by lightning. Facing the window stood the Contessa, the glass bottle in her right hand glinting as she lifted it towards her lips. In the silence Esme could even hear its contents running down the Contessa's throat. Then, prising the bottle from her mouth, came a great sucking pop.

Esme stood, rooted to the spot, praying that Digger wouldn't give either of them away. But he was far too nosey and jumped up at the Contessa to say hello.

'Ugh – get away!' she shrieked. She flapped at the dog, pushing him down.

But Digger was far too forgiving. He rolled over and exposed his tummy, as though asking to be stroked.

'Oh, for God's sake,' she slurred. 'Now she's... done it. That little... How dare she let you back in?'

A deep rumbled escaped her throat as she kicked Digger sharply. The dog let out a squeal, before scrambling upright.

'S-serves you right...' she mumbled, the mixture of alcohol and saliva dragging out her words.

Digger yelped in pain as the Contessa kicked him again. She took another great glug from the bottle. The moon illuminated her face, twisted in bitterness.

Esme heard the crack of an object against bone and saw her dog drop to the floor. She stood, frozen in fear.

'Digger,' she whispered.

The Contessa's shoulders began to shake violently. Esme wondered if she was laughing but then she began to make a terrible retching sound and put her hand over her mouth. She bent down suddenly, leaning over the wastepaper basket under her desk, and started vomiting into it.

Finally, she wiped her mouth with her sleeve, retrieved the bottle from the floor and straightened up once more – only to take another swig of alcohol. Just as she tipped her head back, the moon disappeared from view and the room descended into darkness again.

Esme knew this was her only chance. Quick as a whip, she grabbed her whimpering dog and pulled him to safety.

'Who's there?' asked the Contessa, sharply.

Esme flattened herself against the wall but a loose floorboard creaked beneath her left foot.

'Henry?' said the Contessa, reaching out to touch the trespasser.

The stench of nicotine, alcohol and perfume was strong now and Esme could feel the heat radiating from the Contessa; she was close by.

'No,' she said, quietly. 'It's me, Esme.'

'Ahh, the thief,' the Contessa cackled, suddenly sounding more composed. 'I think that mongrel of yours might have broken something.'

'You…' Esme's voice faltered before erupting from her, unleashing an all-consuming rage. 'You nasty, *horrible* lady!'

'What did you say?' asked the Contessa, menacingly.

Esme didn't flinch; her blood was boiling and she heard something new in the Contessa's voice – fear. 'I hate you!' she shouted. Her heart was beating so loudly she could hear it. 'Everyone hates you! Your children hate you. Jimmy hates you. Mrs Bee. Sophia. We all do!'

'How dare you!' the Contessa snarled. 'Listen to me, you ungrateful, insolent little—'

'I won't listen. I *won't!*' she yelled as the moon re-emerged from behind a cloud.

'I know *all* about you... *Esme.*' The Contessa's tone was low and threatening, making Esme's name sound dirty. She brought her face down to Esme's level. Dragging hard on her cigarette, she grimaced as if the corners of her mouth were weighed down by the congealed remains of her lipstick. She flicked her head to the side and exhaled a mixture of smoke and spittle.

'You know nothing about me. You can barely even look at me!' stammered Esme.

'Oh, but I do,' said the Contessa, jabbing her cigarette towards her.

Esme leant back to avoid being burnt. 'Well, I know all about you too,' she said, triumphantly. 'I saw you throw your ring outside – when you told the Earl that there were three people in your marriage.' She paused, then, 'I could tell him the truth!'

The Contessa stiffened. 'Don't be so childish. Anyway, why would he *care?*'

'You're the cruellest person I've ever met. You should be reported to the RSPCA for everything you've done to Digger. If he dies, you'll go to prison.'

'No one will ever believe you,' the Contessa leered. 'You might as well be *invisible*. Your parents are commoners. Your father's ancestry claims are laughable and your mother... Well, you could be anyone's daughter.' She let out a shrill, feverish laugh.

'You're a liar!' shouted Esme.

'Why would I lie to the daughter of a deranged lunatic?'

Something inside Esme snapped. 'Mummy is more of a lady than you will ever be. She doesn't think she's better than everyone else. She's kind and she looks after people. She can't help that she's ill. And I *love* her.'

The Contessa blinked. 'Your mother has ruined my life. If it wasn't for her, I might have been happy.' She paused, then, 'Henry might have been happy.'

'It's got nothing to do with Mummy. It's *you*,' Esme replied.

'Don't you understand, child? Your mother isn't ill, she's insane. A loony.' She grinned manically, her nostrils flaring as she made a spinning motion with her finger around her temple.

'No! *You're* mad. You're nasty and jealous of my mummy!' shouted Esme.

'It's all her fault!' the Contessa snarled. 'And yours, you... *bastard* child!'

Esme gasped at the horrible word.

The Contessa swayed as she attempted to light another cigarette. The unlit match wavered past the tip a few times, until she realized it was dead. She growled, tearing another match off the booklet and striking it successfully. The flame lit up her face – slick with sweat, eyes bulging.

'I've watched you trying to turn Henry against me. I've watched you win his affection. And to think that just because you are a child you can claim some kind of... *innocence*.' She spat the word out, repulsed. 'I'm not surprised your father took your crazy mother away from here and all the way to London. They wanted to get away from *you*.'

'That's not true,' Esme said, her eyes blazing. 'You're drunk.'

'How does it make you feel?' the Contessa asked, ignoring Esme's statement and licking her lips. 'Knowing your mother will try again. Again, and again, and again. She wanted to *leave* you, Esme. She is ashamed of you.'

'Take that back!' Esme screamed, hurling herself at the Contessa, tears streaming from her eyes.

The Contessa slapped her hard across the face and Esme fell back against the wall, the taste of blood in her mouth. Digger started barking frantically, whining and licking his mistress. Esme tried to get up, but the Contessa hit her again, before closing her cold, bony fingers around her neck. White spots danced in front of Esme's eyes as the Contessa tightened her grip, her face contorted with pleasure. The predator with her prey.

'What the *hell* is happening in here?'

Suddenly the room lit up. It was the Earl. 'What in God's name are you doing, woman?' he yelled, pulling his wife from Esme.

'She... attacked me...' the Contessa slurred.

'For Christ's sake, Lucia, what have you done to the child? Is that *blood* on her face?'

'You don't understand! This is what Diana *wanted*. For that child to be here as a constant reminder of your guilt – so you wouldn't forget *her*. But I can't bear it! You are a . . . a... fool,' she rasped.

The Earl ignored her, turning to face Esme, who had managed to get to her feet and now stood, rigid with shock, blood dripping from her nose.

'What the hell were you thinking? She's a *child*, for God's sake!'

'She's evil, Henry. Just like her mother.'

'She's an eleven-year-old girl,' the Earl said, pulling Esme towards him. 'Are you all right, darling?'

Esme nodded, her body trembling violently. She felt numb.

'Let's get you home.'

'Home?' The Contessa looked startled.

'Yes, home, Lucia. Diana is out of hospital, Esme is leaving.'

'Diana... Diana's back?'

Esme was shocked to see tears slipping from beneath the Contessa's dark lashes, rivulets of black running down her cheeks. She was crying.

'But, I thought...'

'You didn't *think* anything, Lucia. You hoped. You prayed from the bottom of your heart that Diana would be out of your life. My life.'

'Please, Henry,' she sobbed. 'I'm your wife. You married *me*. Why was I never enough for you?'

'We were young, Lucia. We were fools in love. Blinded by it. It's what stopped me from seeing reality for so long.'

'I love you, Henry. I'll always love you. *Please...*' She stumbled forward, snagging her heel on the hearth and falling to her knees.

Automatically, Esme stretched out her hand to help her and for a second, their gazes locked. The Contessa's eyes were watery and deadened by defeat. In that moment, Esme pitied her.

'You don't even know what love is,' the Earl muttered,

barely audible. He helped Esme up, then turned to look down at his wife once more. 'I should have done this a long time ago.'

'What? What should you have done a long time ago?' said the Contessa, her voice quivering and frightened.

'Left you,' he said.

The spell was broken. Esme gulped, feeling as if she had come back from the brink of death. Her emotions hit her like an avalanche as she took in the scene. The Contessa, destroyed by her own poison. Digger, still wagging his tail at his mistress. Vomit, oozing out across the carpet from the capsized bin. And Esme, safe in the Earl's arms. She kissed him on the cheek and hugged him with what little strength she had left. She was going home.

'It's OK darling, she can't hurt you any more.'

Chapter Fifteen

It was New Year's Eve. Only Esme, Bella and Lexi remained at the dining table in The Lodge, scraping the last remnants of Mrs Bee's three puddings from their serving bowls. Dinner had been magical. The tablecloth was still scattered with colourful party hats and the carcass of an enormous goose lay on the sideboard. Lord and Lady Findlay had brought with them a great bowl of punch and even the children had been allowed a glass.

The sound of laughter and clinking glasses drifted through from the drawing room and Esme could barely contain her happiness. Her mother was finally home.

'Ugh,' she squealed, as Lexi discarded her spoon and started to use her fingers to wipe up the last smears of pudding from one of the bowls. Lexi grinned back at her, licking her lips.

Bella burped loudly as she finished the dregs from yet another champagne glass.

'Ewwww, Bella!' Lexi and Esme groaned.

'I can sing "God Save the Queen" in burps,' she said. 'All you need to do is ask.'

'You'll be sick and all that delicious food will go to waste,' said Lexi.

Esme giggled and put on a paper crown, choosing a green

one to match her dress. She lifted the carving knife from the table and touched it ceremonially to each of Lexi's shoulders in turn as she curtseyed.

'Arise, Lady Alexa of Culcairn Castle…' said Esme in a haughty voice. 'Oh wait, you're a Lady already!'

'Children, it's time!' came the sound of her father's voice from the drawing room.

'Midnight!' they screamed, racing down the passage towards the throng of adults.

The chimes of Big Ben rang out from the stereo speakers. Everyone stood in a circle and linked arms as they counted down together: 'Five, four, three, two, one…' On the last chime, the smiling faces, flushed with rum punch and far too much champagne, began to belt out the familiar words of 'Auld Lang Syne'. A new year. A new decade.

Esme glowed with hope and happiness. She looked across at her mother, singing along with everyone else. She looked beautiful in her Gina Fratini gown with its butterfly print. The emerald brooch her father had given her for Christmas glistened in the candlelight. She caught Esme looking at her and smiled. Her eyes were filled with love as she unlinked her arm from her husband's and blew Esme a kiss. Esme went over to give her a hug.

'Happy New Year, Mummy,' she said.

'Happy New Year, my darling,' she whispered. 'I love you.'

Esme knew that she meant it.

It hadn't been so much a rapturous homecoming as a gentle nudge back to normality. Diana had returned to The Lodge and when Sophia had flown in early from her holiday, the whole family had gone to collect her from Edinburgh.

Esme knew her mother was glad to be home, but it was a tentative happiness – a delicate balance between a terrifying darkness and feverish joy. Esme saw her as a newborn foal; slightly unsteady but awake to the world like she was seeing it for the first time. She took delight in everyday luxuries: a cup of tea, Mrs Bee's cake and feather pillows.

When Esme had first returned to The Lodge, Mrs Bee had all but finished putting her mother's bedroom back to how it was before the fire. Esme had helped her hang the newly laundered curtains and put away her freshly washed clothes. There was still a distant smell of smoke, but a scented candle masked most of it. Earlier that day, Esme had collected the first snowdrops, and arranged them in a tiny vase on her mother's bedside table.

Lexi danced across the room, squeezing her friend close and shouting 'Happy New Year' over Jerry Lee Lewis, whose voice was now blaring from the record player. The grown-ups paired up and were rocking around the clock, cigars and glasses still in hand. Esme's father spun her mother around with dizzying speed. The two girls held hands and twisted their hips to the music. Bella jumped up and down, whilst

Rollo and Sophia used the rowdy backdrop to get closer in a slow jive.

'Ooh,' cooed Lexi. 'Look at them getting all smoochy.'

Esme laughed and pulled Bella in to join them. She bounced and whirled like a dervish.

'I'm so happy Mama isn't here. I hope her flu lasts *forever*,' Bella shouted, grinning from ear to ear. 'Everybody has so much more fun without her.'

It was true, thought Esme. The atmosphere was lighter. But she didn't care about the Contessa anymore. She no longer needed to be frightened of her. Everyone she loved, except for the Earl, was in this room. Even Mrs Bee and Jimmy were bobbing up and down in the corner.

'It's a shame your papa isn't here,' she said to Bella and Lexi.

'I bet he's having a shitty time with his cousin,' replied Bella. 'I don't even know if they celebrate New Year in Wales.'

The Earl and Contessa never came to the New Year party at the Lodge but Esme knew the Earl would be sad not to see Mummy, now she was back. Secretly, she was glad there were no celebrations happening at the castle this year because it meant that Rollo, Bella and Lexi were invited to theirs. Esme was yet to tell her mother how kind the Earl had been. How he had stood up for her against the Contessa. She hadn't even told Mrs Bee or Sophia what had happened that night; it was something she wanted to leave in the past. She wanted to forget the hateful words and the physical violence but she would hold on tight to the strength she had discovered within herself. If she could stand up for herself against the Contessa, she need never be scared again.

'Of course they do, stupid,' said Lexi, bringing Esme back into the moment. 'He's in *Wales,* not Timbuktu!'

'I know, but Aunt whatever-her-name-is wouldn't know what a party was if it slapped her in the face! No wonder she's a spinster.'

'Oh, who cares! We're having fun and right now that's all that matters,' said Lexi.

And indeed they were. Esme's mother was better, her father was tipsy and dancing like Elvis and Esme was with her best friend, whom she felt closer to than ever. Watching the Contessa finally crack had reassured her that she wasn't the only one who didn't have a 'normal' mother. And despite everything that had happened this Christmas, she would rather have her mummy than Lexi's. At least she loved her, even though her poorly brain got in the way of showing that sometimes. Esme knew that the joy and calm reigning over The Lodge today might evaporate tomorrow but it would never fail to come back; the sun was always there, even when it was hidden behind the clouds.

'I'm just going to see Mrs Bee,' said Esme to Lexi, as she saw the housekeeper slip through the door and back into the dining room.

'OK. Don't be long!' Lexi shouted after her.

Esme ran up behind Mrs Bee and clasped her arms around the housekeeper's waist.

'Happy New Year, Mrs Bee!'

'And you too, darling,' she said, turning to face her charge, her eyes twinkling.

'That was a delicious dinner, Mrs Bee. I loved the casserole and the Baked Alaska was spectacular. I took the biggest piece. Even Mummy ate all hers – did you see?'

'Ay, she's getting stronger by the second, love. What a fright she gave us all, but she's back where she belongs and so are you, my wee angel.'

'You know what, Mrs Bee?'

'What's that, my darling?'

'I am the luckiest girl in the world because I have you *and* Mummy. I love you so, so, *so* much. Almost as much as Digger!'

'Well, I love you more than chocolate – and that's saying something,' laughed Mrs Bee.

'It's been the best New Year ever.'

'Yes it has. You'd better get back to the party, love. Everyone will be wondering where you are.'

But Esme didn't go back into the drawing room. She collected Digger and went into the garden to look at the stars. Venus's usual brilliance was softened by a milky haze. In the distance, the outline of the castle jutted out against the skyscape – a dense black shape, devoid of life.

A drop of water fell onto her head from the guttering above; the snow had finally begun to melt and tiny spears of grass pierced the white-covered lawn.

An owl hooted into the vacant night. Cupping her hands around her lips, Esme hooted back. Her breath no longer appeared in puffs before her, instead disappearing instantly, and she imagined waking up to a brown-and-green day tomorrow. The morning would wipe clean a Christmas submerged in icy sorrow and conflict. She released a sigh of gratitude. Her newfound independence was liberating and she would do exactly as she pleased, after the snow.

Acknowledgements

My writing career would never have happened but for the faith of some inspirational people.

I would like to thank David Welch, sports editor of the *Daily Telegraph*, for giving me my first break.

To Eric Bailey, also of the *Telegraph*, for providing Trinny and I the platform upon which our career was built.

To Susan Haynes and Alan Samson who recognized that I might have it in me to write fiction.

To Michael Foster for his evergreen rallying and enthusiasm.

To Caroline Michel, my girl crush and genius literary agent. Thank you for your unswerving belief and constant encouragement.

To everyone at HQ, HarperCollins, in particular Lisa Milton and Charlotte Mursell. This book would never have seen the light of day without your bullying, steadfast kindness and forensic guidance. My gratitude is never-ending.

To Gillian Stern from whom I have learned so much.

To my sister, Nits, for her cautious wisdom.

To Desiigner and Starsailor for penning songs that made me write.

To my beloved Trinny for everything.

To Ali McGougan and Becci Bazely for being my ideal readers. Can't thank you enough for taking the time to read the drafts and giving your brilliant feedback. You are my writing rocks and I love you both.

To Stevie Skinner and all at Kasbah Bab Ourika for providing my inspiration and writing haven.

And finally to my darling Sten for his diplomatic cajoling to get me off my fat, lazy butt to write, and for your help in structuring my day, without you, *After the Snow* would never have been finished.